LANDON

The K9 Files, Book 18

Dale Mayer

LANDON: THE K9 FILES, BOOK 18
Beverly Dale Mayer
Valley Publishing Ltd.

ISBN-13: 978-1-773365-57-2
Print Edition

Books in This Series

About This Book

Welcome to the all new K9 Files series reconnecting readers with the unforgettable men from SEALs of Steel in a new series of action packed, page turning romantic suspense that fans have come to expect from USA TODAY Bestselling author Dale Mayer. Pssst… you'll meet other favorite characters from SEALs of Honor and Heroes for Hire too!

Landon, after a tough couple of years helping his navy buddy live out his last years, needed a break. Tracking a war dog named Chico to make sure it was okay sounded perfect. Especially being able to take his three chihuahuas with him. But finding a dog that had been part of a large shipment heading to a rescue across the Canadian border but had gone missing on the last stop before the border – well that was going to be a challenge. Particularly one that had a lame leg and half a paw.

Sabrina had spent years volunteering at a local vet clinic, because all animals had a soft spot in her heart. Finding Landon is trying to track down a missing War Dog, well how could she not volunteer to help him? Still when her world flips upside down, she's more than happy to have Landon close by.

Now if only they could find the dog and figure out who and what was responsible for endangering her life…

Sign up to be notified of all Dale's releases here!

https://geni.us/DaleNews

PROLOGUE

K AT BROUGHT A cup of coffee for Badger and placed it in front of him, then she sat down herself. "So another good ending," she said, with satisfaction.

"I think more than either of us expected in this case," Badger murmured.

"At this point in time"—she chuckled—"I'm expecting the best on every case."

"Maybe, ... it was definitely not a sure thing there."

"And do we have any update on Taylor's military assault case?"

"Yes, the army is doing a full investigation and looking into why she wasn't dealt with fairly in the first place." Badger smiled. "That should shake things up pretty well."

"It needs to happen," Kat stated.

Badger nodded. "It's a sad world where men are allowed to prey on women, no matter what the industry," he noted. He picked up a file sitting in front of him and dropped it in front of her. "Since you were so helpful on the last one ..."

"You mean, on the last couple," she stated, flashing him a big grin.

He added, "I'm only letting you get away with that because I love you."

"I know you are." Chuckling, she opened up the file and asked, "And who is this War Dog?"

1

"Her name's Chica."

Kat studied the picture of the beautiful shepherd Malinois–looking cross. "And what's her story?"

"She was sent down to Mexico and somehow ended up in one of those large shipments, where the dogs go from Mexico up to Canada."

She raised her gaze to him and frowned. "What? How did Chica end up in Mexico?"

"We don't know that, but it looks like our War Dog was adopted by a man out of Texas, who became an ex-pat when he moved to Mexico, where he took the dog with him."

"And then …?" Kat waited.

"We don't know. He's deceased now, and the dog was shipped to Canada. And we're not sure where Chica is."

"They tend to keep really good records on transports like that."

"Sure," he agreed, "but, when the shipment got there, apparently Chica didn't arrive in Canada."

"Crap. Did the shipment touch down anywhere in-between?"

"Some came by plane. Some came by train. Ones with health conditions were transported via a combo of trucking, then flying. A planeload was sent over our northern border with about seventy-five dogs on that flight."

"And Chica wasn't on the plane."

He shook his head. "No."

"So she's got health conditions."

"That's what our assumption is."

"And what about the rest of them in that truckload?"

"Everyone arrived except for three."

She winced. "And of course Chica is one of the three."

He nodded. "The truck driver says that the cages went

missing from the truck on the last leg. No idea how that happened. The other problem is that Chica is not completely whole. She's missing half a paw, and she's had a leg broken in multiple places."

"Which is why, of course, she ended up in the not-so-healthy group."

"That's partly it, but there could be a lot of other things wrong with her now."

"So where did they cross the border?"

"New York."

She stared at him. "That's not exactly a city for a dog."

"Nope, doesn't mean that the dog is even in New York."

"No, of course not. … Niagara Falls, I presume?"

He laughed. "And how did you guess?"

"The biggest border crossing," she said, with a sigh.

"There's a lot of paperwork that has to be done, and there was a problem at the border. Some of the paperwork wasn't quite up to snuff. So they pulled the truck and the dogs off to the side, and apparently they went missing then—somewhere in that time frame, while the handler was taking down the cages, opening them up, letting the dogs out, taking them for walks, putting them back in again."

"And yet he says three of the cages went missing."

Badger nodded. "He didn't know what to do, so he headed on to the next destination with the rest of the dogs and reported it."

Kat sighed. "And Chica could be anywhere."

"That's the problem right now—that's Chica's issue. We still must find somebody who can go track down Chica. That's *our* issue."

She looked over at her husband. "You got anybody in mind?"

"Nope, I sure don't. I've pretty well tapped out everybody we've got locally. You?"

She thought about it and frowned. "I do have one guy, I've been dealing with back and forth. He's from that area."

"Maybe contact him?"

She frowned, pulled out her phone, flicked through her contacts, and when she finally got to the one in question, she said, "I just don't know what he's up for."

"Why is he contacting you?"

"He lost one leg and one hand," she stated.

"How?"

"Bomb squad."

"Military?"

She nodded. "Yes. So chances are he's had some experience with the military animals."

"I'm not even sure that he has. It depends more so on whether he has a soft heart and whether he has any compassion and whether he has any ability to get around right now."

She quickly phoned him, and, when she got him at the other end, there was surprise in his voice.

"Hey, Kat. What's up?"

She quickly explained the problem.

He sighed. "I'm due to have surgery."

"Oh, crap, I forgot. Hey, that's, … that's okay. We'll keep looking."

"Hey, … I've got an idea," he said, "but that depends if my brother would be okay with it."

"And what's your brother doing right now?"

"He was looking after a buddy of his, who just passed away. They were both in the same unit in Iran, and they both got shot up pretty badly. When his buddy started to go downhill, my brother basically stopped his move forward in life to help him out. But now his buddy is gone."

"Oh, good Lord," she said. "That's gotta be hard."

"Pretty devastating for him, yes. And he does have his buddy's dogs now, so I'm not sure whether he'd be free or not."

"What kind of dogs?"

He laughed at that. "You'd think that, you know, somebody like my brother would have shepherds or Newfoundlanders or something huge," he explained. "Instead he's got these tiny, tiny-ass Chihuahuas."

She snickered.

He said, "Right? Anyway let me contact him, and, if he's interested, I'll get him to call you."

"Sounds good." She disconnected the call, looked over at Badger, and shrugged. "All we can do is try."

He agreed. "And we'll keep looking at our end."

At that, they sipped their coffee and went through a bunch of other paperwork they had to deal with.

When her phone rang, she looked at it and said, "I don't know the number." She answered it and found it was the brother on the other end.

"My name is Landon," he stated. "My brother just contacted me, told me about how you're looking for a missing War Dog."

"Yes." She hesitated, then continued. "We just need a little bit more clarity about your experience in this area and would this be of interest to you."

"I'm at loose ends," he shared, his voice roughening slightly. "I could use a distraction."

"Good enough," she replied. "Do you have anybody to keep you from fulfilling this job?"

"No, but I presume I won't die on the job."

"No, I wouldn't think so," she stated, "but I would be remiss in not telling you that some of the previous War Dog scenarios have been pretty rough."

"Yeah, that's life right now," he said. "So tell me more about it."

By the time she put the call on Speakerphone, and she and Badger explained everything, Landon replied, "You know what? I think I heard about these dogs and the job you're doing. A friend of mine, Blaze, told me."

"Do you know Blaze?" Badger asked.

"Yeah," Landon confirmed. "I worked with him overseas a couple times."

"Yes, Blaze is definitely somebody who has helped us out."

"In that case," Landon said, "I guess I can do my part for the War Dog too." He hesitated and then asked, "When would you need me?"

"As soon as possible," Badger said. "The dog's been lost for a while, and now we must find out what's happening with her."

"And what if I can't find her?"

"Then it's a case of *you tried*," Badger noted simply. "So far we haven't *not* located any of our assigned War Dogs, but it could happen. We keep expecting it to happen, but, so far, we've been blessed to find them."

"That puts the pressure on," Landon said, with a wry note.

"And yet we're not doing it for that reason," she jumped in to say.

"No, I got it," Landon confirmed.

Kat leaned forward. "Your brother said you were injured."

"Yeah, I am. Lost a foot just about three inches above the ankle. I've got a prosthetic." Then he stopped and asked, "Does that change anything?"

"No, not in my world."

"Or mine," Badger agreed. "Kat, my wife here, is working with your brother on his prosthetics."

"Oh my," he said, "*that* Kat." He laughed. "Hey, do I get a prosthetic out of this deal?"

"Do you need one?" she asked curiously.

"The one I've got sucks," he stated.

"You have no idea how often I hear that," she murmured. "I'll tell you what. I can't promise anything, but, if we can get this job done, I'll take a good look at it."

"Hey, that'd be perfect," he said, "and I gather there's no money involved in finding the War Dogs."

"No."

"Good. Jobs like this shouldn't require a paycheck to get them done—although I won't be adverse to getting some expenses reimbursed."

"That we can do," Badger declared. "I'll email all this information to you. Let me know what your itinerary is, as soon as you sort it out. And check-ins, please, on a regular basis."

"You got it," Landon said and hung up.

Badger looked over at Kat and grinned. "Not bad," he said. "Not exactly the way we thought it would work, but, hey, we'll take it." And he held up a hand to high-five her.

She smiled and added, "Now if only we get another happy relationship outta this one too."

He rolled his eyes. "Let's get a happy dog first," he said, "and a relationship's secondary."

"It is, until it isn't," she declared, with a smile. "All these guys deserve to be happy, and it sounds like this guy needs it even more than most."

Badger raised an eyebrow at that.

She shrugged. "Not many guys would take time out of their lives to help their buddy on the last of his days."

Badger nodded slowly at that. "You got that right. Guys like that are few and far between."

With that, she closed the file and slid it back to him. "Let's hope he finds somebody who recognizes just how special he is."

CHAPTER 1

LANDON SNOWDEN SAT in his rental vehicle, looking at Chica's file. Good thing he had flown up earlier this month from New Mexico to visit his brother, Harper, before he went into surgery. This trip put Landon so much closer to Chica here in Upstate New York. He had already read the file umpteen times last night, while he was packing up. And then later in bed once again. It was the first thing he looked at when he got up this morning as well, and now, here he was, packed and ready to go. But where was he going? He had texted all his questions to Kat yesterday.

Kat had finally got back home and sent a flurry of her own messages, requesting information. It hadn't taken long before the answers had started to pile in, which she forwarded to Landon.

The first call Landon had made had been to the rescue center behind the logistics of moving all the dogs up to Canada. From that point, the manager had given him the name of the truck driver, who had been at the forefront of losing Chica. But every attempt to contact Charlie had met with no answer. Landon had a home address, but he was looking for another phone number for him. Both he and Kat were on that search, and it might take a while, but, hey, it was faster than going to what may not even be his current home address, located in southern New York State. If the man would answer a phone call, it would help a lot, as, so far, Landon had little to go on.

He'd also asked Badger for more information on the original adoptive family, which he expected soon. As Landon closed the file on Chica and dropped it on the seat beside him, he glanced at his three dogs, all tucked into their bed, then put on his sunglasses.

"What do you think about a road trip, guys?" The three of them started to bark. He chuckled, and then his phone buzzed. He looked down to see Badger had sent Charlie's mother's name and phone number.

"Oh, that's interesting." He quickly dialed it. When an older trembling voice answered the phone, Landon identified himself and noted that he was trying to contact her son, Charlie.

"He's in the hospital," she replied, and tears filled her voice.

"Oh my." Landon's heart sank. "I'm sorry to hear that. Do you know which hospital?"

She told him where Charlie was, even giving the address—not far from here either—and added, "There is some talk they might move him, if he doesn't improve."

"Do you have any idea what happened?"

"No. Nobody does really. He was hit by a car, while he was crossing the road."

Landon frowned at that and asked, "Is he conscious? Any chance I could talk to him?"

"If the doctors let you," she suggested. "I'm too far away and too sick to make the journey, and every time I've tried to call, they wouldn't let me talk to him."

She gave him the phone number to Charlie's room too, and asked Landon to give her an update, if he got in to see

Charlie.

Landon phoned the hospital afterward, thinking he'd much rather do as much as he could with phone calls, instead of making road trips for nothing. However, the hospital nurse he spoke with sounded more encouraging than his mother had. Apparently they were in the process of bringing Charlie out of his medically induced coma, and they were expecting him to have visitors soon. While they couldn't make any promises, according to the doctors, things were, indeed, improving.

On that note, Landon called Charlie's mother and gave her the good news. She was happy to hear that and to be updated. He promised her that he would share any further information he had on Charlie. As Landon thought more about it, he wondered if Charlie would accept a phone call from a stranger. Maybe it would be better to show up at the hospital. He searched his phone for a map to the hospital, finding it near the same area where the dog had gone missing, so, since he needed to visit both places, it seemed prudent to just get on the road.

With that information and his chihuahuas tucked up in their bed on the passenger seat beside him, he hit the road. He was smiling and rocking to the music as he drove. Anything that would take his mind off what had just happened in his life was bound to help. Joe had been a great friend, in the military and out, and to watch him go through the last days of his life was sad and yet heartwarming at the same time. He'd faced death with the same aplomb he'd faced everything in his life.

As for Landon, he knew he wouldn't have done half as well in the same circumstances.

Something was just so vital about Joe that it had been

almost impossible to stay at his side as his body slowly failed him over a span of two years. Landon spent all his time glued to his buddy's side, helping to get him through each day. That had all ended just four weeks ago. A lot of people had asked him why he'd bothered to stay until the end, since it was obvious what would happen. Many didn't understand why Landon hadn't bailed a long time ago.

He wouldn't explain himself because it wasn't his way. When he'd been badly injured some eight years ago, Joe had stayed at his side from the moment of the attack and had helped him to safety. They were behind enemy lines, and it was all Landon could do to make it as far as he had. Without Joe, Landon wouldn't be alive today. He knew that, and it was one unselfish heroic deed he was more than prepared to repay. He hadn't expected it to be this type of a repayment, but he'd never once entertained the idea of bailing, even when Joe himself tried to send Landon away.

Landon had just laughed at his friend and stated, "Like hell."

They'd been best friends forever, and, even now, Landon knew that aching void would take a long time to ease. Sometimes he thought he could almost hear Joe's voice in the back of his head, telling him that he was an idiot and to get back to the world of living, but for Landon? … He was doing the only living he could do right now.

As for this mission, the War Dog needed to be found and assured it was okay. He had a soft spot for all animals, but especially dogs. He would never treat a dog badly, nor would he treat his friend badly, so, to Landon, they were kind of linked. He knew it was foolish, but, hey, somebody had asked him to pitch in and to help, so he would do it, whether anybody else agreed with him or not.

His brother had shaken his head at him and told him, "I know I put your name forward, but you don't have to go."

"Of course I don't," Landon agreed. "But you and I both know I need something else to think about right now."

At that, his brother had nodded once and shut up. "I guess that's why I thought about you in the first place," he noted. "I knew you needed to get out of this rut you're in."

"You're right," Landon replied. "But that *rut* is also something that'll require some time to heal."

"Of course it will," Harper noted in a rough tone. "Joe was a special guy. I often wondered if there wasn't something, you know, closer with the two of you."

He had stared at his brother for a moment, then figured out what he said without saying it. "Well, that's a no. We were always best friends. Then, after he saved my life, no way I wouldn't be there for him."

"I get that," Harper added, with a shrug. "I just wondered, when it went on for two years."

"Death didn't give me a timetable. I didn't care if it was two days or twenty years. I wouldn't bail on him in his final days, unless I died first or went into a coma or something. So who else but me would take care of him in the meantime?" Landon asked.

"You know his parents are gone. His brother was gone. Joe was alone. Now, could I have put him in a VA center somewhere? Sure, I could have. Could I have put him in a hospice facility? Absolutely. Or I could do what I did, ... which was stay by his side, making sure he was getting the best care he could get. This is a man who did everything he could to save my life. I wouldn't do any less than *everything* I could for him."

His brother nodded. "I'm sorry it worked out the way it

did."

"Me too," Landon replied in a rough tone. "This may be just a simple road trip, but it's something else to occupy my mind. I'll figure out what happened to the War Dog if I can, and if I can't? Well, … I can't. The dog could be dead for all we know."

"I know, but I sure hope not," his brother murmured.

"You and me both," Landon noted. "We both have the same love for animals."

"Maybe we should get together and do something with that?" Harper suggested.

"Like what?"

"I don't know. Maybe we could do a rescue or set up some kind of a training center or something?"

Landon looked at his brother, with interest. "We're both walking right now," Landon stated, "not very well and not easily, but it's something we can talk about. I've often wondered about doing something with animals, and I guess, between us, we do have some family money we could put toward a new venture."

His brother nodded enthusiastically. "I wouldn't be against it, you know that," he replied. "Hell, I'd be doing this *rescue Chica* job myself, if it weren't for my surgery coming up."

At that, Landon frowned. "Maybe I should stay here and help you out."

"No, you don't," he disagreed immediately. "First off, I don't know that I'll need any help, and, second, I am not Joe. Even if I do end up falling down a rabbit hole over the surgery, it's not on you to look after me."

He didn't really like his brother's answer at the time or even later, but it was one that Landon had accepted. And now, here he was, ... driving toward a hospital to talk to somebody involved with a War Dog that had gone missing. He shook his head at that. When his phone rang, he turned down the radio and swiped the Call button. "Landon here. What's up?"

"It's Badger," he stated. "I just patched through some more information."

"Good enough. Don't suppose there was a sighting or something like that in any of it?"

"Nope, not yet," he replied, "but we've got a call out to the public, and it's being advertised on the local media in case anybody has seen Chica."

"That might stir up some interest," Landon said.

"Often, if we need to do something like this, just the fact that it's a War Dog now stateside and trying to retire for a few good years is what brings out the sympathetic nature in people."

"Of course," Landon agreed, "and this one is also injured, right?"

"That back leg will never stand her in good stead and of course she's missing a half a paw adding to her mobility issues. She'll always be lame, and we don't know what other problems she might have had more recently, when she was being driven up to the Canadian border."

"Right," Landon noted. "I've been doing some research and reading up on that project, since I agreed to do this job. I'm quite surprised at the number of dogs that go through the country, heading to Canada."

"Hundreds and hundreds a year," Badger stated.

"I'll do my best to find out what happened to her. I'm heading toward the hospital, where Charlie is now."

"Charlie's in the hospital?" he asked, his voice sharp.

"Yes," Landon confirmed. "I found out when I phoned his mother. He got hit by a car a few days ago. I was able to call the hospital, and they are pulling him out of the coma they had him in, as he's doing much better, but it'll still be a while yet."

"So …"

"So, I decided that, since I had to go in that direction anyway to get an eye on the location where the dog went missing and to see if the locals might have seen Chica, I figured I'd run past the hospital as well."

"Ah, so you're on your way to the hospital, and then you'll head out to where the War Dog was last seen?"

"Yes. I mean, there's really no other helpful information so far, is there?"

"No, nothing yet," Badger admitted. "We can hope that something comes from our media program, but it's hard to say."

"It also depends on how well the media handles it, since it's a freebie, I assume."

"Exactly, which means we're at their mercy in terms of being given the right coverage. But again, most of the time, when it comes to something like this, people tend to be very generous."

"That's a good thing. Otherwise, from my online search, I don't see a whole lot of places for Chica to have disappeared to in that general location."

"No, that's not quite true. There are lots of copses, parklands, and the river, so quite a bit of space where she might have initially run off to. What would have happened after that, I don't know. It's a heavily populated area, and she might have been picked up, or somebody might have even shot her. We just don't know any of the details yet."

"Yeah, you're not giving me a whole lot to go on."

"Nope, we're not. Sorry about that," Badger admitted cheerfully, "but that seems to be how it goes sometimes. When you get to the hospital, give us a buzz, and let us know if you get a chance to talk to Charlie."

"So, am I checking in just so you can keep an eye on me?" he asked. "Is it a trust thing, or am I checking in because you want to know how it's going?"

"You're military. We know your brother. Plus, we already checked you out with your former commanding officer."

Landon laughed. "I would expect no less."

Badger continued. "You're golden. You're checking in because we want to know how it's going," Badger confirmed, unoffended. "We're not into looking over your shoulder, but we also need to make sure you're capable of safely doing what we've requested."

"Got it." Then Landon sighed. "For the record, I'm physically capable, and I'm just starting the road trip now."

"Have you got your dogs with you?" Badger asked, with a note of humor.

"Absolutely," he said, "they go everywhere with me, if they can. And, on a road trip like this, it's not a bad idea. They keep me company."

"Not to mention the fact that the War Dog in question might get on better, or be easier to approach, if you have other dogs with you."

"That thought did occur to me too," Landon shared cheerfully. "Got to find her first though."

"Right," Badger agreed. "On that note, I'll leave you to it."

SABRINA WELLS WALKED in and smiled at Angela. "Hey, I was wondering if you had time for lunch today?"

Angela shook her head. "Man, we're really swamped. I'll be lucky if I get lunch at all."

"How about I go pick up something then?" Sabrina asked. "Then you can put me to work when I get back."

She rolled her eyes at that. "You really don't want to say that too loud."

"Hey, I don't mind. I'm done with my shift and tired, but I'm not quite ready to go home and crash yet."

"Says you." Angela laughed. "You'll get home, and you won't even have two minutes to yourself, before you'll be out."

"I'll walk over to the deli right now and get a couple sandwiches, one for you and one for me."

A man in the background asked, "Hey, would you mind picking up a third?" She realized it was Dave, the veterinarian.

"Will do," Sabrina replied; then she headed to the deli. It was busy, being lunchtime, and normally she would prefer to sit inside and to just enjoy the ambience of happy people enjoying a nice break. But, for the moment, that wasn't meant to be. Things at the clinic were chaotic. So many animals were brought in on a regular basis that they had trouble keeping up. Some of the animals just needed veterinary care, but too many others were being dropped off and abandoned. The problem of unwanted animals was frustrating for everyone.

Sabrina had gotten hooked into visiting, when her friend Angela started working here out of the blue a few years back.

Now it was almost standard to come by for a visit to check and see how she was doing. More often than not, Sabrina would spend an hour and take the animals out for a walk, help socialize some of them, whatever needed to be done.

As a nurse, she had a lot of skills, but they were directed towards human patients, not animals. She worked at the local hospital, in the geriatric section, focused on meeting the special needs of that age group. It could be quite stressful sometimes. She came to the animal clinic to unwind and to visit the animals and to take the edge off. She had been best buddies with Angela since second grade, and it was pretty special that they were still close. Since they both worked well over full-time schedules, they both squeezed in time to spend together whenever they got a chance.

Angela had a partner now, whereas Sabrina was still single, something she didn't really mind. Whenever she did finally end up finding somebody, it would have to be someone pretty special who absolutely loved animals because that was pretty important to her. Angela had found another veterinarian as her partner, and that was huge. They were hoping that maybe the two vets—her boss and her partner— would find a solution to current problems at the clinic by consolidating resources.

At the moment they were wrangling over the costs involved of any merger. Sabrina understood that they had a lot to sort through, but surely it would help both vets—the one currently without a job and the one struggling to run the clinic on his own. If they could come to an agreement, they would both get where they needed to be and also help more animals and even remain solvent. It was in the hands of the lawyers at the moment, and Sabrina was no help in that department.

She just hoped it would all go smoothly. But that wasn't her problem. As she stepped up in line at the deli, she noted the guy standing ahead of her, trying to decide on what to order from the chalkboard menu on the wall.

As he asked the woman behind the counter what she would recommend, Sabrina leaned forward and told him, "Everything is good."

He looked back, flashed her a grin, and nodded. "Thanks for that. I've never been here before, but I'll take your word for it."

"Oh, in that case," she added, "you've got to get Marco's specialty."

At that, his eyebrow raised, and he looked at the posted menu, trying to see where Marco's specialty was listed.

Sabrina shrugged and noted, "It's not on the board. It's just something us locals know."

Immediately he nodded and turned to the counter again. "In that case, I guess I need a Marco's specialty." Then he frowned and added, "Make that two."

"That's a good decision," Sabrina said on a laugh. "Sometimes you just can't get enough of a good thing."

After paying, he nodded and stepped out of the way. "Thanks again."

"Hey, no problem," she murmured. She quickly ordered the three sandwiches she needed, as the waitress smiled at her. "Hey, I figured you'd be heading for bed now?"

"No can do. Things are crazy over at the vet clinic," she replied. "I must get back over there and help out."

"You're supposed to be off duty right now," Marco called out from the back. "You think I don't know you work nights at the hospital, and then you go and help at the vet clinic all the time?" He shook his head.

"If I can't have my own rescue," she explained, "I might as well go where I'm needed."

"Yeah, when you could also get some sleep," Marco yelled out.

She winced at that because he was always very loud when he spoke from the back, but she was used to it by now. As Marco walked toward the front counter, she murmured, "You know that I can't walk past an animal in need."

"I get it," he replied, "but you must do more for yourself too, you know? If you always help out for free, they'll never need to look for somebody else."

"I get that too," she said, with a laugh. "We're all doing fine though."

"Says you," he muttered, as he handed over a package to the stranger beside her, and then gave her the three sandwiches in her order. "I made them all to-go," he added, "but I put extra protein in yours, so make sure you get the right one."

She gave him a fat grin. "Hey, I can't mistake mine. You always add double onions and pickles too."

"Damn right," he stated, "it's the only way to have it."

With that, she headed toward the door, almost running into the same man who she'd talked to earlier. She quickly excused herself and stepped around him.

"Hey, it's just me, and apparently my big feet were in the way." He stepped outside with his to-go bag, then sniffed it. "Wow, that smells really good."

"I know. It's all good there," she said, with a smile. "I've got lunch for two other people at the vet clinic, and one of these is for me too."

He smirked. "And, so I hear, you're a nurse?"

She nodded. "Yeah, I work at the hospital, but I'm in

the elder care section."

"Ah, that can't be easy."

"No, it isn't, but I used to do hospice. This is definitely a little easier." Those words struck home, and he grimaced, as if he understood.

"I can't even imagine," he shared. "I ended up nursing a friend of mine for the last couple years, right through until his passing a few weeks back, and nothing was easy about it."

"No, especially when it's a friend," she noted. "Most people don't have any experience with death, until it's right there in front of them, and, without any kind of practical experience to rely on, it can be quite a challenge."

"It was," he agreed, "but I made it through. I know I'm a better person for it, but it wasn't an easy go-around." He lifted a hand and headed over to his truck.

She looked at all the shiny chrome on his vehicle and grinned. "That is such a guy truck."

Startled, he turned and said, "Sorry?"

She laughed. "I was just looking at all that chrome."

"Hey, a truck is supposed to have lots of chrome," he protested, but he was smiling.

"Maybe, but I always thought trucks were for heavy use, not to look fancy."

"This is a rental, while I visit with my brother. However, I have this exact same truck back home in New Mexico, which is covered in dirt." He chuckled.

"Says you," she teased. Then she lifted a hand and waved. "It was nice meeting you. Have a good day." She turned and headed back toward the vet clinic. She wasn't usually quite so friendly, except just something about him appealed to her.

But then maybe ... No, she didn't need to find a partner. It seemed like a long time since anybody had appealed in the way this guy did though. He drove off and honked the horn and lifted his hand. She smiled and waved in kind, watching sadly as he drove away. As she got up to the vet clinic, she stepped inside to find that things were a little bit calmer.

Sabrina smiled as she walked over to the reception desk and announced, "Hey, I picked up the sandwiches. Let me know if Angela has a minute."

"I don't know." The receptionist laughed. "It got a little hairy there for a while, but a couple people just came and picked up their animals, so things have calmed down a little bit. She's in the back, cleaning."

"Do you want to buzz her and tell her that I'm here?"

"Will do," she replied cheerfully.

And, with that, Angela came running out a few minutes later. "Oh, thank God, I'm starving."

"If you would eat a little more and bring a lunch," Sabrina suggested, "it wouldn't be so bad."

"It's just so insane right now," Angela admitted, raising both hands. "I know that next week it could be completely dull, and we'll be screaming for business, but right now? ... Wow!"

"And that's how it works," Sabrina confirmed, with a nod. "I've been here at times, when it's both." She handed over a sandwich to her friend and then one more. "This one's for Dave."

Angela immediately walked it back to Dave, then returned and asked, "Hey, you want to just sit outside for five and eat these?"

"I sure do." Sabrina sighed. "Otherwise, I might as well just go home and eat it there by myself."

"Right, we need to take a few minutes together at least." Angela shook her head and rotated her shoulders. "Sometimes it can just get so stressful."

"It's always the same at the hospital too." Sabrina shrugged. "We do what we can, but we can't always do everything."

Angela snorted at that. "How true." They sat outside on a bench up against the back wall in one of the dog runs. "It seems so funny to even sit here and eat this normally, without being completely surrounded by dogs."

"And you aren't overrun today."

"No, not now," Angela said. "The last one just got picked up before you pulled in. We did get a call about a dog picked up down the road. Apparently it's got an injured leg. The caller was asking questions about it but seemed more worried about the cost than anything," she shared. "I didn't talk to him myself, but that one could come in today."

"Hopefully they can afford it, so they bring in the poor dog."

"But you and I both know a lot of people can't, and if he's just picked up the dog, and it needed some help, that's a different story too. He won't have any loyalty to it."

Sabrina winced at that. "No, I hear you. Hopefully they'll do the right thing."

"Lately it tends to be to just drop it off, and hope we'll look after it."

"Which is exactly what you will do," Sabrina stated cheerfully.

"I know, but these two vets need to get their shit together and make a decision on what they'll do about the clinic," she snapped. "With a second vet working here, we could certainly hire more staff and do a lot more business, and, if we set it up properly, we might be able to, you know, … do more of the charity work."

"Yeah, you say that"—Sabrina laughed—"but I highly doubt that Dave wants to do more unpaid work."

"He's okay to do a certain portion all the time. It just seems like half the time we're on the run and overwhelmed with people. The rescue calls are the same way. We'll get no calls for two or three days, and then we'll get twelve all at once, and that kills us. It depends on what else is happening at the time as to how much we can handle. Lots of times it's a case of just having them brought in for evaluation and do the best we can. A real rescue could do a lot more."

"Sometimes all you can do is all you can do, you know?" Sabrina declared, as she stared down at her sandwich.

Angela looked over and winced. "Hey, I'm sorry. I'm just rattling on, without a thought about what you're going through."

"Don't worry about it," Sabrina said. "We've known for a while that Grandma would go sometime soon. When it happens, I'll get through it."

"I know, but I also know that you went into that department because your grandmother was there."

"Sure, but I'm not exactly telling people that because I don't necessarily want to get kicked out either."

"What will you do?"

"What can I do?" she replied. "I'll carry on the same as I always have. If it's her time, it's her time, and I'll make her passing as easy as I can. And then I …" She just stopped, shrugged. "I don't know what I'll do after that. Maybe change departments again."

"You don't like the department you're in any more than you liked hospice."

"No, both are pretty rough, particularly when you know the people."

"I'm surprised that you're still there."

"You know why I'm there," she replied, "because of Grandma. Yet her time is coming to an end, so, when it's over, I'll figure it out from there." She took another bite of her sandwich, hoping that her friend would get off the subject. As Sabrina looked around and sighed, she added, "There was a really cute guy at the deli today too."

"Ooh, he must have been," Angela noted, giving her a look. "Anything that gets your attention is huge."

"I didn't think I was quite that picky," she said, laughing.

"You didn't?" Angela asked, with a big grin.

"You grabbed the only good guy I've met recently," Sabrina teased. "So what are the rest of us supposed to do?"

"Nothing, except wait for the right guy to come along."

"Yeah, well, I'm a little tired of waiting. Besides, most of them don't like animals quite the way I do."

"Right, which is also why Jason is perfect for me," Angela murmured. "I wouldn't be at all upset if we had our own clinic. But I've already seen how much work it is, and we'd have to hire a ton of staff, so we're much better off to buy into something like what Dave has got going on here."

"So, what's the hold up?"

"Mostly the money. Dave wants more than we can really afford, and fair enough. Jason wants to talk to his father about it. Maybe they could come up with a little assistance to help get Jason started."

"That would be lovely if it happened," Sabrina noted.

"Jason would prefer that it happened another way, so he didn't feel indebted to his father, but everybody needs help sometimes."

"That is so true," Sabrina agreed. "So, if it's offered, I would take it."

"I think he probably would, but it's not been offered yet."

"Right, so it's a matter of waiting and hoping. And who knows? Maybe Dave will get to a place where he realizes he could go a little lower as well."

"Until then, we're stuck in that financial limbo," Angela shared. "You would think for the amount of business that we have here that Dave would be doing okay. Yet, of course, the amount of business just makes him think the actual partnership would be worth that much more."

"Of course he does," Sabrina said, with a smile. "I mean, he is human. He's also getting on in years and shouldn't be doing anywhere near as much as he normally does, I suspect."

"Yeah, but I wouldn't mention that if I were you."

"Learned that the hard way, did you?" she asked, laughing.

"Yeah, I did, as a matter of fact," Angela admitted. "He took immediate offense."

"Of course he would. He prides himself on this clinic that he has built from the ground up."

"Which I think is where the problem is," Angela guessed. "You know, he's very possessive and really wants to stay here and do what he's doing, but he also knows that it's getting harder to do solo."

"That makes sense."

"He's torn. There's that side of things that's looking very much like he wants to go forward with a partnership because he can see the value, but the other part of him doesn't want to let go of his baby or even share it, and that is holding him back."

At that, Sabrina could totally see how Dave was struggling with the concept. "More days like this—where it's crazy and overrun and chaotic—should help him to see the value of getting some extra help."

"That's the thing though because Jason doesn't want to just work for him. He wants in on a partnership."

"So, what about working for him to start?"

"Jason does come in every once in a while, but he doesn't really want to just be a vet. He wants to have an investment in the company."

Sabrina shrugged. "Hopefully you guys will work it out."

"Yeah, I just hope everybody can be sensible and not get too wound up about it. I just don't want it to be awkward, and I'm kind of in the middle, you know?" she pointed out.

Sabrina didn't know what to say about that because she could imagine that this could get very uncomfortable for her friend. "Hopefully you guys can figure something out," she said calmly and let it go. She finished her sandwich, then hopped up. "You know what? I think I'll do the right thing for a change and head home to get some sleep."

At that, Angela looked up and smiled. "I'd really like to see you do that. You don't take care of yourself very well sometimes."

"I've got my dogs at home to take care of too," she added, with a smile. Then she headed back into the clinic. After she collected the money from Dave for the sandwich, she headed back out with a wave goodbye to everybody.

CHAPTER 2

S ABRINA WAS WITHIN walking distance from her home to both the hospital and the vet clinic, and that made life a little easier for her too. She headed into the small home that she had owned since she bought it from her grandma a few years back. It needed a lot of work, but, hey, it was home, and it held a lot of good memories for her. Her grandma was currently in the last stage of her life at the same hospital where Sabrina worked.

Deaths in her family had happened once before, when her parents were killed in a car accident. Sabrina never thought she'd survive that, but she'd moved in with her grandma, and life for her had improved tremendously. Her grandma was always there for her, something Sabrina really appreciated, but, at the same time, she had grown very dependent on her and knew she would have a terrible time when her grandma passed away. How could she not?

She loved her dearly, and it meant everything to her that she could be there for her now, the same as her grandma had been there for Sabrina for so many years. But that didn't make this process any easier. It would be tough, no matter what.

One just didn't let go of an era and somebody you cared about without feeling that pain of loss. Everybody kept telling her not to get involved with her patients, but this was her grandma. There was no not-getting-involved in this case. She was already involved and had been all her life. She had no intention of stopping now.

When she got into her house, she quickly took her dogs, Snowball and Patches, out for a walk around the yard, wishing she had more room, while getting some quality time with them before she crashed. There was a large field not too far away, but she wasn't up for going over there just now. Thankfully she had a doggie door for them, what with her crazy schedule. And the automatic food dispenser was great, as was the water fountain for the dogs, directly connected to her plumbing. If she ever needed to leave town for a weekend, technically her dogs would be all right for a couple days. However, her best friend Angela could be called upon to check on them under those circumstances.

Calling the dogs back, she headed back inside to go lie down but got a phone call from work.

"Any chance you can come back in?" her supervisor asked in a hurried voice.

Sabrina closed her eyes and pinched the bridge of her nose, then murmured, "Damn."

"I know, right? You and me both," she replied. "We're swamped, and I just found out two nurses are sick and cannot come back this afternoon."

"Crap," Sabrina said, "I was just heading to bed."

"Yeah, about that. … You didn't go to bed as soon as you got home, did you? Otherwise you would've gotten a whole five minutes," she pointed out in that same dry tone. "So, is it yes or no?"

"Yes," she muttered, for a couple reasons. "I need the overtime. I've always got those animals to help out."

"That's one of the reasons why I'm calling you," her supervisor admitted. "You spend the money wisely for good and don't just fritter it away, like some do. But, if you're too tired, you can't do another shift."

"Is it a full shift?"

"I might get by with half a shift. I'm still making phone calls."

"Okay, I'm coming." She headed back to the hospital. At least she got lunch this time. Lots of days, she didn't get even that. As she reached the hospital parking lot, she saw the huge beautiful shiny truck she'd seen earlier. Surprised, she watched as the man paced around in the parking lot, talking to somebody on the phone.

She didn't have time to wait because she needed to get inside, but he put away his phone just as she was walking by.

He turned and looked at her in surprise. "Hey."

She smiled. "Hey, I didn't know you were coming here."

"I didn't know you were either." He frowned. "But I guess it makes sense, as you said you worked at the hospital."

"Absolutely. Are you here to see somebody?"

He nodded. "Yeah, a guy named Charlie. He came in a few days ago."

She winced. "I don't know anybody in the other areas of the hospital, but you can get the room information from the nurses' station."

"I'm working on it," he stated. "We're all waiting to see if we can get the doctor's permission for visitors. Charlie woke up this morning, after being in a medically induced coma for a few days. So I'm not sure if he's in any kind of shape to talk."

"Ah, and I just got called back for a second shift."

"After you've already done one?" he asked, his gaze locking on hers.

"Yeah, but two staff nurses called out sick, so they're very short-handed."

He nodded slowly. "And, of course, quality of care requires bodies."

"Warm bodies that can do something, hopefully." She laughed. "Even if they can't do much, they're still warm, and our patients need that."

"Good luck with that. I've done lots of missions where I didn't get my quarter of sleep, and it sucks, and the longer it goes on, the worse it gets."

She stared at him. "Military?"

"Navy." He smiled.

She nodded. "I get it. Good luck with your friend."

With a wave, she quickly raced up to her department, knowing it would be a really long and brutal day. But she'd agreed to be here, so nothing to do but her very best to provide full and quality care because that is who she was and that was what every patient deserved.

WITH BADGER'S HELP, Landon now stood at Charlie's doorway. Landon had finally been given permission to go in and to talk to Charlie, who was staring aimlessly around the room. "Hey." Landon knocked gently on the doorframe.

Charlie's head immediately turned, as he looked at him and asked, "Do I know you?"

"No," Landon replied. "I'm here for the war department. I need to know about the lost War Dog, Chica."

At that, Charlie's eyebrows rose high. "Yeah, I wish I knew what the hell to say about that," he replied, as he relaxed back on the bed. "It was a pretty scary time, when I realized they were gone."

"So three went missing at the time?"

"Yes, although we have since found the other two."

"That changes things slightly," Landon noted in relief. "I'm glad to hear you have those two back. But nothing on the other one, *huh*?"

He shook his head. "And Chica was pretty easy to get along with too. She was a beautiful dog, and all I can think of is that somebody stole her from the truck."

"That's possible," Landon noted. "It's certainly not unheard of in any case."

"No, it happens way too much," Charlie admitted. "I just feel responsible, since she was in my care at the time."

Landon nodded. "You didn't see anybody hanging around?"

He shook his head. "No, I didn't. The whole thing was kind of a mess. I was approaching the border crossing and realized I was missing some of the paperwork I needed. I was all flustered and was trying to get ahold of people to figure out what I was supposed to do, in between taking dogs out to stretch their legs and to go to the bathroom, since they were transported in those cages. I didn't have a place to let them all out." He raised his palms. "So it just wasn't a good scenario. And then, when something like that happens, ... I felt even worse. Well, never mind that." He gave a wave of his hand. "I don't need to bore you with details, but obviously it wasn't a good scenario."

"Got it," Landon replied. "I would like to know anything you can tell me about what happened that day. And where were you exactly, and what were you doing when?"

"I was at the border," he began, "and I was in this big parking lot, trying to figure out what to do about the paperwork, still waiting for a callback. I took all the dogs out to stretch their legs and to go to the bathroom. Put them all back into the truck. I was stressed to the max, but I headed over to the closest restaurant, where I grabbed some food for me and bought a bunch of burgers for the dogs. I was trying to figure out what to do next, when I got back to the truck and found I had three dogs missing.

"They were the last three cages in the truck, and that just made it worse. Because they were the only ones that someone could potentially see. For all I know, it was some do-gooder who thought the dogs were headed for some horrible life. If it had been only one gone, I would have wondered whether I had left the cage unlatched or something, but not three. Somebody opened those cages. I don't know who was involved in it or why," His frustration was evident in his voice. "Believe me. I've felt like shit ever since."

"I'm not here to blame you, Charlie," Landon stated. "And obviously you're in a situation right now where you really need to focus on your health."

"Right." Charlie sighed, as he relaxed into his hospital bed. "It's not like I needed this either."

"So I gather you continued on to Canada."

"Yeah, so I finally got a callback, and they ended up texting me photos of the paperwork I didn't have. So, with still no sign of the missing dogs, I figured I better deal with the ones I had, and I went ahead and crossed and got the rest of the dogs delivered."

"That makes sense," Landon replied.

"Two days later, I got a call from somebody with immigration at the border station, saying that they'd had a report of a couple dogs being sighted in the area. So I headed back, and, with some help from some locals, I managed to recover the other two that were missing. All the reports had been of two dogs together, so it seemed like Chica wasn't with the others, at least not for long. Anyway, with no luck finding her, I took the two others across to Canada, but I never got a chance to go back and try to find Chica."

"So, out of over one hundred dogs, only the one is missing."

He nodded. "Yeah, but that one is one too many," he said.

"Where did all these dogs get collected from?"

"All across the United States," he replied, sounding surprised. "Often we get them coming in large groups from one particular place, but, in this case, they were coming from multiple locations because we do all the vet checks and passports and get all the shots in order to get them across the country. Then we take them up to Canada, and this time, for some reason, we had a problem, although I've done this exact same trip what? Maybe five times already." He flung up his arms in frustration, and he immediately winced. "Wow, I really shouldn't be moving around so much."

"Yeah, I understand you were hit by a car?"

"I'd parked on a street, and I guess I was tired and wasn't watching and stepped right into traffic," he reported miserably. "Now I'm trying to get back on my feet."

"I'm really sorry to hear about that," Landon replied.

The guy shrugged. "It was my own damn fault, but it's a bummer because I was hoping to head out between trips and see if I could find the dog."

"That's exactly what I'm planning on doing," Landon stated. "I'm really hoping I'll track her down."

"What will you do if you find her?" he asked, puzzled.

"Not sure yet," Landon admitted. "However, once I find

out what her status is and how she's doing, then I'll report back to the boss." He wasn't exactly sure what Badger would do at that point in time. Landon hadn't asked about such a contingency, which was kind of foolish on his part.

"At least the dog will get some care then. That foot of hers is kind of buggered up," Charlie noted. "And, while I didn't have much time with her, her other leg is lame, like from an old injury or something."

"How lame? Like could she have run for ten miles?"

"I don't know," Charlie replied. "Maybe she's got better training than I do, but, with that leg in that kind of condition, I think it would be painful."

"Painful doesn't mean they won't do it though. Did you get any intel on what her history was or anything?"

He shook his head at that. "No. She was dropped off as one of the animals to go to Canada, but, when I tried to find out more about her, all I got was that somebody had dumped her off, saying that she was no good. I mean, how could anybody do that?" he asked, anger in his voice. "Every animal is good, and just because this dog had some health issues didn't mean it wasn't worth saving."

"Of course not, but I imagine it's easier to move healthier animals across the border."

"Sure, but we move animals of all kinds across the border," he stated. "To be honest, that's one of our best avenues of placing them." Charlie lowered his voice and said, "The Canadians take hundreds, hundreds of them every year. I would make that run ten times a year if I thought I could. We'd eventually have more problem finding people to adopt them, but, so far, we've never gone up there and not had all of them get homes," he shared. "It might take us a little bit longer in some instances, but we've done really well there."

"It's kind of sad that you must go to Canada in order to place these animals, especially ones that have worked so hard for our country."

"I know, right?" Charlie agreed. "Just so many animals in the US don't get the proper medical attention. They don't get fixed, and then we have this overrun problem, and nobody seems to care." He shook his head. "I know that's a harsh judgment because lots of people care. However, when I move approximately five hundred a year across the border to find people willing to foster or to adopt them, it breaks my heart. At the same time," he added, "I don't want to do anything to jeopardize the process because it works, and we can save all kinds of lives. so it is what it is."

"Got it," Landon noted. "So you don't really know where the dog came from, and you're not exactly sure where it went."

At that, Charlie winced. "And that sucks, doesn't it? It sounds like I'm making it all up."

"Are you?" he asked.

"No, no, no. I'm not," he stated earnestly. "I just feel shitty about it."

"I got that, so I'll need to talk to your boss. I just want to confirm all the details that you've given me," he explained, "so I can move on from here. I'll take a run up to where you were when they went missing, so if you want to give me the details on that, I'd really appreciate it. And, hey, what about the War Dog's personality? What was Chica like? Anything you could think of to make it easier for me to get her to trust me?"

"You really think you'll find her?"

"I sure hope so." He stared at Charlie. "That's my intention. And sure, maybe it's a long shot, but I've got to give it a try, right?"

At that, Charlie smiled. "In that case, let's see if I can draw you a map."

"Do I need a map?" he asked curiously.

"I don't know but maybe," he told him. "I'm a little rattled, and who knows if I've given you all the details. My head is buzzing pretty badly."

Landon nodded and guessed that Charlie was probably in his early sixties. "Sounds like that hit-and-run rattled you pretty good too."

"It sure did," he agreed and then yawned and frowned. "Honestly I'm struggling to even stay awake now."

"Yeah, and I promised the doctors I wouldn't stay too long," Landon shared, "so let's get this done. Then I can run up and see what I can find."

"Will you let me know?" he asked.

"Absolutely, but I must find her first to tell anybody anything." Quickly grabbing pen and paper from the nurse's station, Landon came back to see Charlie struggling against sleep. Landon got the information he needed from Charlie and a crude map. "You rest now, Charlie. I'll contact you as soon as I find out anything."

And, with that, he stepped back out of the room. Charlie had yawned several times, even as Landon stood in the doorway studying him, but Landon didn't find any deceit in his voice or in any of the information he'd provided.

He hoped it was accurate. Nothing worse than trying to make a plan for your next step with bad intel. He obviously knew what his next step was, but he didn't want to go through all that trouble of searching an area if this Charlie guy had something else going on.

Landon really hoped not, but it was always one of those

decisions that felt a little sketchy. He hated when he wasn't exactly sure what he should do. He still had that lingering sense of doubt, but, as he studied the man shuffling in the bed, trying to get comfortable, Landon realized that Charlie was probably exactly who and what he seemed to be.

Stepping into a waiting room, Landon made a quick call to Charlie's boss, who confirmed what the injured man had told Landon. She didn't have any more information on the location of the dog but did add that it had been a last-minute solution to put Chica on the truck going up to Canada. She also confirmed that the cross-country transport was a common practice and that they did it several times a year. He shook his head at that because it just seemed crazy that Americans weren't looking after their own, but apparently the Canadians had been doing this for years, and it was a system that worked very well.

She was really anxious that nothing mess it up because they had hundreds more already looking toward the next load.

And, with that, Landon contacted Badger to give him an update as to how far he had gotten, as he slowly wandered down the hallway toward his truck. By the time he put away his phone, he realized he must have taken a wrong turn, and he was in a completely different part of the hospital.

He frowned, did a full turn, and just as he went to walk up to a counter to ask for directions, a woman stepped up and then chuckled. "Okay, now three times can't be a coincidence."

He looked back to see the woman from the sandwich shop. He smiled at her. "I was talking on the phone with my boss, and I completely lost track of where I was, and now ... I'm lost."

"That's easy to do in this hospital," she declared, with an eye roll. "You're not the first person."

"So how do I get back to the parking lot?" he asked, raising his hands. "It seems foolish to admit I got lost *inside* the building."

She grinned and took him to a window at the end of the hallway, then pointed out where the parking lot was.

Landon frowned. "I know I was talking and walking for a while, but, jeez, I didn't think I'd managed to travel that far."

"A hallway connects the two buildings," she explained, "so if you ended up there, you wouldn't even have realized that you left one building for another, but you would have already been heading in this direction."

"Okay, but this doesn't bode well for my trip though."

"What trip?" she asked. "Did you get to see the guy you hoped to see?"

He nodded. "Yeah, I came here because Charlie was taking a load of dogs up to Canada, and one of them, a War Dog, somehow got lost."

Her eyebrows shot up. "Lost?" she asked cautiously.

He winced and nodded. "Yeah, lost. Apparently anyway." Then he explained the little bit that he knew about the situation.

"Oh my, I hope you find the poor thing."

"That's my intention." He smiled. "I just don't know what all will be involved in getting there."

She nodded. Pointing down the hallway, she began to escort him to his truck. "I volunteer at a vet clinic here in town," she added. "That's who I was getting all the sandwiches for this morning. Animals get dropped off there all the time."

"How can somebody do that?" he asked, staring at her. "I have three dogs of my own out in the truck right now."

"Three?" she repeated, her eyebrows shooting up again.

He nodded. "Chihuahuas." She gave him a tiny smirk. "Don't say it," he warned her in good humor, even as he narrowed his gaze at her.

"Say what?" she teased, obviously trying hard to keep a straight face.

"That I don't look like a guy who would have Chihuahuas."

She nodded. "You said it, not me." She gave him a huge smile. "But, hey, at least you've got dogs."

"Always had dogs," he confirmed. "Love them. Absolutely love them."

"So do I. I have two at home myself, and I'm absolutely thrilled that you're searching for this poor dog," she stated. "Since I work for free at the vet clinic, I can't volunteer any of their services, but I know that we're always more than happy to help out, if you end up in a spot of trouble and the dog needs somebody to look after it."

He shrugged. "I hope not. I don't know what the score will be. Chica's been lost a couple months now, so not sure what she's already been through since then. Plus, she had her own war wounds to heal from. So I'm really hoping somebody has been good to her in the interim."

She nodded. "If you do find Chica, let me know."

"How will I do that?" he asked, looking at her. "You haven't given me your number."

"In the interest of helping out an animal, I can do that. This is for the vet clinic."

"What about afterhours?"

She nodded. "Fine, here's my cell. Don't abuse it."

He grinned at her. "Never. Unless it's a case of a dog that needs help."

At that, her smile fell away. "If that's the case, you call me. Where was she lost? How far away is it from here?"

He shrugged. "Not too far. I just got a location at the Canadian border where it was last seen."

She frowned at that. "You know what? I feel like I heard rumors about a wounded dog being picked up somewhere near here."

He stared at her. "I don't suppose you have a way to chase down those rumors?"

She shook her head slowly. "No, but now it'll really bug me until I figure it out."

"If you do"—he pulled out his phone again and quickly sent her a text—"that's my number. I'm Landon. Let me know if you hear anything."

"Sure. And I'm Sabrina. What'll happen to the dog if you do find her?"

"First off," Landon noted, "we need to make sure that she's okay and gets whatever medical treatment she needs. It's missing half a paw already, so it's very distinctive. Plus, she's also had multiple breaks in her back leg, so she limps."

"Right, and there's a fine distinction with that too."

"She's also a highly trained War Dog. She's used to being in difficult situations and still going strong, so she won't necessarily look like she's injured or down to that extent."

She stared at him for a long moment. "Kind of like you, huh?"

He winced at that. "Is that really how I come across?" he asked in mock horror. "Like I'm a lame dog, one step away from being put down?"

She frowned, then burst out laughing. "*Uh*, no, that's

the last thing I would say about you." Still snickering, she explained, "You're more like a junkyard dog than a retired War Dog, and you look like you've seen better times in your life."

"Yeah," he agreed. "I'm still dealing with losing that friend of mine."

At that, her smile sobered. "I'm sorry. I deal with loss at my work all the time, and it's never easy, even when you haven't gotten to know them very well yet."

"Nope, not easy," he confirmed, "and, just when you think you've got a handle on it, something comes out of the blue and throws you for a loop."

"Agreed," she replied, "but you're doing really well."

He smiled at her. "How would you know that?" he asked in a teasing manner.

"Hey, I can see that you're doing well," she stated. "I have really good instincts."

"I hope so," he said. They had reached the front door, where Landon had entered. "And, if you do hear anything about the dog, let me know."

"Will do." And she stood at the entrance and watched as the most interesting man she'd met in a very long time got into his vehicle and drove off.

CHAPTER 3

WHEN SABRINA FINISHED her shift—which ended up being more like half a shift thankfully—she was exhausted but couldn't stop thinking about the man, Landon, whose number she now had in her phone. It was unlike her to give her number to anyone, and it worried her that she'd offered it so easily.

Maybe he was on the up-and-up, or maybe not, but it wasn't like her to trust someone like that so damn fast. She sighed as she headed back home.

"You're an idiot, and you know that," she muttered. Once home, she wanted to contact Angela and ask her if she'd heard anything about a War Dog or about a dog with a missing paw. Landon had been right in saying that it was a very distinctive injury, so, with any luck, somebody might have seen it and recognized that something was off about it and maybe would get the dog some help for it.

As soon as she got home, she had a quick shower and put on some loungewear because, after a double shift, she was too tired to do more than that. Slumping down into her chair, she quickly contacted Angela.

"Hey, what happened to you?" Angela asked. "You sound thrashed."

"I am thrashed," Sabrina murmured. "I got called back in for another half shift."

"Damn it, girl," Angela muttered. "You've got to stop doing that."

"How can I?" She yawned. "When people need me, you know I have a problem turning them down."

"But do they need you *specifically*," Angela asked, "or do they just call you first because they know you'll end up going. I worry that sometimes they take advantage of you."

She winced at that. "I won't argue over semantics, but listen. Remember I was telling you about that guy I met at the deli?"

"How could I forget?" she replied. "That's the only guy I've seen you excited about in a very long time."

"I know, right? Anyway I saw him again at the hospital."

"What? Oh my God, did he follow you?" she asked in a sharp voice.

"No, of course not. He was there to see a man who was in a car accident a few days ago."

"Wait, so how did you happen to see him again? That's not anywhere near your department, is it?" she asked, still confused.

"First in the parking lot and later, he took a wrong turn and was lost in the hospital."

"*Sure* he was," Angela muttered, once again in that doubting voice.

"Hey, it happens more than you'd think," Sabrina argued. "You have no idea how many people get distracted and wander off and need help finding their way back to where they belong—or just out of the building. I mean, I know that last hospital expansion was necessary, but it sure made things a lot more confusing. Especially where the signage is concerned."

"They're supposed to get those fixed, aren't they?"

"Supposedly, but I feel like it's on this giant list of things to do, but the priority won't ever be high enough for it to get done, you know? And that simple step would save all the staff so much time. It boggles the mind what they consider important."

"Good point," Angela muttered. "Anyway, so what's this about the guy?"

She quickly told Angela about the War Dog.

Angela cleared her throat. "You don't happen to have any way to verify what he said, do you?" she asked slowly.

Sabrina winced at that. "No, and could you just once not be quite so cautious?"

"And could you once not be quite so gullible?" she snapped back immediately.

Sabrina groaned. "I don't want to fight with you. I was hoping that you would take into consideration the fact that this could be the real thing. So, if you hear anything about the dog, let me know. I didn't even ask him what breed it was, and I don't know anything besides its injuries."

"If it's a War Dog," she noted, "it could suffer from anything."

"No, you're right. I'll text him and find out."

"Whoa, whoa, whoa. No way. I'll call you right back." And she hung up.

Sabrina winced because she knew her best friend would be more upset at her for contacting this guy, but, as soon as she had an excuse to text him, she was more than willing to. And that said a lot about her own headspace too. Quickly typing a text, she asked him about the breed of the dog. The answer came back pretty fast too. She smiled when she got his response.

Malinois, a dark shepherd-looking dog.

And, if that wasn't enough, she ended up getting another text, and this time with a picture. Her heart softened immediately when she saw the beautiful animal on her phone, yet the dog also looked like she'd had better days.

She whispered out loud, "Hey, sweetheart. I hope you can be found." She sent Landon back a text. **Thanks. I was looking for something to send to the vet's office, so they could keep an eye out for her. The chances of her being brought in here are pretty slim though.**
Stranger things have happened.

She wasn't sure what that meant, but she was willing to keep an open mind about it. Then she phoned Angela back.

"You texted him, didn't you?" Angela asked in an ominous tone.

"Yep, I did, and I'm sending you a picture. It's a Malinois. The look in her eyes is breaking my heart."

"Yeah, so you know about those creepy guys in the van with the candy for the kids? Well, in your case, it'll be the lost puppy in the field."

She smiled at that. "He didn't try to lure me into his vehicle. There was nothing like that."

"Sure, *this time*," Angela replied, "but you're really bad about this."

"I am not," she said crossly. "Just stop it. He's gone to the border, trying to track it down now, so it's hardly an issue at the moment."

At that, Angela was slightly mollified. "Yeah, but you've got to watch out for yourself, if he comes back."

"Maybe so," she stated. "On the other hand, I'm not against having a chance to get to know this guy."

At that, Angela gasped. "Seriously? You don't even know him."

"How will I ever get to know him if I don't *get to know him*," she said in exasperation. "I get it. You're worried about me."

"Yeah, remember the last guy?"

She winced at that. "Sure, of course I remember. How could I forget? He was two bricks short of crazy," she muttered. "But that doesn't mean that every other guy I meet will be like that."

"No, maybe not," Angela mumbled. "I just don't want you hurt again."

"I don't want to get hurt either," she muttered. "So let's just keep things under control."

"I'd feel better if you hadn't given him your number."

"I gave him my number. I didn't give him where I lived or anything else," she explained. "I can always block it if he bothers me."

At that, her friend went quiet. "Fine, but I don't think it'll be enough."

"What do you mean, it won't be enough?"

"I think he's already caught your interest."

"I've already told you that he has, but that doesn't mean I'm such a desperate idiot that I'll go crazy over him."

"Maybe not," she agreed, "but you have this tendency to fall quick and to fall hard."

"Yeah, in high school," she snapped in exasperation.

"Yep, I know. Please just be careful." And, with that, her friend rang off.

Sabrina texted him back, unable to help herself. **Lovely dog.** His reply surprised her in its speed, but then maybe he felt about animals the same way she did.

Beautiful animal. Now I just need to find her, but I don't have any guarantee that she's still anywhere near

the same location where she was first lost.

Sabrina frowned at that, meaning the War Dog could be anywhere by now. She quickly responded back. **I contacted the vet's office to warn them in case anything like her shows up here.** Expecting either a text or nothing in reply, she was surprised when her phone rang.

She answered it hesitantly, then he immediately said, "Thank you for doing that."

She smiled. "Hey, anything for an animal, right? No problem."

He chuckled. "Yeah, I'm the same way, which is why I'm out here doing what I'm doing."

"Considering you've spent a lifetime in service, it makes sense that you would still be serving, one way or another," she murmured.

He paused for a moment. "I did tell you about being in the navy, didn't I?"

"Yep, you sure did. So you don't think this Charlie guy has anything to do with Chica's disappearance?"

"It occurred to me before I saw him, but I didn't get that kind of vibe from him while I was there," he stated cautiously. "That doesn't mean that I haven't been fooled before though."

She winced at that. "That's life, kind of, isn't it?"

"It is, unfortunately. Just when you think you've got a good handle on humanity, you come up against somebody not so great."

"But what would be in it for Charlie to take her?" she asked. "I mean, as long as it's well cared for and has a home, that's all that matters, right?"

"Exactly. Getting these dogs to a good home that will tend to their needs is all the war department cares about," he said. "They are really good animals and can be trained further, although in her case, she needs a pretty leisurely life, due to her injuries."

"Right." Sabrina frowned. "She needs a special home."

"I'll check in with Charlie again in a little while anyway," he murmured. "But first off, he needs to heal up a bit and maybe consider the fact that the war department is here checking up on Chica. If his story stays the same when I show up to chat with him next time, I'll feel better."

She stared down into her phone. "I didn't think about that," she noted. "It's a little disturbing to think that somebody might have deliberately had something to do with this."

"Somebody definitely did, but we don't know if the dog was just let out of the cage to run free because somebody thought that maybe they would like her and she would be better off with them." He stopped then and added, "Honestly there's any number of scenarios that could apply. And the parking lot where the dog went missing had no cameras. We may never know who started this chain of events."

"Got it. I'll try not to worry, now that you've put the poor thing in my head."

"I'm working on it."

"I know. If I hear anything, I'll let you know." And, with that, she hung up, but the smile stayed on her face. She whispered out to the world around her, "Chica, wherever you are, girl, somebody is coming for you. Just stay healthy and stay strong. He'll be there soon."

IT WAS TOO much to hope that the dog would be anywhere

in the neighborhood of where she went missing, but Landon also had no way to know what she'd do, since it was a new location for her. She may have stayed around, hoping that somebody she knew would come back and get her. Or she may have also hated being in the cage enough that she didn't want to be anywhere close by.

He wandered around in the woods backing up the parking lot for a while, then stopped off at the coffee shop and asked if anybody had seen the dog.

The owner shook his head at the photo of Chica, yet frowned at Landon. "You know what? Somebody came through here, asking about a lost dog a week or so ago," he replied. "It never really occurred to me that anybody would still be looking for it."

"We're always looking for War Dogs," Landon replied in a strong voice. "This animal has already done enough time in rough wartime circumstances that she deserves whatever chance for a good life we can give her."

The owner nodded. "I'm not arguing with you there. I served myself, and honestly it was shitshow from start to finish."

Landon nodded. "Unfortunately we see that way too often."

The owner added, "Look. If you give me your number, I'll give you a call if she shows up here or I hear anything. So, nobody has seen any sign of her then?"

"No, but I did hear that somebody was talking about having picked up a dog that was injured. Supposedly he's a trucker who apparently goes back and forth in this route a lot of the time. I'd still like to talk to him," he added, "to check it out, in case that's the dog I'm looking for."

"I suspect I know who you mean," the owner noted.

"He comes through my place pretty regularly. And I did see him recently, walking a dog. Didn't really look like your photo though."

"Got it," Landon replied. "I'm here to try and pick her up and to do whatever we need to do to get her medical attention, if she needs it. I was really surprised she was in that group that went to Canada as it was."

The coffee shop owner nodded at that. "Me too. I mean, I get that it looked a little bit on the lame side, but it didn't look injured when I saw it, just walking her on a leash." He walked a few steps away and then pointed outside. "Guess what? That's the guy right there." And they watched as a delivery truck drove up.

"Got it," Landon agreed, "I don't want to lose track of the only lead I've got."

"No, of course not," he murmured. "A War Dog deserves our best effort."

"It absolutely does," Landon said, as he stepped outside and watched as the man pulled up, got out, and left the vehicle. "Doesn't look like he's leaving anything inside."

"A lot of guys with dogs just come in, pick up a few things, and then head back out again, without letting their dogs out."

"Right. While he's in here, let me go take a quick look at the vehicle, and then maybe I'll come in and have a talk with him myself."

"You'll need to make it real quick. He generally doesn't stay around long."

"Good enough." Landon dashed outside, heading around to the parking lot where the man had left his truck. As he walked up to the side of the vehicle, he watched as the other man headed into the coffee shop. Then Landon checked around the vehicle and inside, looking to see if there was any sign of a dog. But nothing stood out. Frowning, he headed back toward the coffee shop. As he walked in, the owner was talking to the trucker.

When Landon stepped inside, the owner pointed. "This is the guy who's looking for that shepherd."

At that, the trucker turned, looked at him, and frowned. "What difference does it make about a shepherd?" he asked, puzzled.

"It's a War Dog, and the defense department is trying to find out what happened to it."

The other man's eyebrow shot up. "A War Dog? Really? I mean, she's pretty lame."

"Which is exactly why we're trying to find out what happened to her," he replied. "So any help you can give us would be appreciated."

He shrugged. "Yeah, I picked up a dog a while ago, but it took off on me."

"It ran off, you mean?"

"Yeah, I stopped to take a leak, and, man, it bolted."

"Any idea where you were?"

"Sure do." He motioned down the highway. "Back down there, at that first halfway big town."

Landon stared at him. "I just came from there."

"Well, you better go back because that's where I was."

"Did you try to get her back in the vehicle?"

"I tried calling, baiting her with food, but she didn't look too interested. I couldn't get anywhere close." He gave a shrug. "She never really settled down in the truck either."

"Yeah, if they'd had her in cages for a lot of that traveling," Landon noted, "she might not take kindly to being cooped up again."

The trucker winced and nodded.

"So how was she doing?"

"She was friendly enough, but she looked like she was suffering. I fed her what I had for her in the truck, but I didn't have anything else really to give her. Then, once she bolted, it was all over. She seemed like a damn nice dog though," he said, with a second shrug. "I tried to get her back, but she wasn't having anything to do with it."

Landon studied the man for a long moment and nodded. "If you could tell me exactly where you saw her last, I'd really appreciate it."

"Sure, no problem." Then he proceeded to describe where he'd been, when the dog had jumped from the truck.

"Thanks for the help," Landon replied and looked over at the owner of the coffee shop. "You too."

The trucker just nodded, and the owner added, "Good luck. I really hope you find her. She's been to hell and back already and doesn't need any more bad news."

"No, I hear you there." Landon frowned. "She needs a few good comfortable years, not more trouble." On that note, they all agreed, and Landon took off for his truck at a run.

"Hang on, girl. I'm coming," he mumbled as he ran. *Right back to where I was*, he thought to himself, *but, hey, at least we have the last-known sighting, and it seems to be Chica.* As soon as he got into the truck, he quickly phoned Badger and gave him an update.

"That's good news," Badger said. "How long ago was this?"

"A week or so," he replied. "It sounds like she bailed the second she got a chance, so I'm wondering if she was reacting to a long trip in a cage with a truckload of dogs all that time. There's a good chance she won't be in much of a hurry to get caught and put back in another cage."

"No, I don't imagine she will, but she also could be very hungry at this point."

"Maybe," Landon muttered. "Although there's also a damn good chance that she's well past that. She may be hunting just fine on her own by now."

There was silence for a moment from Badger's end. "Yeah, that's possible too, though that's not exactly how we want it to go."

"No, but she's got to eat, and I don't begrudge her the chance to feed herself."

"Yeah, but anybody with livestock will have a whole different take on that."

"Got it, and I'm on my way." With that, Landon hung up the phone, started up the truck, and headed back in the direction he was hoping to go when this was all over. He really wanted to see Sabrina again. For a five-minute interchange, she had made quite an impression, and he was definitely interested. Although he was out of the dating scene and not all women liked dogs or that he had three of them.

Then he grinned and quickly found her number and hit Dial. "Hey, I don't know if you've had a chance to connect with anybody about whether that dog could be there or not, but I spoke to a trucker who picked her up where I'm at, near the border. Chica bailed on him and bolted at a stop down around your neck of the woods, just a week ago," he shared, "so any sightings that come from down there are likely to be valid."

"Oh, wow, so she could be around here."

"She could," Landon agreed, "and I need to find her, if she is. It doesn't sound like she's in great shape."

"I did phone my friend at the local vet's, but I can also contact a couple other vet clinics and send out an alert. I do have a rapport with a lot of locals, just because I volunteer in the industry so much," she noted. "I go and pick up animals from different places and all."

"That's good to know because this girl definitely could use somebody on her side."

"Oh, I'm on her side all right," Sabrina declared. "The question is, what does that mean for her?"

"What do you mean?" he asked.

"I guess I'm a little disturbed at how she ended up on the cross-country transport truck in the first place, then missing. What happened to her in the meantime? How is it that she slipped through the cracks?"

"Her legal owner died," he noted, recalling the sparse details in the dog's file. "And when the son got to town to take care of business, there was no dog. She'd been in the backyard, and, as far as anybody can tell, she took off when nobody was there for her."

"Oh my goodness," she cried out, "that poor girl."

"Yes, but at the same time that *poor girl* is quite capable of looking after herself to a large extent," he explained. "We just have to make sure that she's safe."

"Again, that brings me back to what you'll do with Chica when you find her."

"The same thing I would do for anybody. I'll make sure she's well looked after, one way or another." And, with that, he hung up.

CHAPTER 4

S ABRINA STARED DOWN at her phone, surprised that
Landon had called, yet, at the same time, not surprised
at all. The fact that the dog could even be in the area at this
point in time was kind of scary. She knew what he meant
about the dog taking care of herself, but, if the dog was
limping and was potentially in very rough shape, she could
be a target herself.

She frowned, wondering if she should text him back
about that, then realized she really needed to phone around
to the local vets and see if anybody had heard anything. She
had a good rapport with the other vet clinics, as they often
shared cases and medicines, if need be. As she sat here at
home, she made four different calls in the local area, and, on
two, she left messages because everybody was really busy, but
the receptionists at each place promised to get back to her, if
anybody had heard anything.

Then Sabrina phoned Angela back again. "So guess who
called me?"

Angela gasped. "Oh my God! He's a serial killer."

Sabrina snorted at that. "A serial killer who's looking for
a dog?"

"But you don't know that for sure, do you?" her friend
asked, sounding worried.

Sabrina stared down at the phone. "What I don't understand," she murmured, "is where this is all coming from? What is the deal with you?"

"It's just that you haven't had a relationship in a long time," Angela said, "and I don't want you to get hurt."

"Calling the guy a serial killer is hardly the same thing as me getting hurt," she murmured.

"I know. I know." Then she sighed heavily. "Let's just say, I would much rather have you bordering on the side of caution."

"There's caution, and then there's being stupid," Angela stated, not understanding really where her friend's problem was in all this. "Obviously I won't do anything stupid."

"Sure, but you've already offered to help him, haven't you?"

"Yeah, I made a few phone calls," she said. "Does that make me stupid?"

"No, I'm not saying that," Angela stated immediately.

"Maybe you're not saying that, but it sure sounds that way," Sabrina noted. "Look. I need to just get off for a while." And, with that, she hung up on her friend, wondering when the last time was that she'd done something like that.

Sabrina and Angela hadn't ever had a problem between them before, not one that couldn't be talked through in five minutes and handled immediately. So she didn't understand why Angela was all of a sudden so protective or crazy about this. Sure, Angela hadn't met Landon, and Sabrina didn't know much about him. Maybe Sabrina should have asked him for some sort of reference, but is that what you did these days? She knew she'd been out of the dating scene for a while, and that was kind of a joy in one sense because she didn't deal with all that implied, but she hardly felt like things were to the point where she needed to do a background check on Landon before going out for coffee with him.

Yet, having put the idea in her own head, she now had to wonder where Angela's concern was coming from or whether her friend was just being the foolish one. But, as long as Sabrina's contact with Landon was just a phone call, and ... *potentially a coffee*, she thought to herself, then where was the harm?

Besides, how was Sabrina ever supposed to meet anybody? Angela was always telling Sabrina to go out and to get to know people, but how was Sabrina supposed to do that if, the minute someone came into her life, her best friend immediately started tagging them as potential serial killers? The fact that her friend had even jumped to that extreme kind of bothered Sabrina. And Angela was much too stern and foreboding about the issue to pull it off as some joke.

Granted, Angela spent most of her time at work or with Jason, so Sabrina didn't interact as much with Angela now. Was she freaking out because she was one step removed from Sabrina and now Landon? She just shook her head. It made no sense to her. And Angela's paranoia came from left field. Granted, this was the first man Sabrina had taken an interest in, and it had been a few years, so there was that.

Determined to not let it get to her, Sabrina headed to bed and crashed. She knew that morning would come faster than she wanted and so would her next shift at work.

As it was, she was wakened by a phone call. She glanced down to see it was Angela. Sabrina groaned, wondering if she should even answer. She checked the time, noting it was six, only a half hour earlier than her alarm would go off, considering she was on a morning shift today.

Finally she decided to answer, but what the hell? "Why are you calling at this hour?" she asked, without preamble.

Angela sobbed. "I'm sorry. I'm so sorry."

"For what?" Sabrina muttered, still trying to shake the sleep from her eyes.

"Because I sounded like such a bitch."

Sabrina frowned at that. "Well, yeah, you did," she agreed. "And I'm not exactly sure where all this is coming from, but wow. Could you just get a grip? I mean, you tell me to get out there and to meet some guys and to get a life, but then, when I do find somebody who's kind of fascinating, look at how you've acted?"

"I know. It's just the way that it came about," she replied. "It put all my nerves on edge for some reason."

"Your nerves are on edge?" she asked. "Why? For one thing, it's not your life. For another, it's not your nerves. It's more like paranoia. And the *way it came about*? If I go to a bar, who will be there for me to meet? Someone who just wants a one-night stand. Will that be a better way to meet people? I met Landon at a sandwich shop. Remember?"

"Sure," Angela replied, "but then at a bar, at least you know what to expect."

Not sure her friend's logic held together, Sabrina asked, "How is that even helpful? I'd much rather *not* be in a position where I meet somebody at a bar, when I don't like to hang out at bars myself to begin with. Bars are just hook-up joints, not really made for long-term relationships, in my opinion. It's never made sense to me to go to a place like that to meet people when doing that is so far removed from who I even am."

"Yeah, but that's how you meet people," she argued, "and then you figure out what you'd like for a type."

"I already know what I'd like for a type," she said in exasperation. "It's not as if I haven't ever dated before. I'm not some innocent here, so I don't know what the hell you've been telling yourself about me all this time." She started to get angrier.

"I don't know," Angela admitted, then stopped, took a breath. "Look. I'm sorry. I called to apologize."

"Yet you woke me up, knowing I had to go to work this morning."

At that, Angela stopped. "I thought you were off today," she said in a small voice.

"Wow. So you thought it a good idea to wake me up at dawn on my day off? Oh my God. So, if you don't mind, I'll forget this conversation ever happened because this is not how I want to start my day."

Hanging up, she stared down at the phone, wishing she hadn't answered it. Sabrina acknowledged that Angela was trying to apologize and had probably had a sleepless night, but right now everything she said was hitting Sabrina wrong. After a quick shower, she got dressed. She wondered how much of her argument with Angela was about Sabrina's own need to check on Landon's story, or was it just the fact that she really liked the little bit she knew about this guy and hadn't wanted any kind of harsh reality to interfere? "What reality though? A serial killer? Come on," she muttered. "It's just a guy looking for a dog, and he hadn't done anything to warrant being suspicious of ... yet."

Of course the *yet* worried her. Maybe he was a good guy. Maybe he wasn't. She didn't have any way of knowing, and, with Angela's doubts ringing in her ears, it was hard to even think about it rationally. Sabrina finished up a quick breakfast and headed into work, a little on the early side.

Thank you, Angela.

Her supervisor looked up. "Wow. What's with you?"

"I couldn't sleep," she replied briefly.

Her supervisor stared at her and then shrugged. "Do you ever think about just ..." Then she shrugged again and headed to the coffeepot. "Or are you just out of coffee at home?" her supervisor joked.

Sabrina smiled at that. "No, I've got lots of coffee."

"Ah, so something's on your mind."

She shrugged. "I didn't sleep all that well."

"Obviously you could use a bit of a break," she noted, "but whatever. ... You're here now." She sat down and did a briefing of what happened on the night shift, outlined what needed to be done during today's shift, and shared how the patients were doing. This was necessary, but it was also the most difficult task in some ways because Sabrina heard specifics on the patients who had made it through the night, the ones who were being moved, the ones who were doing well, and the ones who were not. Including her grandma.

She'd learned to be more detached to it all, but that didn't make it any easier. Making it harder was the reality that a lot of these patients would never go home. A lot of them were just putting in time, hoping for an easy end. Yet, for so many of them, no easy end was in sight.

By the time her briefing was over, it was still on the early side, but Sabrina got to work, hoping that would completely change the mood of her morning. By the time lunch rolled around, she had been so busy that she hadn't had a chance to even think about the rough start to her morning. That was perfect. She checked her phone, something that she kept off during the day, and noted one missed call from Landon.

She stared down at it, unable to stop the happy surge she

experienced when she realized he'd called her. But it would have been about the dog, of course, so there was absolutely no need to get too excited. She stepped away from some of the noise around her and listened to the message. He was back in town at a hotel close by and would head out to touch base with the nearby vet clinics.

He was basically calling to see if she'd heard anything. She didn't respond right then, but it was a perfectly reasonable phone call for him to have made. It made her feel better and, at the same time, made her wonder if she was just being foolish. After all, although this guy was temporarily in her life, it didn't mean he wanted anything to do with her.

She probably shouldn't have said anything to Angela about it in the first place, but Sabrina also hadn't expected Angela to go off the wall in a panic. Sabrina still didn't even know where that was coming from. Angela was many things, but a worrywart wasn't one of them, or at least she hadn't been until now. But Angela had a partner of her own now, so who knew how that had changed her perspective. It didn't make any sense that it would cause her more stress, but obviously something was up with her.

Sabrina had heard of other longtime friends breaking up once a significant other showed up in the picture. Could it be as simple as that? Possibly. Sabrina just never thought it would happen to her and Angela.

Pocketing her phone and finishing off her lunch, she headed back to work again. She could do nothing about Chica or Angela or getting some sleep or any of it, until she was done for the day. Besides, there wasn't exactly a call to action on that phone message from Landon either.

By the time she was done with her shift, she felt a tremor starting inside. It happened, just from the fatigue of the day, after having done the shift and a half the previous day, plus not getting as much sleep as she should have. It's not like she wasn't used to it, but, at the same time, she was obviously a little more stressed than she had expected to be over the state of her relationship with Angela.

Sabrina left work and slowly headed home. One of the benefits of being off work and working so close to her home was that she could walk, and, by the time she got home, usually some of the stress of her day had died down.

The problem was, she still needed to deal with Angela, her friend for so long that, whatever the problem was, they both just needed to get over it and to move on. Easier said than done though this time. At the moment, it wasn't as if Angela had any really good reason to get angry at Sabrina, and it was just frustrating. Sabrina shook her head. When she got home, she would make herself a cup of tea and sit on her deck.

As she neared home, she heard a horn honk behind her. She turned suddenly, and a large truck pulled up beside her. She stared in surprise, as Landon grinned at her from the driver's seat. She moved closer to the passenger side, and he automatically rolled down the window. Almost immediately she was greeted by three of the smallest Chihuahuas she'd ever seen. Her heart immediately melted.

"Oh my God." She laughed, as they tried to jump out the passenger side window to get cuddles. She reached a hand over and gently greeted them—as much as she could without getting them more excited than they already were.

He tried to calm them down and then sighed. "Honestly, at this point," he said, "I really don't have a hope in hell of getting them to calm down."

She burst out laughing. "That's not necessarily a problem."

"Maybe, maybe not." He shrugged. "They are who they are." She watched as he immediately called them by name—Larry, Curly, and Moe.

When she heard their names, she burst out laughing. "Oh my, that's absolutely too perfect."

He grinned at her. "Hey, you got to do what you got to do, and these three are pretty inseparable."

"So how on earth did you end up with three of them?"

He frowned, then looked at her with a sad smile. "Because I'm such a big sap. Their mother was my friend Joe's dog. I was already taking care of him, and the loss of Ginger was devastating to him. When she was hit by a car, I raced her to the vet, but she didn't make it. However, she was pregnant, and they were able to get the babies out. The vet didn't have the facilities there to look after them, and they were unsure about my buddy wanting them—but he did. So I took them home. I think having the puppies gave Joe extra joy in his final days," Landon noted and then stopped, deep in thought. He shrugged. "I hand-raised them, bottle-feeding all three around the clock, and that's how it goes, I guess. When Joe died, I knew I could never let them go."

She nodded immediately. "Especially after bottle-feeding them," she murmured. "They just become too much for your heart."

He nodded slowly and grinned at her. "So, when we saw you walking this way, I couldn't help but stop. Sorry about the horn. I didn't mean to scare you."

"No, it's fine. I just wasn't expecting to see you."

He shrugged. "I was at the hospital, talking to Charlie again."

Her eyes lit with interest. "Right, did he have anything

else to offer?"

He shook his head. "He was surprised the dog ended up down here but not terribly surprised in a way. I don't know." Landon hesitated. "I'm not sure how much I believe him now."

"Oh?" She frowned at him. "In what way?"

"I don't know. He just seemed a little cagey today."

"Maybe not feeling well?" she asked. "Sometimes people tend to get a little bit more secretive when they're not quite up to snuff."

"I hadn't considered that," he admitted, pondering it. "I guess that's a possible explanation, but I don't know. Most of the time, anybody I've known who wasn't feeling well was pretty blunt about it. You know, like, 'Get out of my face, and I'll talk to you later,' or something like that."

She nodded. "I've seen people with long-term health issues who are like that," she agreed. "So maybe give him another chance to talk to you later."

"I told him that I'd call back or talk to him another time, and he just waved me off, as if he didn't want to deal with it."

"And really, if he's sick or if he's dealing with something other than the car accident, even the medical bills alone," she noted, "that's certainly something to consider. However, you aren't entitled to know all of his medical history, so that's a missing piece for you too."

"I hadn't even thought about that being part of it," he said. "I just spoke with him moments ago, so I'm still mulling it over in my mind."

"I get that too. Just keep an open mind."

He smiled at her. "I was just about to go pick up a coffee, then find a park or something. I need to let these guys run for a while. Any interest in joining me?"

She couldn't stop the skip of her heartbeat, as she nodded immediately. "I'm just off work, so that's good timing for me too."

"Where's your vehicle?" he asked, looking around.

"I walk to work," she replied and then immediately winced.

"Hey, that's okay. I'm not trying to make you uncomfortable. Don't come if you don't want to."

At that, she looked down at the animals, who were still chasing each other and their tails in the front seat of the truck. "Honestly, it would be lovely to get a coffee," she said, "and a park is just over on the next block here."

"What about a coffee shop?" he asked, curiously looking around. "There's got to be a place close by."

"I think that's some kind of a required standard in life these days, isn't it? A coffee shop on every corner?"

"Most of the time," he admitted instantly. "I just need to find one with a drive-through."

At that, she hesitated and then suggested, "Or you can go over to the park with the pups, and I'll put on a pot myself and bring it over."

"Oh no," he said immediately, "that's not necessary. Just a drive-through will be fine."

She shrugged and pointed out the closest one.

He nodded. "Perfect, and I'll find the park right after that." Then he drove off.

She watched him go, realizing that there really were nice men in the world. And, with that thought, her mind returned to Angela and her fears. Sabrina probably should have asked him for some kind of reference as to what he was doing for the War Dog, since she was making phone calls and contacting people. She didn't want to find out afterward that this was some scam, and that thought now wouldn't leave her alone.

Still, she headed toward the park, knowing she would play it safe regardless. Yet also knowing that the chances were good she would fall helplessly for this guy because something was so very appealing about a guy who had nursed three Chihuahuas from birth.

Then again she was a sucker for anybody who loved dogs. Well, actually she was a sucker for anybody who loved animals of any kind. In this case, it just was even more accentuated because of who he was. At least who he said he was. She had to keep reminding herself of that, and yet did she really have to go through life always so worried about everybody else?

It was a hard way to operate, but Angela had set Sabrina on edge, and there was just no getting away from her friend's fears now, ... at least for the moment. As Sabrina walked over to the park, she looked around and found a picnic table that overlooked the river; then she sat down and waited.

Almost immediately her phone buzzed. She looked down, and it was a text from Angela.

Coming by after work?

Sabrina hesitated, then sent her a message. **Nope. Having coffee in the park.** Then she shut off her phone—in case Angela started calling in a panic. When Sabrina heard a heavy-duty engine, she turned to see Landon pulling into the parking lot. And realized she hadn't even considered asking him to pick her up a coffee. But, when he hopped out, holding two cups, she groaned, raced over, and said, "I didn't think that you were buying me a coffee."

"Of course I am," he replied, frowning at her. "I'll hardly invite you for coffee and then not pick up the tab."

She shrugged. "I wasn't thinking of it along those lines," she murmured. She took the two coffees from him, so that he could let the dogs out. As she watched them jump all over each other to get out, she laughed. "They really are rambunctious, aren't they?"

"Yeah, the vet told me that they would calm down as they got older, but it sure hasn't happened yet."

"How old are they now?" she asked curiously.

"Not quite two," he said proudly, with a smile. "I've gotten used to their antics, but not everybody handles it the same way."

"I love animals, especially dogs."

"If nothing else they're good company. It's like they're crazy, overly rambunctious, and all kinds of things," Landon said, "but they're family."

And, with that, the last of her reservations fell to the wayside, and she nodded. "That is *exactly* how I feel about them," she agreed. "Not everybody does though."

"Is that why you help out at the vet clinic?"

"That and the fact that my friend Angela is there, and they always seem to be short-handed."

"That's a good strategy on her part, to get her friends in to help for free." He chuckled.

"I know, right?" she murmured. "I don't normally mind though. Depending on my days off and how much time I have, if I can get over there and give them a hand, I do."

"Not today though?" he asked curiously.

"No, not at the moment," she replied but didn't elaborate. She walked back over to the picnic table and set the coffees there. "Is this okay?" she asked.

"Yeah, this is just fine. And considering that these guys

have been cooped up for so long," Landon said, "I'll take them along the shore here for a walk."

She immediately walked up beside him and nodded. "That's a good idea. It's nice to see you out here with your dogs."

He looked at her. "You must be used to people with animals."

"I am, yet at the same time, I'm not." She laughed. "Just when you think you know what people are like, they turn around and surprise you."

"Oh, I definitely get that."

Then an awkward silence fell, until she remembered one of her calls today. "I did hear back from another one of the vet clinics, but they hadn't heard anything."

He nodded. "I am more or less expecting that all along the line," he admitted, "but I won't give up hope yet."

LANDON TRIED TO not make it look obvious that he was staring, but something was very fresh and appealing about Sabrina. Something about that wholesome girl-next-door look that he hadn't seen enough of to become accustomed to. He also knew that saying anything about it would likely make him sound creepy. And, considering the scenario, she might already be thinking that way.

"I should have given you one of my business cards before," he said. "It would have maybe given you a little more validation, if anybody asked questions."

Shuffling the leashes on the dogs, he pulled out his wallet and handed her a card. "I had it made up for this job," he explained. "I mean, obviously I'm doing this on a humanitarian basis," he added, "but, if you have any questions or any reservations about what I'm doing, feel free to call my bosses, Badger or Kat."

"Badger or Kat? Interesting names."

He nodded. "Kat is a prosthetic specialist," he noted. "She's pretty amazing in her field."

"Interesting," she murmured, and then she looked over at him. "Oh, do you have a prosthetic?" Then she realized what a personal question she was asking. "Oh, gosh, I am so sorry. That was very rude of me."

He looked at her and grinned. "Actually I'd much rather people ask outright than hide it." He lifted his pant leg, and she saw an ankle made of metal.

"Wow," she said, fascinated. "That's not something you see every day."

"It is in my world," he noted, "and definitely in Kat's world."

"Is that how you came to do this work finding Chica?"

"Somewhat, yes," he replied. "I was a little bit lost after my friend died. I'd been taking care of him for a couple years, and then he was gone. I was casting about, trying to figure out what to do with myself. My brother was asked to help out with Chica, but he's having surgery, so he suggested that I might want to do it for them."

"So, you're like fully vetted with the war department or the War Dog division or whatever?" she asked, reading the card. "How does that even work?"

He gave her a little bit of the history that Landon knew from Badger of how these cases landed at Titanium Corp from Commander Cross's desk.

"It's nice of them and you to do this without getting paid," she murmured.

"It's just such important work, especially for anybody who has seen what these dogs did for us. So getting paid isn't really a consideration when it comes to this kind of stuff," he explained. "Everybody is more concerned about making sure that we find the dogs involved, and we can confirm they are in good health, well taken care of, and happy."

"Me too," she murmured. She looked at his business card again and asked, "Will you get offended if I call this number?"

He looked at her and shook his head. "That's why I gave it to you, so why would I get offended?" He smiled. "Besides, you really shouldn't be spending time with strangers without checking out their credentials at least a little."

She burst out laughing. "Yeah, one of my friends already ripped me over that, asking me a ton of questions that I couldn't answer. So then she kind of read me the riot act."

"Of course she did, but the good news is that I'm not a serial killer," he said immediately and then grinned at her.

"Wow, it's almost like you heard the conversation." She chuckled.

He looked at her with raised eyebrows. "No, really? Was she that worried?"

"She was, but I don't know why. All of a sudden she has become much more nervous, when she never used to be."

He tilted his head. "It's always better to be safe than sorry anyway," he said, with a shrug. "Feel free to call them. Like I said, I won't take offense."

She nodded and smiled. "Glad to hear that. Enough people are out there that I manage to offend without even trying." At that he looked at her, and she shrugged. "Just second nature in some ways."

He grinned at that. "If you don't suffer fools, it's not

that hard to have it happen."

"Right. I thought it was just me who had that problem."
She chuckled.

"No, it's pretty easy to get people pissed off at you."

"And here I wasn't trying to do anything but help a
dog," she complained, "but Angela took it badly for some
reason."

"She's not an animal lover?"

"No, she totally is. As a matter of fact, she's the one I
help out at the vet clinic."

"Oh, well, that's a surprise," he replied, looking at her,
frowning.

"That's what I thought too, but maybe this story just
surprised her. I don't know."

"Whatever," he said, "but I can't say I'd want that number passed around indiscriminately. However, by all means,
use it at your discretion."

"Thank you. … Hopefully I won't need it at all."

"But, if you do, use it," he encouraged her. "I have no
intention of upsetting the applecart in your world. If people
are unhappy or upset, then use it. That's what it's for."

She pocketed the card and suggested, "Should we go
grab our coffee? It should be cool enough to drink now,
right?"

He looked at her and turned to look back at the table.
"Yeah, and we better get it before somebody else does."
Horrified at the thought that someone would be so rude, she
turned to see two crows, hopping along on the top of the
picnic table, looking at the cups curiously.

"Oh, good point," she said, laughing at his joke. She
headed over to the table and brought them back his way.
"We can just keep walking if you want or sit if you prefer,"

she added, handing him his cup.

"Walk?" he asked. "It's a beautiful day."

At that, they fell into step and strolled along the path. "Have you got another line of attack figured out for where to go next?" Sabrina asked him.

"No, not yet. … I keep thinking about what the trucker said, and I do have the truck stop where he picked up fuel and lost her in the process, but I haven't been there yet," he admitted. "I was just coming back from seeing Charlie, and I don't have anything else to work with."

"Right, it's too bad that Charlie couldn't give you any more help."

"Yeah. And I don't know that there's anything terribly suspicious about what he said this time. It just seemed that when I was asking questions about how the dog ended up in his hands, things got a little dicey."

"So, I guess finding that out would help, wouldn't it?"

"Yeah, it would, if you think about it. I mean, it would be nice to not have this happen again."

"I guess things can always go wrong, especially considering how many dogs a person is trying to handle at one time when transporting them through those adoption service channels."

He nodded. "Absolutely, and they seem to work off the honor system, checking with veterinarians, who take these animals in. And you never really know what these people told the vets, as they were dropping off a dog and never came back for them. So, when something goes wrong, it's not really a surprise to me," he said. "The recordkeeping is typically really good, from what I hear—I guess because a border is crossed and because this shipment was of dogs in need of medical help. However, in this case, the whole reason Charlie made an unexpected stop was to get some missing paperwork. So what are you supposed to do?"

"So, how badly is Chica injured?" She stopped, and he looked over at her curiously.

"I don't know that she's *newly* injured—or she wasn't when she was first loaded on that transport," he replied. "But now? With her missing for weeks? That'll be something that we'll find out more about as I get closer to her."

"My question relates more to how she'll handle feeding herself if she's hurt or even has an old injury from before."

"That's something that I'm trying not to focus on too much," he admitted. "I'm not at all sure how she'll do along that line. Charlie did say that she was moving okay, but that she seemed to be suffering somewhat with her steps. I don't know if she really was suffering or if just the way she walked made it look painful. I mean, as somebody who walks with a limp myself, people often misinterpret how I'm doing. People tend to assume that whatever is wrong with me is something that can be instantly fixed, and so I just need a moment to rest or something."

She stared at him. "That's an interesting conundrum because a lot of times people don't know how to speak to people who have a disability."

"And most of us who have a prosthetic don't consider ourselves disabled," he replied and then smiled at her. "Don't worry. I'm not trying to tell you to speak a certain way about it with me. I just know that, when you've had a lot of people in your world who view it in a way that's less than nice," he added, "you tend to get a little more defensive."

Immediately she nodded. "And the other thing that I notice and struggle with sometimes, and certainly with my friends, is that the socially acceptable phrase changes so quickly. It's as if the minute you think you've got the right terminology down, you find out it's changed again, and what you've been using is suddenly offensive. For example, should we say *handicapable* this week? Is it *prosthetic-enabled* or what? I mean, what's the current use of language?"

At that, he stared at her to see if she was joking, then burst out laughing. "I have *no* idea." Landon chuckled. "But don't ever say any of those again."

She grinned at him. "Right, I'm sorry. So how do you figure out how to use language in a way that doesn't offend people? I mean, I wouldn't want to be insensitive, but it's pretty easily done."

He nodded. "I get that. I really do. It's kind of interesting to consider how the language has changed over the years, but, when you think about it, most of the people like me, military types, are not the kind to take offense, one way or the other." He shrugged. "We're all sturdier stock and coming to terms with our situation, and, as much as that might set off a flurry of raw feelings because we're now in a situation we never expected to be in, we're also damn thankful to be alive, so we may not be so quick to take offense."

"That's good news," she said, with a sigh, "because I certainly wouldn't want to offend anybody."

He asked, "You worked in hospice you said, didn't you?"

"I did. I'm now working in long-term care."

"Right," he said, "so not quite the same thing."

"No, not at all. Hospice was pretty tough though. I found that I was always watching my language, always whispering, always trying not to offend anybody or take offense when people were less than happy, especially with how we defined *quality care* because their loved one was dying, and there's just nothing more any of us can do."

"Oh, yeah, I can see that. I just hadn't considered it."

"And once you take a certain amount of criticism and what some may view as abuse, all because a loved one is dying," she shared, "you get to the point where you almost have to protect yourself."

He nodded. "The same thing applies if you've had people calling you names too often," he noted. "It's not that we expect to have anybody treat us that way, but it does happen, and you try to minimize the impact on yourself, just so you can carry on, you know?"

She smiled. "You seem to be very well-adjusted."

"*Hah*, it may appear that way, but it isn't necessarily the truth. My buddy Joe, the one who passed on recently, was the most well-adjusted person I know. It often made me really angry that he was the one who died, since he was the one who had adapted to life so well."

"So well in life but not so well in health, *huh*?"

"He ended up with cancer," he said. "We did everything that could be done, but, when it came back, it came with a raging roar and took him away."

"I gather he was a really special friend."

He looked at her sharply, then smiled and said, "Not in the way that you may mean."

She flushed. "Hey, totally not what I meant. I'm sorry. Jeez, I seem to be apologizing a lot, right?"

"You don't need to," he replied, with a dismissive hand wave. "We had a special bond because he saved my life on a mission behind enemy lines. No possible way would I have survived without him dragging me to safety, and it wasn't something I would let go unnoticed. If there was anything I could do to make his life easier, I would be right there for him."

"I'm sure he appreciated it."

"Maybe. He also told me that I was an idiot, time and time again." Landon laughed. "He was always telling me to go off and to live my life and to stop wasting it helping him."

She grinned at that. "I think I would have liked him."

"I'm sure you would have. In fact, everybody did. He was a guy just full of heart. The trouble is, just because you follow your heart doesn't mean that you get a chance to live. I … For the longest time I was really angry about the whole thing. But, even as he was the one it was happening to, he helped me to put it all in perspective and to realize that sometimes bad things happen to good people, and there's just nothing you can do about it."

"I hear that a lot too," she murmured. "Working in hospice lets you see another side of life that we're not always ready to see. That whole death and dying part is something a lot of people never have any exposure to, not until something happens out of the blue, and then they don't have any way to deal with it."

"Well, in my case," Landon explained, "I knew he was sick, but I hadn't realized how bad it was, and he wasn't talking. That made it even more difficult. I tried to get him to open up, but he didn't want me to know. So when he did finally tell me, I told him exactly what I thought about him trying to keep it all a secret. I moved in pretty soon afterward."

"And he didn't have a problem with it? Some people don't want their loved ones to see them at their worst, physically, much less dying in front of them."

"No, I think he felt a certain amount of relief that he wouldn't be alone, you know?"

"I don't think anybody should die alone," she said. "I've spent many an evening, sitting with patients who didn't have anybody else, just so they weren't alone. It did take a toll on my heart, and it's one of the reasons I changed departments. My grandma is currently in long-term care, and that made it even easier to switch."

"Right," he murmured, "but that can't be easy either."

"No, it sure isn't," she agreed. "She's the only living relative I have."

"Ouch. That's tough," he murmured. "So that's where you need to be."

"Absolutely. For the moment anyway."

He grimaced. "Does she still know who you are?"

She looked at him and slowly shook her head. "Not always. And not recently."

"Have you two always been close?" he asked.

"Too close, unfortunately. But you know what? It's one of the reasons I go work with the animals afterward. I just … It makes it easier."

"Did you see her today?"

"I should have, but she was in getting tests done. So the answer to that question is no."

"How close is she … ?"

"I'm not sure. It's the kind of thing that nobody is ever willing to give a time frame on," she noted. "I would say myself that it's probably not more than a few weeks, but it's hard to know."

He nodded. "She's very lucky to have you."

"I'm lucky to have her. I just wish she would recognize me at this point."

"I don't know that it helps though," he suggested. "Watching somebody die is painful, no matter what. It hurts on all levels. Especially when they're young and supposed to be so vibrant and full of life. It seems like such a waste."

"Yeah, there is that aspect to it," she agreed, "but it's no easier watching someone die, like Grandma, who is old and has had her time, if there is such a thing."

"I don't think we're ever ready, are we?" he asked curiously.

She took a sip of her coffee, and, as he studied her face, he saw the compassion, caring, and likely a lot of pain that she hadn't dealt with yet. She replied, "No, it's an ending that we're not ready for. I don't care what the situation is, it still hurts."

He nodded, and they walked along in silence for a long moment, until he murmured, "We somehow got into a very maudlin topic."

She chuckled. "Death will do that to you."

"Got it. That is something that I hadn't really considered."

She looked over at him. "No, but you're still grieving, aren't you?"

"Absolutely," he replied. "Joe was a really good friend of mine, and he was one of those larger-than-life guys, even right up to the end."

"I'm sure he really appreciated everything you did for him," she said.

"I'm sure, but he rebelled as he got sicker and sicker. He kept telling me to take off and to have a life of my own."

"And now you will," she stated.

He smiled at her. "That's exactly what I kept telling him. He didn't really appreciate it though."

She chuckled. "I hardly see you as a pushover."

"Nope, I'm not. Especially since I was bound and determined to do everything I could for him. Now that he's gone, … well, it's up to me to figure out what I want to do next. And while I'm figuring it out," he added, "I'm bound and determined to find a missing War Dog. At least, if I couldn't stop Joe from dying, maybe I can stop this one from suffering any longer."

CHAPTER 5

A<small>S SABRINA WALKED</small> back home from the park—after Landon had left with just a friendly *See you around*, no promises or plans made—she felt kind of let down. When her phone vibrated, after she turned it back on, she saw it was one of the other vet clinics. She quickly answered.

"Hey, Sabrina. Somebody did mention that they saw a dog like that, but it was a couple days ago."

She stopped in her tracks. "Do you know where they saw it?" She turned to look back at the park, but Landon was already gone.

"Over on Willoughby Street. I don't have anything more than that. They wanted somebody to run out and take a look, but, I mean, it's not as if we can do that," the woman said in frustration.

"No, I know. Everybody is so busy, and it's not as if you can just get up and walk away to look for a dog."

"I think they tried to call a rescue, but I'm not sure if anybody ever found it.'

"I wonder which rescue they would have called?"

"I don't know, but you should probably phone around to a few of them, I imagine."

"Will do." Then she looked again to see if there was any sign of Landon. Of course the phone call came after they had gone their separate ways. She hadn't really wanted to end their time at the park because it was really nice to spend time with somebody so interesting. But now she had information for him, so quickly she placed a phone call.

"That was fast. Miss me already?" he asked in a teasing voice.

"You said you were heading out to search for the dog, right?"

"Yeah, to the place where she got away from the trucker. What's up?"

"I just heard from a vet clinic not too far from here. They reported a sighting fairly close by. She gave me the address, though apparently it was a couple days ago."

"Okay. Let me punch that into my GPS, and I'll see how close it is to where I am. I'll take a drive around and see what I can find."

"She didn't say anything else but sounded quite frustrated, as the caller seemed to think that she should leave her post and run out and find the dog."

"In a perfect world we could do that," he admitted, "but believe me. Nobody is blaming anybody at the moment. It's just a matter of trying to find Chica and making sure that she gets taken care of."

"Right," Sabrina said in relief. "Let me know if you find her."

"Will do." And, with that, he hung up.

The trouble was, she found it impossible to leave it at that. He was doing everything he could, and, sure, she'd done what she could do to a certain extent as well, but she hadn't phoned any of the rescues. She'd only called the vets.

So, when she got home, she quickly pulled up a list of rescues that she often contacted on behalf of her local vet clinic, usually when they were checking to see who could take any animals. She went through the top three numbers with no luck. By the time she got to the fourth one, the woman said, "We had a phone call about a dog wandering around, reported as skinny and really shy. Nobody could get close to it at all. We did send somebody out, trying to see if they could spot it, but they didn't have any luck."

"Okay," Sabrina replied, and she got the details of where the animal had been seen and where they had gone looking for it.

"I can't guarantee it's the same dog," the woman noted cautiously. "Yet it sounds like a might be. This one was definitely limping on a back leg, and she's got a problem with a front foot."

"That sounds like her," Sabrina said excitedly. "Look. I'll tell Landon, but he might need to call himself."

"That's fine. We have gone out a couple times but, so far, with no luck."

"If you do spot her, please let me know." Sabrina quickly provided the number for her and for Landon. Hanging up, realizing what she'd done, she winced and called him back.

"Wow, this is fun," he greeted her.

She chuckled. "In a way it is because the dog was spotted, and a rescue was contacted," she relayed in happiness. "So let me fill you in on this report." As soon as she managed to get all the details shared, she added, "Now I did something that I feel guilty about, and it's kind of why I'm calling. ... I gave them your number."

"Good," he said immediately. "That's excellent. Let's hope that we can find her now."

"The trouble is, they went out to the reported location, and, although they apparently saw her the one time, they couldn't get close to her, and she was looking really skinny."

"That could make her a little more aggressive too," he noted, "though it might also make her a little easier to catch, if we have food."

"I get that," she said, worrying. "I hate to think of her suffering like that."

"Me too," he replied immediately, his voice gentle. "Look. ... I'm heading there now. I'll let you know." And, with that, he hung up.

LANDON WASN'T SURE why fate was smiling on him, but meeting Sabrina when he first got to town turned out to be a godsend. As soon as he made it to the location of the most recent sighting, he stopped, hopped out with the other dogs, and wandered the area. He had dog food, and he was determined to leave some behind, but he needed to select the best location for it. He also wanted to set up cameras but knew that probably wouldn't be allowed in a public place. The things that he could do while he was in the military and on active duty were a whole different story than what he could do now as a civilian.

Still, it was frustrating to know that the dog was here somewhere, and, more than that, Chica was suffering. Plus, so far, nobody had been able to bring her in out of the cold. That's what Landon's entire goal was, to save her from this rough life she was caught up in. And, if she was even further injured, that would hinder her ability to survive even more.

He didn't want her getting into trouble for killing livestock or other animals. Chances were, she was digging through garbage as much as anything. Particularly if her leg was injured. But she could also become easy prey for other animals and couldn't hold her own in a dog fight. Worrying, and with his three dogs on leashes, he told them, "Come on. We've got to find her. If you guys want a new friend, we need to bring her in."

At that, the dogs barked and headed off, their noses to the ground. He grinned at that because it was almost as if they understood. Although how they could, he didn't know. This was all about making sure a War Dog, at the end of the day, could come home, safe and sound.

He had no clue what he was supposed to do with her then and figured it didn't make one bit of difference at the moment. It was all about making sure she had a chance at a better life. He wandered the entire area, looking for any signs of her.

But everything was concrete. Sidewalks were everywhere, and it was hard to even imagine that Chica would be caught up in this area. Where had she been that she would still be struggling to find her way though? And yet this wooded area nearby with city-installed trash cans made more sense than anything else he had searched. He stayed out quite late, the dogs at his side, always happy to go on an adventure. But even they were starting to lose their enthusiasm.

"I know that you guys need food too, don't you?" However, he had thought of that. He sat down on a small hill close to a wooded area, and he slowly hand-fed the dogs. They weren't so much used to this, but they weren't objecting to it either. They were fun-loving dogs, and they trusted him. They'd been with him since birth, and he'd never let them down.

And he never would.

As he sat here, he watched and waited, and suddenly he sensed a gaze behind them. He frowned at that but didn't move. He called out calmly, "It's okay, Chica. … You can come in. I have food for you too."

He didn't sense anything at the time, but it seemed like that gaze just stayed on him. If she'd been through a couple rough patches, it would make sense that she was reluctant. Maybe she was completely against cages, which was something he was against himself, but he knew a lot of people swore by them. For some dogs, they were probably a really good answer, if they had a need for a calm space of their own. He'd just never had any opportunity to use them with an animal that didn't fight it.

Maybe it would have been better in some cases to have worked through it, but he never had to, so it wasn't an issue for him. He sat here, calm and quiet, just talking to his dogs. He also tried talking to the dog behind him—the dog that he hoped was Chica and that he hoped was still behind him. For all he knew, if he turned around, it would be something completely different. He almost smiled at that because his dogs hadn't given any kind of alert, but then they weren't exactly guard dogs.

Still Curly lifted her head and sniffed the air around her. "It's okay," Landon told her. "We've got somebody out there that needs a friend."

She looked at him, and her tail wagged. "That's right. We need to bring her in and give her a hand," he explained gently. "So you just be you. Be friendly and we'll see if we can get her to come a little closer." He still didn't have a clue if it was even the dog he was looking for—or if it was even a dog at all. But Landon stayed in place and just kept gently talking to his animals and to the stray one that he hoped was behind him. When his phone vibrated, he checked his screen. It was Sabrina, so he answered the call. "Hey."

"So, does that mean no luck?" she asked instantly.

"I'm still out here. I can feel eyes on me from behind, but I'm not sure if it's the same dog. I'm trying hard not to spook her."

"Oh my," she said excitedly. "But you think it's her?"

"I have no clue," he admitted in a quiet tone. "I've got my dogs out here with me, and I'm just handfeeding them. I'm hoping I can at least get some food to Chica, even if it means walking away."

"Right," she replied, all business now. "Look. If you need a hand, let me know."

"I definitely would take you up on that, if I knew what I could use a hand with," he teased. "But, at the moment, I just want her to know she's not alone."

"Right," she said, her voice lowering. "In which case, even if I came and joined you, it wouldn't be a help."

"Not necessarily," he replied. "For the moment we'll just leave it as it is, giving Chica whatever time and space she needs."

"Right." Sabrina sighed. "In that case, I guess I'll just wait for you to give me an update later." And, with that, she hung up.

He smiled down at the phone. "Look at that, you guys. We have somebody really concerned about Chica too." No doubt Sabrina's concern was real, and he had to appreciate that. The fact that anybody could hurt an animal was always beyond Landon's ability to understand, but likewise, every time he met somebody like Sabrina, it blew him away that there were people with that level of concern for a stranger or even a lost animal she had never met.

"She's definitely an animal lover." Of course, to him, that was everything. Finally, after a few more minutes of the dogs just munching along beside him, he shifted ever-so-slightly, so he could see behind him. He couldn't see anything, but he still felt that gaze and that presence.

"It's okay, girl," he called out behind him. "Honestly, we won't hurt you." She may have had just enough interaction with humans that she didn't trust anybody at this point. And he really couldn't blame her. Not everybody was like him and definitely not like Sabrina. He could only hope that he could find a way to get close to Chica before she was suffering too badly.

He understood her need for food in a big way. The comfort that a full stomach brought made everything in life a whole lot easier to deal with, and animals were no different. Chica desperately needed food, and she needed to know that she would be okay, but he had to get close enough to her for that trust to begin to grow.

He sat here and waited until the sun went down; meanwhile Larry, Curly, and Moe were all dozing beside him. With careful movements, he stood and left a pile of dog food where he had been sitting. Moving slowly and carrying his sleepy dogs, he walked back to his truck. Once he got the animals inside, he hopped in and just sat here, waiting. And, sure enough, out of the shadows crept an animal. It was just far enough away and dark enough that he couldn't quite see her, but he had high hopes that it was Chica.

When he heard gentle sounds of eating, he smiled. "I hope it's you, girl, but whoever it is, you needed a meal, and, for that, you're welcome." He sat here for a while longer and waited, wondering if he had a chance to go out there. Leaving the dogs in the vehicle, he hopped out and walked over to where he'd left the food. There was a sudden rush into the darkness.

He nodded. "Not trying to hurt you," he murmured. "I just want you to get used to me. We'll be spending time together," he told her in that same calm voice. "The sooner you get used to me, the sooner you'll get regular food." As he stepped by the pile of food, he saw it was mostly gone, so he carefully emptied out a bit more for her. And then he called out, "I'll see you tomorrow, girl." And, with that, he headed back to the vehicle. He still hadn't seen her, so couldn't confirm anything, but, in his heart of hearts, he figured it had to be Chica.

He just wanted to make sure that he was the one who ended up finding her and talking her down from whatever nightmare she was still caught up in because that trust was something they would need going forward. As he headed back to his rental, another vehicle pulled into the parking lot. He watched as a guy got out, looked around furtively, saw him, and hid something in his hand. Landon watched him with a sinking heart. "Hey, what are you up to?" he asked in a casual voice.

The guy looked at him, startled, and said, "Nothing, just here for a walk."

"So what's in your hand?"

The guy glared at him. "Nothing to you, so just fuck off, old man."

Old man? Wow, that was a new one. Landon was a whole thirty-four years old. But this kid looked like he was a punk. "It better not be that dog you're trying to shoot," Landon said.

The guy stiffened in the dark. "It'll be you I shoot next," he threatened, "if you don't fucking leave me alone."

"I'll just sit here and wait and see what you do," he told him. "I've put cameras out to make sure the dog is okay. I'm trying to bring her back in, and I sure as hell don't want a punk-ass like you scaring her."

"That bitch deserves a bullet. I tried to put a rope on her, and she bit me."

"What, so you come back here with a gun?"

"Not really a gun," he said in the scoffing tone. "It's just a BB gun. I'm allowed one of those."

"Sure you are," Landon replied, his heart sinking. "Is that all you do? You just spend your time sitting here, shooting defenseless animals?"

"Did you hear what I said? She bit me," he snarled. "She's dangerous. I even told the sheriff that too."

"*Great*," he noted, with a hard sigh. "So now I must talk to the sheriff about you?"

He looked at him, startled. "Who the hell are you anyway?"

"Somebody who came here to collect the dog. Somebody who doesn't want to deal with punks like you getting in the way while I do it."

He snorted. "What do you know about it? It's not even your fucking dog."

"No, it isn't, but she does belong to the war department, and that is who sent me."

At that, the kid froze, turned slowly, and stared at him. "What are you talking about?"

"Doesn't matter what I'm talking about." For whatever reason Landon wasn't willing to give the kid any more airtime than necessary. "But I'm telling you, fair and square, leave that dog alone."

"Or what?" he asked, with a sneer. "You won't do anything. You're one of those law-abiding kind of citizens."

"I guess you didn't get a close look at my eyes then, did

you?" he stated, adding a deadly note to his voice. "Because nobody who did would make that mistake."

"What, so now you'll break the law for this damn dog?" he asked. "I told you that she's dangerous. She bit me."

"Yeah, and you probably hurt her in the first place, making it much harder for me to get closer to her."

"Good. She deserves it."

"No, that's not happening," Landon said. "I'll head over to the sheriff's office right now to file a complaint against you." And, with that, the kid hopped into his vehicle and drove off. Landon quickly texted Badger an update with the news. Badger called almost immediately, and Landon explained the encounter. "Yeah, I don't know quite what happened, but that punk kid came out of nowhere."

"He wouldn't be the first punk kid who thinks he's got some kind of power over everybody," Badger noted. "Chances are, he could be related to the sheriff."

"That would be about right, wouldn't it?"

"I wouldn't be at all surprised."

"God damn it," Landon muttered. "Just when I was making some progress."

"I suspect the sheriff will be on his way to see you anytime now."

"Good. Do I get to pull any power plays on him?"

"Yeah. You can send him to us right off the bat," Badger stated cheerfully. "Believe me. Even if we don't have any power over him, you can bet that there'll be a stink with his voters when they find out."

"Yeah, maybe not though," Landon said. "This kid was pretty sure the guy was on his side."

"Which just goes along with the theory that the sheriff is his relative or something of that nature."

"Maybe, it still sucks though."

"Absolutely it does, but what you need to do is to stay calm. Don't let him get to you."

"Yeah? What about my temper?"

"It would be nice if you held off on that too," Badger stated, with a chuckle.

"A vehicle's coming. What do you want to bet it's the sheriff?"

"Depends on whether it's the sheriff or a deputy," Badger suggested.

"I'll let you know in a few minutes." He sat here and waited, as the vehicle parked right beside him.

Instead of the sheriff himself, it was a deputy. The man got out of his vehicle and walked over. "Hey, we got a complaint about you."

"Yeah? You don't even know who I am," Landon replied, already getting pissed off.

The deputy's eyebrows lifted at Landon's attitude.

"You're here because of that punk-ass kid who came to shoot the dog, aren't you?"

At that, the deputy frowned.

"Is this town full of pieces of shit like him?"

"Hey! Whoa now, no need for that kind of language."

"It depends on what your relationship is to that kid," Landon stated, and the deputy started to get angry.

"We protect all of our citizens here. Particularly the ones who are family," he declared, with a nod.

"Got it. And you apparently don't look after the animals that need help either," Landon added.

"Oh, so what do you do? You some sort of animal lover?" he replied, with a sneer.

"So, you know about the dog then, right?"

"Yeah, I know that a dog bit him."

"I can't help but wonder what he did to the dog before it bit him," Landon replied, staring at the deputy, his temper back under control. "And, of course, you must wonder what kind of a kid would come here with a BB gun to shoot the dog, though I guess you don't need a license to be an asshole."

At that, the deputy started to get angry again. "Hey, that's enough of that kind of talk. We don't need your kind of riffraff around here."

"That's interesting," Landon said, "because it seems to me that you and that kid have already been allowed in town. What difference does one more make?"

"I won't tolerate that coming from you," he declared.

"Yeah?" Landon asked, his temper rising. Anytime somebody hurt an animal it always pissed him off. "Before you start making accusations, you should be talking to the war department."

At that, the deputy stopped dead in his tracks and asked, "The what?"

"You heard me," Landon stated. "That dog was a War Dog, and I'm here to rescue her. She was legally adopted via a binding contract between the US Government and the vetted adopter, but the owner died suddenly, and she got loose while being transported and ended up in trouble. I'm on her trail right now to make sure that she is recovered and gets home safe and sound."

At that, the deputy looked at him and scoffed. "That's a bullshit story if I ever heard one."

He held out his phone and said, "Hit Redial, and they'll provide you all the proof you need."

At that, the deputy hesitated.

Then looking at him with death in his eyes, Landon ordered, "Go on. You'll want your name and badge number to show up saying what side of this fence you're on, so go ahead." Landon prodded him further. "Believe me. The war department and the US government in general have a very long memory when it comes to people hurting military service animals. Particularly one of their own."

"No call for that now," the deputy replied, as he backed up ever-so-slightly. "Besides, the kid didn't mean any harm."

"Didn't mean harm?" Landon huffed. "I've seen kids like that a lot in my lifetime. Entitled bullies who think they can push around everybody else. So, if you expect me to back down, you've got the wrong guy in front of you." Landon was still too irritated and trying hard to calm his surfacing anger. "You better keep your son or your nephew or whoever he is on a leash over this, and just give me a chance to rescue the dog, so we can both get out of your lovely town."

The deputy frowned.

"What was your name again?" Landon asked him.

"I didn't give you my name," he retorted.

"Yeah, I know," Landon confirmed, "and now I want it, so I'll have it for my records."

"Why?" he asked, backing up yet another step.

"Because I want to know who this asshole kid is," Landon told him, "and I figure I'll find out pretty damn fast, once I have your name."

"Now, come on," the deputy protested. "All I asked you to do was get moving."

"Yeah, that's not quite the same thing," Landon argued, "and your nephew or whoever he is pissed me off with his attitude, coming out here to shoot a dog."

"It's an injured dog, and it's dangerous," the deputy said.

"And we sure as hell don't need any strangers coming in to take care of our own."

"Yeah, I hear you. You want to bring on that fight, you go for it." At that, he lifted his phone and took a photo of the deputy's face.

Immediately the deputy protested. "What the hell?" he asked.

"Yeah. What the hell is right. I'm already trying to figure that out, when I look at you guys. You keep your family away, while I take proper care of this War Dog, you hear me?"

The deputy frowned.

Landon then handed over his card and stated, "I'll be running your face through the databases too, to make sure you're on the right side of the law. I don't care what *elected* position you think you have here, but, if I've got any reason to throw the book at you, I damn sure will."

At that, he got in his vehicle, turned on the engine, and backed out of the parking lot.

Still pissed off, Landon took several deep breaths, getting his control back. His grumbling stomach reminded him that he hadn't eaten in a while, so he told Chica goodbye and left. Shortly thereafter he pulled into a drive-through and ordered several burgers to-go, then headed back to the hotel he'd booked for the night.

As he walked inside his room, he dropped onto the couch and devoured his burgers, with all three dogs staring at them, as if to say they should have some too.

"Oh no, you guys ate earlier," he reminded them. But their gazes were all over him, looking for that extra bite to top off their earlier meal just perfectly.

With a sigh, he broke up the last bite into three small

pieces and gave it to them. With that, they immediately curled up on the bed and nodded off. He had one last call to make, … somebody who might know the punk-ass kid. As he pulled out his phone, he sent a text to Badger and another one to Sabrina; then he called her.

CHAPTER 6

S ABRINA LOOKED AT the phone and saw a picture of one of the deputies in town, and then saw that the message came from Landon. Even as she was trying to figure out the connection, her phone rang. "Hey. You sent a picture of a deputy?"

"Yeah. Do you know this guy?" he asked.

"Kinda," she muttered. "He's one of our deputies, I think, but I'm not really sure. I don't have too much to do with law enforcement."

"Right, I wasn't sure if you would know him or not. I had quite a run-in with him and somebody in his family."

"Oh," she said, with a long-drawn-out sigh. "That would Deputy Smith's son, I believe. His kid is a bit of a troubled one in town. We've had some problems with him before."

"Yeah? Doing what?"

"He's got a pellet gun or a BB gun maybe, whatever the hell they call it. We've had quite a few animals in the clinic that have run into young Mr. Smith," she relayed, anger spiking in her voice. "The sheriff won't do anything because we can't tie it to the deputy's son, and the people who bring in the animals are already traumatized and don't want any more trouble."

"Wow. They may have a fight whether they recognize it

or not," Landon declared, "because no way in hell am I letting that punk hurt Chica."

"Is that what he was doing?" she cried out in horror.

"As far as I could tell, yes. He showed up there at the park, while I was waiting, while Chica ate, and, yes, I think it was her, though I never got a good look at her. He got out with that gun of his. We had words, and he took off, and the next thing I know, this deputy shows up."

"Yeah, that would explain it," she replied. "I didn't recognize him from the picture. But I know that we've made several phone calls on behalf of vet clinic, complaining about somebody with a BB gun shooting animals, and it never seems to go anywhere."

"Of course not, but things like that just piss me off."

"If you can do anything to stop this kid, I'm all for it." Then she hesitated and added, "As long as you don't hurt him."

"I'd like to shoot him right in the ass with that BB gun of his and see how he likes it," he admitted in a dark tone.

"You and half the neighborhood," she said. "But again, you need to stay out of trouble."

"I do, but I also don't need to be fighting somebody like them to keep the War Dog alive."

"Oh gosh no, that's terrible. And where are you now?"

"At the hotel. I've just filled in my bosses on all that happened today."

"Do they get upset about something like that?"

"They'll back me up, if that's what you're wondering, but the problem is more about making sure that we can rescue Chica first."

"Did you get even a glimpse of her?"

"No," he said, "I got close enough that I could hear her

eating, but I wanted to give her room so she would continue to eat. I was just about to go back out and talk to her, when this punk kid pulled up, and he was holding something in his hand, trying to hide it from me. I wasn't sure what it was, but I figured he was up to no good."

"Yeah, he's up to no good all right," she declared in disgust. "It doesn't seem to matter who complains. It never changes. He's just always up to no good, one way or another."

"Something like that can't be allowed to continue," he stated calmly.

"Maybe not, but it's also not the easiest thing to put a stop to."

"No, I know. I'll have to think about that. But the first thing I need to do is get the dog, so I can at least bring her in for treatment and hopefully save her life."

"That would be great if you could do that. ... I just wish we knew how bad off she is."

"I don't know, but the kid said she bit him, when he tried to put a rope on her, so you can bet the deputy is all about her being injured and dangerous and needing to be put down."

"Of course he is." Sabrina groaned. "That's really not what we needed to hear right now."

HE GRINNED AT her use of *we*. "I'm glad that you're on board with this whole project, and I'm not trying to ruin your life, by the way."

"You're not, and I don't care one bit about that kid or the deputy," she said. "We've had enough of those kinds of run-ins from the vet clinic end of things. I don't have anything to do with them other than that, so I'm not the one to talk to about it. But plenty of vets are around who would be quite happy to see that kid get leashed. I know I sure would."

"Yeah, you and me both," Landon agreed. "I'll think about how to corral that loose cannon."

"You just take care of yourself and don't get involved," Sabrina warned. "They can be pretty ornery here."

"Really?" he asked. "So now I should worry about an ambush too?"

"I don't know about that," she replied, surprise in her voice. "I'm just giving you a heads-up."

"Yeah, I get it," he said. "But, whenever there's an underdog out there that needs backing, especially when some asshole bully is involved," he stated in a gentle voice, "I'm the man who'll jump up and help."

"You're also injured," she pointed out, as if trying to be the voice of reason.

"No, I'm not," he declared. "I'm recovered. This is as good as I get. But, if you think it isn't good enough for the job, you don't know nearly enough about me."

"No, I don't know you, not hardly at all," she noted. "I would like to get to know you better, but I also need to know that you won't go off half-cocked and get yourself thrown in jail or something."

"No, that's not my style," he told her. "And, on that note, I would suggest maybe meeting for breakfast."

"Breakfast?" she asked.

"I'm not sure what time you go to work, but I'm flexible," he added.

"I'm off work tomorrow," she murmured.

"Good, I really like the idea of that, as long as you don't have anything against breakfast," he teased.

"I don't have anything against breakfast," she stated immediately, still in her serious mode. "Just tell me that you won't do anything stupid, right?"

"No, I won't do anything stupid," he reassured her. "Don't worry. That's really not me at all," he repeated. "But I do want to make sure that Chica is safe, and I won't be pushed around by some punk-ass bully, hiding behind his daddy's badge."

"What time then?" she asked. "And where would you like to meet?"

He thought about it and then said, "How about sevenish? Or is that too early, considering it's your day off and that you've been working extra?"

She laughed. "No, that's fine. My days off are often way earlier than that."

"That's what I figured. If seven works for you, that's great. I should be back by then."

"Back from where?" she asked.

"I'll head up to the park first to make sure Chica gets breakfast. Then, if I can get close enough to talk to her and if I am really lucky," he added, "maybe I'll get her on a leash."

"Wow, that is positive thinking."

"It needs to be," Landon stated, "because I don't trust that asshole kid at all."

"No, none of us do," she said. "That's something this town has lived with for a long time."

"And the deputy never does anything?"

"No, and neither does the sheriff. When I asked him about it once, he just shrugged and told me, *Kids will be kids*, then added something about him growing out of it."

"That's the trouble, because he won't. He'll only grow *into* it," Landon declared. "People like that are abusers, one way or another. Either it'll manifest as domestic violence toward a wife or a child, who bears the brunt of it, or they'll end up even worse and lash out at the community and beyond, thinking that the world owes them and that they can do whatever the hell they want without any kind of restrictions or accountability or consequences placed on them."

"Oh, I think he's already there," she said. "Enough about him. So we'll do seven in the morning. That's perfect. Any preference on where to go?"

"Nope, I'll go with your recommendations on this one."

She picked a restaurant just around the corner. "That one is really nice for breakfast."

"Good. I'll see you first thing in the morning." And, with that, Landon rang off. With a smile and with the dogs curled up all around him, he turned in for the night.

CHAPTER 7

SABRINA WOKE AFTER a rough night. There was no reason for her not to sleep, but she kept waking up, checking her surroundings and then going back under again. She'd be a liar if she thought that Landon hadn't played a part in her dreams, because he certainly had. But it was also intermixed with danger and that stupid kid with his air rifle, BB gun, or whatever the hell he'd graduated to, just to attack dogs.

All she saw was Chica, starving, injured, and looking for a home, and it broke Sabrina's heart every time she caught an image of the War Dog in her dreams. It wasn't fair, but life was like that so often, and she saw plenty of it at the hospital and at the vet clinic. She didn't need to see what people did to each other because she already worked with those who neared the end of their lives, but to see what people did to animals? Well, … that was just too much.

Finally she got up around 5:30 a.m., then had a shower and sat out on her deck with a cup of coffee. By 6:15 a.m., she was wishing they'd made the plans for breakfast earlier, but she also knew that it was too early to accommodate Landon's plans. Besides, this being her day off work, she had really hoped to get some good sleep, especially since she'd scheduled herself out of the chance to sleep in earlier this week. But that was just the way of life.

She instinctively knew that Landon was already up. Most certainly he'd gone out looking for Chica. Hell, she was half tempted to go out herself. As she sat here wondering, she got angrier and angrier. Finally, taking a chance and noting it was 6:30 a.m. now, she texted to see if they were still on for breakfast.

The response was a little slower to come than usual, but he did eventually answer. **Absolutely.**

With a smile, she hopped up and texted, **Good, I'm going for a walk then, and I'll meet you there.**

He sent her a thumbs-up and added, **I might be a little bit late, but I'll be there.**

She frowned at that. **Should I hold off?**

Instead of sending her yet another text, he phoned her. "I'm out with Chica," he explained. "I caught sight of her, but I can't get close to her yet."

"Did she eat the dog food?" Sabrina asked excitedly.

"It looks like it," he murmured, "but she's very touchy."

"Of course she is. I wouldn't be at all surprised if she's fully aware of who is after her."

"And that wouldn't make me happy either," he noted.

"But hopefully she is smart enough to avoid that crazy kid. As long as she knows that he's not you. We don't want that idiot to come along and take advantage of her, as she becomes a little more neutral to people because of the food. Then that punk could get close enough to shoot her."

"I know," Landon acknowledged. "I'm trying to give her enough food that she'll be full up and not take any chances on getting fed elsewhere because she's so hungry. But I also don't want to leave her alone too much."

She immediately suggested, "Look. We can cancel breakfast, so you can stay there."

"No, not necessary at all," he replied. "I also need her to know that I'm coming back and forth. The issue will be if that kid comes back here."

"I wish there was a way to know," she muttered.

"Are there any cameras around here?" he asked.

"I don't know," she said. "I've never even thought about that. But it's a park, so I really don't know. I don't think we have the budget for things like that."

"No, maybe not," he agreed, but his tone was thoughtful. "Maybe I'll set up something myself."

"Can you?" she asked curiously.

"I don't have the equipment with me, but I wouldn't need much," he stated. "Let me think on it. I'll meet you at the restaurant in twenty." With that, he hung up.

She frowned but was willing to meet up with him and to continue their conversation. She hated to be so anxious about Chica—and Landon—but the whole thing had set her on edge. It would be nice to just scoop up the poor dog and bring her home, but she was so untrusting at this point in time. Landon was right in that they didn't want to do anything to jeopardize the progress he was making. Neither did they want somebody else to take advantage of that progress for their own purpose. It would really hurt to have this asshole kid get close enough to Chica to really hurt her, all because of the work that Landon had been doing.

But it was also the way of the world sometimes, with often no way to separate the good from the bad. She headed in the direction of the coffee shop, even though it was a tad early, so she would likely have to wait for Landon. She made it a slow walk, so she didn't get there too early. Just a few minutes before seven, she walked inside.

She took a table in the far corner, so she could see when

he arrived. The waitress came by, and Sabrina just ordered coffee, adding that she was expecting someone to join her. With her coffee cooling, she sat here on her phone, aimlessly scrolling through the news. Then she quickly shut it down, weary of the steady stream of depressing news and negativity.

There was just no end to the bad news out there. She wished there was a website or a news media outlet just devoted to good news. She knew the odd heartwarming story was handed around, but the bad news seemed to dominate. While she understood it on some level, she also found it depressing. She didn't do much social media for the same reason. She looked up, when something caught her attention, to see Landon striding toward her. She smiled up at him. "Hey, you weren't late after all."

"A few minutes maybe." He sat down across from her, looked at her coffee, and nodded. "I'm glad you got coffee first."

"Are you kidding?" she joked. "Coffee is my life, imperative for my existence."

He chuckled. "I hear you there."

"What about your dogs?" she asked.

"My three are in the truck." He pointed toward the window beside her.

She saw his truck but no sign of them in the window.

"They'll probably just sleep for a while," he noted. "They had a pretty busy morning. We've been out there since four-thirty a.m."

Her eyebrows shot up at that. "And here I thought I was an early riser."

"I was just tossing and turning," he explained. "I couldn't get Chica out of my mind. So, as soon as it was light enough, I headed out there. The dog food I left her was gone, so I added more. Then I sat there and waited, just talking to her and the other dogs."

"Do you think she's injured?"

"From the view I had, I couldn't see a wound or anything, but she wasn't moving very well," he noted. "So I don't know if it's from her old injuries or something new. As soon as she realized I left more food, she gobbled it up pretty quickly."

"Did you leave her extra?"

"You know it." He smiled. "As other people and traffic started to pick up, she shifted into the shadows around me, but she's definitely there. Now I must find a way to get close enough to get a leash on her."

"That'll be the trick," she noted.

"I know, but I'm determined to get her. Especially now that I can see her," he murmured.

She smiled. "So what did you decide about a camera?"

"Oh, right. I sent a message to my boss about it to see if there was something I could do. It must be battery operated, and I don't know what kind of distance we can get from it."

"Where would you put it, and what would you be trying to take a picture of?" she asked curiously.

"I'd put it close to where I've got the dog, and I'd want it pointing toward the parking lot."

"Ah, to get the kid on film."

"Yeah, because that kid is a damn nuisance. It would be one thing if he truly were a kid, but I don't think he fits that classification anymore. I'm pretty sure he's an adult."

She thought about it and nodded. "Yeah, I think he's got to be like twenty-one, twenty-two-*ish*."

"Definitely an adult," he said.

The waitress returned just then, with menus and a coffeepot in hand. He turned over his cup and nodded. Thanking her, he grabbed a menu, and they both quickly ordered, thanking the waitress.

Landon continued their conversation, as if no interruption had been had. "That's the thing about being up at four-thirty a.m. I'm definitely hungry by seven."

"I woke up at five and didn't quite know what to do with myself. I was tempted to go out and look for poor Chica myself," she admitted, "but I knew I'd be interfering with whatever you were doing."

"Yeah, I am trying to keep it down to just one of us at the moment," he murmured, "so I appreciate you holding back."

She nodded. "I just really hate the idea of Chica suffering."

"She's got food at the moment, and lots of water is around there too. I'll go back after breakfast," he shared, "unless I can arrange to get some security."

"If you could gain her confidence and could win some support from her, you might get her out of there before the need for that."

"That would be nice," Landon agreed, "but I'm not sure it will happen that fast. I don't know if the trucker treated her all that well either because she's very skittish."

"And it could be nothing to do with the trucker at all," she replied calmly. "We've seen lots of animals come in with old anxieties that flare up when faced with new stressors, and it's heartbreaking."

"I get it." Then he smiled at her. "So what will you do on your day off?" he asked. "I don't imagine you get too many of them, if you're called in for double shifts all the time."

"I don't, and I'm really hoping I don't get called in today," she admitted, "but I'll take it if I do."

He cocked an eyebrow at her. "Are you short on cash?"

"No, I'm not, but there are always animals to help, if I do happen to have extra."

He studied her for a long moment and saw the sincerity in her face.

At least she hoped that's what he saw.

Then he nodded. "It's nice to know good people are out there, working hard for animals who need help."

She chuckled. "I was thinking the same thing about you earlier. It's a sad world when we look at everybody around us and wonder which side of the coin they fall on."

"Right," he said, with a shake of his head. "It's kind of a sad world in so many ways."

"Yet I guess some of us choose to hang on to the good things and just keep moving and doing what we can."

"Absolutely," he agreed. "As long as we keep the balance weighted more to the good than to the bad overall, we're doing okay."

"I hope so," she muttered. "But, as for what I'll do today, I don't know. I have grocery shopping to do, and the usual errands to run—a parcel to mail and things like that." Sabrina shrugged. "Normally on my days off, I would head to the vet clinic and help them too, but not today."

"Because you're on the outs with your friend?"

That was a shrewd understanding on his part, and, while Sabrina wasn't sure how he came to that conclusion, she replied, "Maybe."

He nodded. "Not sure what the problem is, but I hate to see good friends on the outs. Particularly when animals are involved. If your time at the vet clinic is needed, I would hate to see a hiccough in your friendship changing that."

Sabrina pondered that for a moment, and thankfully the waitress came back to refill their coffee, so she had an excuse to park the conversation until the waitress left.

And Landon, he picked it right up afterward. "Besides, do you show up to help there for the animals or for her?"

"Both really," she noted, "and for me as well, but it's nice to have a break sometimes too."

"Absolutely," he agreed. "Mental health is really important, especially when you're dealing with a stressful job, and yours would qualify, would it not?"

"It's hard to not get attached to the patients," she said. "So many times I end up with so much admiration for them, as they go through very difficult times, still with their heads up and a grace that amazes me. I keep thinking that, if I were in their position, I'd be screaming and kicking the walls, railing at the injustices of life, but they handle it so well."

"Not all of them though, do they?"

"No, definitely not all of them. But the ones who do so gracefully are those you remember the most," she noted, with a smile. "You want to remember them all, but I can't. It's a day-to-day business, and, at some point in time, the patients become a blur of need. Some of them I only see for a day, before they are moved. Some of them I see for weeks and others for months." She shrugged. "And I can't remember them all, although there are definitely those who really hit the spot."

"Of course." He nodded. "I'm sure it's the same at the vet clinic. You can't remember all the animals, but a few will touch your heart."

"Yeah, but the problem is, you get to the point where you just want to take them all home."

"I don't know how you don't." He laughed.

"Lack of space and time," she admitted. "I realized at some point that it wasn't fair for me to have all these animals, when I am away so much at work. Also I've had some neighbors who haven't been happy with me as well. So now I have my own two dogs and tend to focus more on fostering instead, bringing them back when they're healthy, more socialized, and a little more adoptable."

He shook his head at that. "You'd think that the neighbors would be happy you are helping out."

"Nope, they just don't want animals around. You're either an animal lover or you're not, it seems, although a lot straddle the fence and sit in the middle."

"I never understood that either," Landon declared, as he stared out at his truck. "That's how I ended up with those three out there." He smiled.

"Of course, and you love them, and together you're a family."

He nodded. "I can't imagine all these people who have a pet for however long and then just dump it, even though the animal has been part of their life and given them its trust and its best years."

By the time they had finished breakfast, she'd learned a whole lot more about him. And, so far, she found nothing not to like.

As they ordered refills on coffee, he sat back. "Thank you."

Sincerity filled his voice, but she wasn't exactly sure what he was thanking her for. "For what?" she asked. "For help tracking down Chica or for breakfast?"

"I was hoping to pay for breakfast, so I won't thank you for that," he replied, with a note of humor. "But for coming out with me to have breakfast together, that is a definite yes. Even with my three little buddies out there, sometimes life can get a little lonely."

"Isn't that the truth." She thought about all the hours she spent on the job, where sometimes she just wanted to be held, just wanted to know that she wasn't alone. That's also why she stayed and spent time with so many of her patients because they were in the same boat. Not everybody had somebody in this world, especially not somebody they wanted at their side when they were dying. She smiled at him. "So I presume from here you're heading back out?"

He nodded. "Yeah. I'll swing by the pet store and pick up some more groceries for her."

She nodded. "I'll head home, and, with any luck, I can get my laundry and housecleaning caught up, then get those errands that need to be done." She sighed. "If you have any success, give me a shout and let me know, will you?"

He nodded, as he smiled. "I will." As they both stood, he added, "I'll take care of the bill."

"Thank you for that. … It was lovely to spend some time out in the world, instead of just being at work or home."

"Ditto," he said, with a laugh.

"Maybe we can do it again sometime?" she suggested hesitantly.

He turned toward her. "I'd really like that. I'll let you know how things go today," he said, "so maybe we can meet up tomorrow."

"Perfect," she replied, and, with that, she walked out.

LANDON WATCHED SABRINA go, as he now sat and sipped away at the rest of his coffee. She was hands down one of the nicest people he'd met in a very long time. When the bill came, he paid it and then headed out to his truck, where the dogs greeted him with joy. He spent a moment just loving on them and then said, "Okay now, settle down. We're going to a pet store."

With that, their ears cocked, and they immediately tucked into the dog bed. He figured that they understood those words even more than terms like *sit* or *walk* or even *treats*. He set his GPS for the local pet store, and, when he got there, he put the dogs on their leashes and walked them inside. He let them each pick out a toy, and, with another bag of dog food for Chica and the Three Stooges to share, he headed to the cash register.

The cashiers were oohing and aawing over the dogs while he paid. By the time he got everybody back out to the truck, he'd garnered quite a bit of attention. He was used to it though because the dogs were very cute. And, when they were carrying toys—which in the one's case was a big teddy bear—it was too adorable for words.

But Landon was on a mission, and it didn't include time for the gawkers. He had a War Dog that he was trying hard to bring in from the cold, even if Chica didn't realize she had such an option. He wanted to make her know that it was safe for her to reach out to him. By the time he parked at the site, Badger had gotten back to him.

"You can put up something temporary," he relayed, "unless law enforcement has a problem with it."

"Yeah, well this deputy is likely to have a big problem because it's his son I'll catch on video."

"Then you definitely need to do it," Badger confirmed

instantly. "I can airfreight some supplies to you."

"I don't need much, so how about I just go to the local electronics store, pick up what I need, and charge it back to you, when I turn in my mileage and all."

"That works," Badger stated. "Just make sure you keep it on a low-budget plan."

"Yep, no problem." Landon walked back to where he'd been feeding Chica but saw no sign of her. He put down more dog food and called out to her, "I'll be back in a little bit." After that, he headed to the local electronics store, which turned out to be perfect timing, as it was just opening. He walked in, picked up a handful of things that he needed, then headed back out to Chica.

With his dogs loose and running around, he set up the camera in the area where he had the dog food laid out for her, but angled in a way that would also get anyone walking up this way. He needed to know if she was eating all the food or if another animal was eating some. He didn't begrudge anybody a meal, but he wanted to make sure that Chica got enough to sustain her. Then he sat at the picnic table and worked away on a simplified report of what he was doing.

He sent an email to Badger, with a picture of the receipt. That done, he yawned a couple times, then looked around at the dogs and suggested, "We could just lie down here." The dogs looked at him sleepily, and he nodded. He headed over to the bank and stretched out, his eyes closed. He wasn't sure whether he slept or not, but he definitely dozed in and out, which was pretty typical for him.

His leg was sore but not bad enough to do anything about. He needed to get more talcum powder somewhere soon, and then he would change the way he put on the prosthetic, so it was a little easier on the skin of his stump.

Then a balm would help too. But again, it wasn't a big deal, just one of those little irritating things that happened when you had prosthetics. At least he could drive and do everything that he needed to do.

Although, as he thought about Sabrina, some of the things he would like to do would be more of a challenge. He had yet to have a serious relationship since his injuries, but he'd been pretty darn sure that the ankle would scare off most of them. Yet Sabrina didn't seem to be too bothered— maybe because of her medical training. He didn't know for sure, but then not being too bothered was a long way from wanting to be in his arms. Of course she hadn't seen the ugly reality either. It wasn't so bad when he was fully dressed, but, under the clothes and the prosthetic, was a different story.

He could hope that it would all work out, and he knew he would certainly give it his best shot, but it would take somebody who was open and accepting. As he lay here, one of the dogs started to growl. He reached a hand down and placed it on her head. "It's okay, Curly." She was, by far, the more nervous of the lot.

He put it down to being female and just more protective. He shifted ever-so-slightly, so he could look behind him, and, sure enough, there was Chica. She was limping a bit and staring at him, obviously wary.

"It's okay, girl," he repeated to Curly, his hand on her. And then he called out to Chica, "Hey, Chica. It's been a pretty rough go, huh, girl?"

She lowered her head and sniffed the air around him. He knew Chica would have already picked up the scent of his dogs. But that shouldn't scare her because his dogs were small and generally very friendly, and they'd been here before. Although the three of them were looking at her a little more apprehensively than he was expecting, and Chica was injured and scared, which made everything a little bit different.

She shifted another step forward, and he kept talking to her calmly. "It's all right, girl. I brought you more food. Did you get breakfast?" Right then a vehicle backfired nearby, and she took one look and booked it in the opposite direction. She certainly could run, but he knew that would exhaust her. She had an odd gait, which indicated she was using the one leg quite a bit less than the other. But then, if it was broken and hadn't healed quite right, that would explain it.

Many people wouldn't do elective surgeries on dogs just to fix something like that. As long as the dog didn't seem to be suffering, they would leave it. Plus, if the dog had a protected home environment and wasn't out trying to fend for itself, it was probably fine in the long run. Still, in this case, it obviously hindered Chica. Something he would take a look at, if he ever got to the point of getting close enough to handle her. Knowing it would be a while before she came back, he got up, then walked over, checked on the dog food, and saw plenty was left, then went back to his spot on the ground, hoping for a little nap.

He fully expected to spend the entire day here. When another vehicle pulled up, and Landon heard raucous laughter in the background, he sat up and spied the same kid that he had had the run-in with the other night. The big grin on the young man's face fell away when he saw Landon.

"What the hell?" he asked. "What are you doing here again?"

"It's a public park, so no reason I can't be here," Landon stated in a calm and reasonable tone.

At that, the kid scowled. "You're just being nosy, hanging around. I told you that dog was a menace."

"Yeah, you keep telling me that, but I'm pretty sure other people are telling your father something different."

At that, his eyebrows shot up. "What's the matter? Did you run to the police with a complaint about me?" he asked, with a mocking grin.

"Nope, I can't be bothered with that," Landon stated. "You've been crossing the line for years, and the law has never done anything about you yet, so it's not likely they'll start now. It'll take a different kind of law to do that."

"What's that?" he asked in a mocking tone.

"If you don't know, I won't bother telling you." At that, Landon stood up.

That's when the kid got a look at his ankle and laughed. "Jesus, I didn't even notice in the dark, but you're only half a man as it is."

"That's fine with me," Landon replied, quite accustomed to punks like this. "Half a man is still plenty more than you are."

At that, the kid snarled. "What the fuck? I don't have to take that shit from you."

"No, you sure don't," Landon agreed. "A *big man* like you, making fun of a war vet. Yeah, that's about your style, isn't it?" Landon taunted, his own tone mocking.

"I'm not so stupid as to go fight in the damn war. Nobody wins." He laughed. "And you come home, looking like you're some busted-up hero, but nobody gives a fuck."

"I get it," Landon said cheerfully. "Good thing I didn't go into the service for that reason then, isn't it?"

A woman appeared from out of the passenger side of the kid's truck. She looked nervously at Landon and then back at the kid. "Come on, Jared. Let's leave."

"No," he snapped. "I told you the dog is here."

"I don't care about any dog," she wailed, with a nasally whine. "I just want to leave."

"I'm not leaving." He glared at her. "What the hell is the matter with you anyway?"

She shrugged. "You know how I feel about confrontations."

"This isn't a confrontation," he snarled at her. "This is just a broken-down excuse of a man." He turned to sneer at Landon.

At that exchange, Landon looked over at her. "Seriously? This is the best you could do for yourself?"

She flushed at that.

"Really? That's what you'll go with?" Jared laughed. "I'm rich. All the women go with me."

"Ah, so that's the reason. I was wondering. You can only get a woman because you have money." He shook his head at that and told the young lady, "You realize there's a hell of a lot more to life than a douchebag like this, right?"

She stared at Landon nervously, then turned to Jared. "Come on, Jared. Let's go."

"Fuck off," he yelled at her. "You can fucking leave if you want, but I'm not leaving this asshole here, thinking he owns the place." She took a step back, obviously used to his temper. "Yeah, just fuck off. I don't give a shit. I don't want to spend the day with you anyway."

Landon watched the hurt cross the young woman's face. He nodded. "Look. You're probably better off if you do go," he suggested. "Your buddy here is looking for a well-deserved ass-kicking anyway."

"Really, like you'll do that?" Jared asked, as he pulled out his BB gun.

"Oh yeah, right." Landon laughed. "I forgot you're a big-ass hunter who uses a BB gun on innocent people, aren't you?"

"It's an air pistol, asshole."

"Jared, put that away," she said. "You know what your dad said."

"Shut the fuck up," he yelled, turning toward her. "I told you to take off, if you don't want to be a part of this."

She hesitated, biting her tongue.

Landon looked over at her. "You know what you need to do," he said. She hesitated, but it was obvious that she was torn. He understood that it was hard to buck the bully in the sandbox, but somebody had to. "Go ahead. It's better if you can leave."

She shook her head. "You don't know what it's like when he gets like this."

"I don't need to know," Landon stated. "I've faced idiots like this many times. Bullies in the sandbox just grow up to become bigger bullies, when they're out in the real world."

She winced at that. "Still," she murmured.

Landon looked over at Jared. "Nice to know you're so well-thought-of around here."

"You don't know anything," Jared snapped, as he quickly checked that his gun was loaded.

"Are you planning on shooting me with that thing?" Landon asked, a note of amusement in his voice. "That would not make me happy." It would also likely turn Landon's temper into a raging storm. If this kid thought he would get away with something like that—not to mention the fact that shooting Landon would be well past the bully stage, stepping down a very murderous lane. It's not as if the air gun would hurt him. Well, it would hurt, but it wouldn't hurt him as bad as a lot of more lethal weapons could. It was proof of where this kid was heading in life and how this asshole thought he could get away with this because his father and the rest of local law enforcement had always allowed him to.

"Do you really think your dad will turn a blind eye when you start shooting people with your little paintball gun?" Landon asked. "You think he can protect you from the lawsuits coming from this when you start shooting an unarmed war vet?" he asked, with mockery in his voice.

At that, the kid hesitated. Immediately his girlfriend took advantage of the moment. "He's right. You know that. Come on. Let's go."

Jared looked back at Landon. "I don't give a fuck if he's right or not. Nobody talks to me like that."

She was already back at the truck, but, instead of the passenger side, she got into the driver's seat and turned the vehicle on.

Jared roared, "Get the fuck out of the driver's seat, you bitch," racing over to his truck.

He pulled up to the door and hauled her out, sending her spinning to the ground in a fury. He got into the truck and yelled at her, "You can fucking stay here!"

With that, he slammed it into Reverse and peeled out of the parking lot and headed down the highway.

Landon walked slowly toward her and helped her up to her feet. "Are you okay?"

She took a shaky breath and tried for a smile. "Yeah, I'm okay." With a shaky hand, she brushed her hair off her face. "I'm sorry about that. When he gets like that, it's impossible to talk to him."

"So why are you with him?" Landon asked bluntly.

She shrugged. "I don't know. Sometimes I wonder."

"You need to be asking yourself a lot more as the days go on," he suggested. "You already know that he's abusive, so the question is, why are you still with him, particularly when you know he'll only get worse?"

"Is he though?" she asked, a note of desperation in her voice. "I was hoping I could change him."

Landon shook his head at that. "You and every other female in this world says the same thing about the abusive guys they hook up with. The one who beats the crap out of them and shoots the dogs in front of them and beats up the kids in order to make the women in their life behave," he stated, his voice hard. "Let me tell you something. There's no changing them. The die is already cast. Could he change if he chose to? Sure. But that's clearly not what he's choosing. He likes the power play too much. The best thing you can do is go home and make a major change in your life."

"He won't let me do that," she muttered. "He's angry right now, but he'll be at my front door in no time, and he'll get all pissed off if I don't go out with him."

"Then maybe you need to do something about that," he stated.

"What do you think I can do? You don't know what he's like."

"You're already afraid of him, aren't you?"

She hesitated and then nodded. "A little bit, yeah. He's been like this for years, but now? … He's just getting worse."

"Of course he's getting worse. There's literally nobody out there to curtail him."

She swallowed hard. "He's just mean, like the way he was talking to you. That's how he treats people in town too."

"His dad doesn't do anything about it, huh?"

"His dad was the same. He used to beat up their mom pretty good. They say he suddenly stopped, but I don't know anything about that. Maybe he thought about his son. I don't know, but he protects his boy, so Jared's never had any consequences."

"Yeah, I get it," Landon noted, "but I really hate bullies."

"He'll hurt you," she said. "Couldn't you just leave town and maybe not get into it with him?"

"And why do you think I would do that?" he huffed, staring at her.

"Maybe to preserve your life?" she said instantly.

"Is he going to kill me?"

She winced. "I don't want to say that, but, when he's angry, and he's got a mad drunk on, it gets really ugly."

"Wow. Nice warning. Too bad his dad doesn't do anything about it."

"Jared's been warned multiple times, and he needs to smarten up, but I don't know where it will end. The sheriff is pretty pissed at Jared's behavior and at his dad for protecting him. They've all gotten into arguments themselves. Honestly, I wouldn't be at all surprised if the sheriff isn't a little afraid of both Jared and his dad." Landon stared at her in shock, and she shrugged. "Like I said, the whole family is kind of messed-up."

"What happened to the mother?"

"She kind of disappeared a few years back."

Well, crap. Just how ugly was this family? "*Kind of* disappeared?"

"Yeah," she said. "We figure she got up in the middle of the night and was smart enough to run away."

"And this was after his dad supposedly changed his ways?"

"Jared didn't treat her very well either."

"Tell me again why you're still with him?"

"I don't know how to get away," she whispered. "Most of the time he's great. I mean, he's fun to be with, and he's generous and kind, but then there's the rest of the time." And, with that, she shrugged and added, "Anyway, I'll get out of here, before he comes back. I'm hoping he'll calm down, before he comes back my way again."

As she went to leave, Landon asked, "How old are you?"

She looked at him. "I'm twenty-two. Why?"

"Do you understand that you may not make it to twenty-three like this?"

Her skin flushed bright red and then paled dramatically. "I hope you're wrong. I hope he's not that far gone."

"You know what? I'd feel better about Jared if I knew where his mom was," Landon stated, "because the chances of his dad or Jared killing her are pretty damn high."

She stared at him, her eyes wide, then her bottom lip trembled. "You shouldn't say things like that."

"Really? And why not?" he muttered.

"Because, if they hear you, they'll be really upset."

He just stared at her, with that flat look in his eyes. "Bring it on. There is no room in the world for people who act like that, especially if it's led to at least one murder. And you need to get your shit together and to get the hell away from him."

She gave him a sad smile. "I think it's already too late for that." And, with that shocking answer, she turned and started to walk down the road.

He raced after her and asked, "Hey, look. Do you want a

ride somewhere?"

She looked at him, saw the big truck still in the parking lot, and shook her head. "No, if he sees me in your truck, then he'll get even angrier, so it's much better if I walk. That way, when he comes looking for me, I'll be alone. If he thought I'd hooked up with you, that would be more fuel on the fire, you know? And I don't know at what point in time he'll blow."

"When was the last time you saw him blow?"

"With the dog," she replied. "He was sitting there, throwing some pieces of a hamburger on the bench, and making a big joke about it. When the dog got too close because he'd deliberately put the meat there, he gave it a hell of a whipping," she said, with tears in her eyes. "I didn't think it would make it. But it took off, and now he's determined to kill it."

"Did she go after him?"

"She was fighting for her life," she shared. "She got away, but he got bit in the process. But it wasn't like she attacked him or anything."

"Right, so he deliberately teases a starving dog with food, then beats it for trying to eat, and now he wants to turn around and kill it. That's a nice guy you've got there."

She nodded. "Like I told you, he's got a mean streak."

"You never told the sheriff about what he did to the dog?"

She shook her head. "Nobody asked."

"Of course not, and I suppose, if the sheriff does ask, you won't tell the truth either?"

She looked at him, her eyes wide. Then slowly she shook her head. "No, I don't dare."

He nodded to himself. "I'm not going anywhere. That

dog is very important to me, and I'll be here every time that asshole Jared comes back."

"Then you better camp here because Jared won't stop."
And, with that, she turned and walked away.

CHAPTER 8

B Y THE TIME Sabrina was done running errands and got home, it was time for a cup of tea. She put the kettle on as she put away the groceries and transferred her laundry to the dryer. When she finished with that, she sat down on her small deck, periodically checking her phone for an update from Landon on the dog.

When her phone rang, she quickly snatched it up, without even looking at the screen.

"Hello?" It was Angela. Sabrina's heart sinking, she frowned. "Oh, hi."

Silence came on the other end, and one long moment later Angela replied, "I guess I've really blown something between us, haven't I?"

"You certainly crossed a line that I'm not terribly impressed with, but, hey, whatever." She tried for nonchalant indifference, but it was hard. They had been friends for so very long.

"Look. I get that you're pissed off and upset with me, but we're really short-handed today. I was wondering if you would set aside your differences with me and come give the animals a few hours. I know it's your day off."

Sabrina wasn't sure what to say to that because she really didn't want to go in. She wanted to be free and available in case Landon called. "I guess I can come for a couple hours," she replied reluctantly.

"Oh, good," Angela said. "I really am sorry."

Sabrina didn't say anything because *sorry* goes only so far on something like this. She didn't want Angela to think she could keep saying things like that. "Whatever. I'll be there in an hour. I'm just having some tea."

"O—kay," Angela said, as if she were aware that things were still not good between them. Then after an awkward silence, she added, "I'll see you when you get here." And, with that, she hung up.

Sabrina stared at her phone, wondering why she was being contrary because there was no reason not to move past this. No matter how much she really liked Landon, she didn't even know if she would get a chance to see him again.

She wanted to spend any time she could get with him, and, if there was an opportunity, this was it. Still, she also wanted to be there for the animals, and, as he had alluded to earlier, trouble in their friendship could have a negative impact on the animals. Of course that should never happen, but, all too often, relationships did affect things like that.

So, by the time she got to the vet clinic, the receptionist was looking pretty harried. "What do you need me to do?" Sabrina asked her.

"Thank God you're here," Cindy exclaimed. "Can you take out some of the dogs? They haven't had a break, not even to go to the bathroom, much less to run around or to get any attention."

"Yeah, I can do that." Sabrina then headed into the back and found quite a few of them here. "Why so many dogs?" she asked the vet, as he passed through.

He frowned. "A rescue group just came through. They're moving to the next state, but they needed a place for the animals overnight, and some of them were not doing so well traveling. Therefore, we've got them here for the day."

With a nod at that, Sabrina quickly moved the dogs outside to the dog runs to give them a break. Most of them were stressed but happy to be outside and more than happy to see somebody. She spent quite a few minutes just cuddling each one and letting them run around, all the while knowing it would break her heart when she had to take them back to their cages again.

But at least they were heading to better homes, which is more than she could say for an awful lot of the animals they saw here. By the time she was done with that, she turned around to see what else was needed. And it was usually cleaning cages. As she caught sight of the vet again, she asked, "What next?"

He looked at her, distracted. "Would you mind asking out front? I have no idea." And, with that, he was gone again.

She headed out to the receptionist and asked her, "What do you need next from me?"

Cindy looked up and tried to refocus. "Our clean-up girl didn't come in today," she noted hesitantly. "How do you feel about cages?"

Sabrina nodded. "That's what I figured would be next. It looks like they haven't been touched in a while." She went back and began the process of cleaning the cages. The rabbit and cat cages all needed new bedding, and, depending on the condition of the animals, they all needed to be scrubbed down too. She worked her way through cage after cage, wondering why she even bothered coming in. It was obvious they needed her, but, if they were doing well as a vet clinic, why didn't they just hire somebody? Sure, today somebody had called in sick, but it was still something that nagged at Sabrina.

Maybe she shouldn't be quite so willing to help out. She always worried that the animals would suffer if she didn't come, but, in reality, it would force them to do something about solving their ongoing staffing problems. By the time she was done, she was more than ready to head back to her place. Stopping out front, she asked, "Isn't it about time you guys hired some staff?"

The receptionist nodded. "That would be nice, but they keep putting it off."

"Maybe if I quit coming in, they'll quit putting it off," she replied.

At that, the woman looked at her in horror. "Please don't do that. When it gets tough in here, it's the animals that will suffer."

"Yet they shouldn't. And the vet needs to address that situation, not me," she declared, her voice growing louder. "There should be enough staff here to get the cleaning done every day, regardless."

"We're still trying to work a deal with the second vet," Cindy noted.

"But that's just an excuse and, even if the second vet comes on board, it'll just make it even busier in here," she murmured. "Where is there any relief for the rest of these jobs?"

"I don't know." Cindy lowered her voice and added, "There's definitely been some issues."

"Yeah, I know because I'm coming in every day on my day off and lots of other days too."

"I know, and we really appreciate it."

"Yeah, but how much is everybody else helping out on

their time off?"

The receptionist winced. "We're not ... in a way. I stay late every day, but not everybody here is doing overtime, and I don't see anyone volunteering time."

At that, Sabrina stopped and asked, "What about Angela?"

Cindy gave Sabrina a sideways look and then quickly shook her head.

"She's okay to call me in though," Sabrina snapped.

Flushing, the receptionist looked around. "You didn't hear that from me. *Please.*"

"No worries. Anyway the cages are cleaned up, *for now*, so I'm leaving." And, with that, not even attempting to see Angela, Sabrina walked out. And she had to admit that the whole thing bothered her.

She suddenly realized how messed-up this situation was and how Angela had been taking advantage of her. Her supposed best friend went home to her boyfriend, while talking up Sabrina to give of her time off from her nursing job. It was hurtful to find that things may not be as they seemed between them. Sabrina had kept going along, giving of her free time to the clinic all because of the animals—and Angela—but something wasn't right.

Sabrina wasn't even sure what to think at this point. So she walked outside, and she stopped to smell the roses literally and just took a few minutes to breathe deeply. It had been a chaotic day, and it was already three o'clock. Realizing she hadn't heard from Landon, she frowned, and she stared at her phone, wondering if she should do something. Just then it rang, and it was him. With a smile she answered, "Hey, I was wondering if I would hear from you."

"I'm still here with the dog," he said, but there was a

fatigue in his voice that she hadn't heard before.

"Are you okay?"

"Yeah. I had another run-in with Jared, the punk with the BB gun. This time he brought his girlfriend and that attitude, and he ended up fighting with her. He literally tossed her out of his truck and onto the ground and then drove off, leaving her stranded."

She stopped and stared at her phone. "Seriously?"

"Yeah, seriously. I had quite the conversation with the girlfriend. I ended up telling her that she needed to get the hell out of that situation while she still could. Apparently Jared's mother disappeared sometime back. Like here one day, gone the next."

"I vaguely remember hearing something about that. Somewhere around that time he was up on nuisance charges or something. His mother leaving made everybody feel like he was just acting out."

"Oh, he was acting out all right, but I'll tell you, after talking to the girlfriend, I'm not so sure something much more sinister wasn't going on."

She shook her head. "Like what though?" Sabrina asked.

"I don't know," he replied, "but I'm really tempted to find out."

"You're really bothered by it, aren't you?" she asked. "It's odd. That kid's a jerk, but I didn't think something like that would get to you."

"Besides the fact that he's a useless piece of hot air," he added, "I'm pretty worried about the dog. He came back with the girl, intending to shoot Chica. And, with me working to get on better terms with her, I'm worried she'll let him get close to her again. Although she apparently did attack him last time but rightfully so. He had teased her with food while she was starving, then, when she got close enough to get the food that he was supposedly giving her, he kicked her really hard several times. Chica bit him, and that's when the asshole decided that Chica's a danger."

"Oh my God." Sabrina stared blindly at the street around her. "I hate that."

"I know. ... I'm sorry. I wasn't even sure I should tell you."

"No, no," she disagreed, "of course you should. I just wish I knew how to help you right now."

"Where are you?" he asked curiously. "Sounds like you're outside."

"I'm on the street, just coming back from the vet clinic."

"Oh, good," Landon said. "Did you patch things up?"

"No, I didn't see Angela, and honestly—" She stopped and thought about it. "No, it's fine. You've got enough problems to worry about already."

"Sure I do, but that doesn't mean there isn't room to hear about what's going on in your world."

She hesitated, then said, "It seems stupid, and I'm not even sure if it's an issue."

"It's definitely something because it's bothering you," he replied. "So what happened?" Then she explained the conversation she'd had with the receptionist. "Now that is interesting," he noted. "So they expect you to volunteer your time off, knowing how much you work already, but they aren't staying late or doing anything extra themselves? Talk about selfish and cheap."

"Yeah, something like that. I just—for the first time to-day—I started to wonder if I was being taken advantage of."

"You are, in my opinion. However," he added, "*if* you are being taken advantage of, in the end, you have to put your foot down because you're allowing it each time you say yes."

"That does *not* make me feel better."

He chuckled. "Nope. So do things on your terms. That's the only way to make sure that what you're doing has value and that you're not being taken advantage of."

"*Great,*" she muttered. "I'm still not sure about that."

"Granted, I think they are being totally selfish to ask you to put in extra time when they won't do it themselves. I don't see them even considering that you have more than a full-time job already. However, playing devil's advocate, seeing things selfishly from the clinic-only point of view, maybe they are lamenting how they're there all day long, and, chances are, they have only so much left to give," he explained. "You probably have volunteers at the hospital, don't you?"

She stopped at the front gate to her place, then stepped inside, closing it behind her. "We do," she admitted.

"And, although you do extra shifts at the hospital, you get paid for them, right?"

"Yes."

"Maybe the clinic wants that hospital system in place over there. That mind-set still totally fails to consider how you have your own job, with what? A fifty-hour workweek?"

"Sometimes more," she muttered.

"And right there, right now, you're feeling like it's too much *because it is.* So maybe you need to just change how you react to the clinic's calls for help."

"It's just frustrating when they are chronically short-handed like that. It's one thing to fill in because someone calls in sick or there are emergencies, but this is pretty routine. I feel like it would be much more efficient to just hire more help, so everyone isn't burned out all the time."

"Is the problem that they can't get anybody decent," he asked, "or is it a case of not wanting to spend the money?"

"I have no idea," she said.

"Maybe that is something you need to find out. At least if you had those answers, you could make fully informed decisions about when to help or not, after you are armed with that knowledge."

She chuckled. "When did you get to be so wise?"

"Somewhere along my many experiences called life," he replied. "The punk today had an awful lot to say about me being a broken-down half of a man," he shared. "It's something I've definitely heard before, but I'll admit it was kind of odd to hear it again today."

"That's ridiculous," she said. "So what if you're missing a foot? I mean, even with that, you'd still be more than enough for that blowhard."

"I told him something along those lines." Landon chuckled. "I don't think he liked it."

"No, he's all ego," she stated, "and honestly you probably need to watch your back."

"Do you think he'd come after me?"

"Yeah. He's not used to people standing up to him. So, not only is he likely to come after you, he's the type to shoot you in the back, without any warning."

"*Great*," he muttered, "just what you want in your town."

"I know, right? Nothing I've ever seen of his handiwork was anything to be proud of." Then she stopped and asked, "Do you really think he might have done something to his mother?"

"I'm thinking somebody might have. Apparently his

father, the deputy, was quite the wifebeater."

"Oh, crap, so the kid takes after his father then. So very typical," she muttered.

"Yep, and you know that's where Jared's headed next in his own relationships. That's why I told the girlfriend to get the hell out. She told me that it was already too late. She was only twenty-two but already looking like life had beaten her down."

"Guys like that are frightening, and I'm pretty sure these women feel like they're stuck with them, until they get dumped because the guy doesn't want them anymore," she noted. "Where are you right now?"

"I'm heading to the truck," he explained. "Quite a few vehicles are coming up the road right now, and I've got my dogs with me, so I want to get them up and out of the way, just in case Jared returns."

"Did you get a camera set up?"

"I did," he confirmed. "I'm also not so sure that kid won't come back with some friends. His girlfriend said Jared was quite the mean drunk as well."

At that, Sabrina felt fear sliding down her spine. "Hurry up and get in the truck then," she said, "like really hurry and get out of there."

"I am, but I'm not planning on leaving," he said. "What's the matter?"

"I don't know. … I'm just feeling nervous right now. You can't trust that kid."

"Does he have a whole gang he runs with?"

"No, I don't think so, but he may have a couple friends who are just as stupid as he is."

"*Great*," he muttered. "*And* it looks like they just arrived." At that, he said, "Gotta go."

He hung up, leaving her standing here, staring in shock at the phone, wondering what she was supposed to do.

WITH HIS THREE little dogs safely stowed in their bed inside his truck, Landon turned to face the newcomers, studying them as they all hopped out of the same vehicle. The punk was the gang leader, and two others were with him. Jared was a problem, but, when you had somebody like this bully—who needed backup to take on Landon—then Jared had even bigger problems. It's one thing if you had somebody with the confidence and the bravado to make an attack on his own, but when asshole Jared had to bring in two friends for backup, Landon knew that he was a weak-ass punk on the inside, and that made him even more dangerous because he probably needed guns to back him up too.

Landon watched as they sauntered toward him. He closed the truck door and turned to lean against it. "Back again?" he asked in that calm voice that he'd used many a time to diffuse problems when he was out on missions.

The punk nodded. "Sure I am. My girlfriend says you gave her a hard time."

"The same girl you pushed out onto the pavement before you drove off? Come on. We both know you're lying, just looking for an excuse to throw a punch," Landon stated. "If that's what you want, no need to lie, just fly at it."

At that, the kid stopped and looked at him. "What?"

"You heard me," Landon declared. "You brought your lackeys here to back you up because you're not man enough to do this on your own. You've got no real beef with me, and you're just trying to drum up some reasons in order do what you want to do, which is to take out your little BB gun and shoot people with it."

At that, his friends stared at him.

"What the fuck is wrong with you?" Jared asked. "You're damaged. You can't even handle a fair fight, and yet here you are, mouthing off at me. Don't you get it? I'll pulverize you to the ground."

"And then shoot me up with your little BB gun?" Landon asked in a mocking voice. He didn't shift from where he stood, his arms crossed over his chest, as he watched Jared like a hawk. "I've seen guys like you before, Jared. You never got into trouble because Daddy was always there to bail you out," Landon said. "But you can bet that my camera system is taking care of this right now and live-feeding it right back."

"Back where?" he asked, stopping in his tracks. "That's bullshit. No camera can do that."

"But what if there is?" asked one of his buddies.

"Yeah, what if there is?" Landon turned his gaze to the others. "Are you guys really that hard up for friends that you've got to hang around with this loser?" Landon asked, shaking his head. "Nothing better in your life to do but pick on people? Like war vets?"

"You're not a war vet," Jared stated. "You were probably just in a fucking car accident."

But one of the other guys noticed his prosthetic. "Man, you can't beat him up. He's only got one foot."

Landon added, "But that won't stop your friend at all. He's out for blood. He needs something to make him feel like a *big man*."

"You know, if you were smart," interrupted the third guy suddenly, "you'd keep your mouth shut."

Landon looked at him insolently. "Yeah? And you'll make me?"

"Sure I will," he replied.

"Yeah, that's what I mean," Jared yelled, stepping forward.

"Meaning that, as long as you have somebody to back you up, you're big and brave?" Landon asked them in a mocking tone. "You guys might want to consider the fact that Jared here is in a lot of trouble already. He's on his last warning, and I'm opening an investigation into his mother's death."

At that, they all froze.

Jared stared at him in shock. "What the fuck are you talking about? My mother ran off."

"Sure she did," Landon quipped. "Do you think I don't know that you beat the shit out of women and that you're the kind of guy who comes from behind and stabs somebody in the back in the dark of night? You're the kind of guy who throws a young woman from your truck to the parking lot when you're angry at her and then storms off and leaves her in the road."

"That's just Caitlin," he said, with a sneer. "She doesn't count."

"I'm pretty sure she thinks she counts," Landon replied. "Or maybe not. Maybe you've beaten that out of her to the point that she has no self-esteem left. Of course that would be typical of you, wouldn't it? I mean, beating up women is something else that makes you feel like a big he-man, right? Somebody who *the world should watch out for*, right?" Landon added, turning up the mockery.

"I don't fucking get it," said the third guy. "Why is he so calm?"

"Why wouldn't I be?" Landon replied. "You might get a couple shots in on me," he admitted, "but so will I. Let's see which ones do the most damage."

At that, the second guy took a step back. "Look. This is wrong," he said, looking at his two buddies, "and you fucking know it."

"I don't care if it's wrong or not," said the third guy. "Since when did you become such a pussy?"

"Hey, we've got no business beating up this guy. He didn't do anything." the second guy replied.

"He is stopping me from shooting that damn dog," Jared snapped.

"Yeah, the dog that you tormented," Landon noted.

"Man, I was never on board with shooting the dog in the first place," added the second guy.

At that, Landon looked at him with interest. "So why the hell are you hanging around with such a loser like this?" Landon asked. "You do realize that he beats up his girlfriends for sport?"

At that, the guy flushed and looked sideways at Jared. "Did you really hit Caitlin?"

The kid just shrugged. "She deserved it."

"Fuck, man, no. That's not cool."

"So what?" Jared snapped. "You can fucking walk away from this anytime you want."

At that, Landon nodded. "You probably should. Things are fixing to get ugly pretty quickly."

The second kid looked at his friends, then said, "Yeah, and, if I walk away, you guys will make my life miserable."

"Yep, we sure will," the third guy agreed, with a sneer. "Believe me. We'll tell everybody what a little baby-ass coward you are."

"A coward? That's interesting," Landon noted calmly. "A coward for walking away from beating up somebody three to one? I wonder what the rest of town will think about that."

"The rest of town won't have any idea," Jared shouted at Landon. "Don't you fucking get it? This is my town. My dad? He's a deputy here, and he protects me."

"He can't protect you forever. Besides, just because you seem to think that you'll walk away doesn't mean that your hell-bent buddy here gets to walk away too."

Jared shrugged at that. "Sure he will. My dad protects all of us." But his tone was less than convincing. He looked over at his friend and shrugged. "Do you really believe that bullshit?"

The third guy frowned and then shrugged too.

Jared continued. "Doesn't matter anyway. I've been in trouble before. It's no big deal. They throw you in the slammer for a couple days, then let you back out again."

"Yeah, well how many times you been in?"

"Twice," he replied almost proudly.

"Guess what? The third one and you'll go down big-time. We'll see how you like fighting off the big boys in prison."

At that, the second guy immediately took another step back. "He's right. You'll be on your third offense. It ain't no walk in the park next time. You could go to prison."

"You don't know anything about it," Jared sneered, turning on his friend. "Like I told you, walk away if you want to be a punk. This is the only chance you get. Walk away or else you stand here, and you'll be part of it."

At that, Landon looked over at the second kid with his doubts and nodded. "You should take that advice."

"You don't understand," he whined. "I live in this town. If I walk away, my life is ruined, as far as these guys are concerned."

"You mean, you can't find any other friends?" Landon asked.

"They won't let me have any other friends," he replied in a caustic tone. "They'll make my life a living hell." He turned to face Jared. "Won't you?"

"Absolutely we will." Jared cackled. "You won't even know what hit you, but, one of these nights, when you least expect it, it will."

"With your BB gun?" Landon asked. "Or do you have *real man guns?*"

At that, he flushed. "Don't worry," he snapped. "That's in progress."

"Great, so now you'll start shooting and killing people. That'll send you off to prison for sure, but you don't care about that, do you? I mean, you guys are big-ass tough-guy types."

"You're right. We are," Jared sneered.

Landon watched as the second guy took a step farther away, but the third guy was circling around, trying to get a hold of Landon. But he was leaning against the truck, directly in line with his two cameras. With both audio and video, he knew the battery-operated camera wouldn't last for too long, but he was hoping his temporary camera setup would capture this much at least. And he had no intention of going to local law enforcement with his tape; he would go over several counties, or maybe he'd just toss it all in Badger's lap.

His phone was also recording video right now, as it sat on his dash. If Landon ended up taking a licking, he would make damn sure he dragged these little assholes down to the ground with him. He had never walked away from a fight in his life, but he also knew his dogs were here, in his truck, and guys like this would think nothing about shooting them too.

Even as he thought this, the three Chihuahuas stood up against the window, clearly upset.

One of the guys noticed and asked, "Jesus, those are your dogs?"

"Yeah, they are," Landon confirmed, knowing what was coming. *Lay down now* he commanded, with a hand signal, and, with one last worried look from Curly, they did.

"Yeah, a man like you has to have those shitty little yappy things." Jared chuckled. "Only real men have real dogs."

"Real men don't go shoot real dogs for fun," Landon stated. "But then you don't really know anything about real men, do you? Your daddy was nothing but a wifebeater, and you are too."

"I don't have a wife," Jared retorted, and, for some reason, he and his more eager sidekick seemed to think that was an absolutely raucous joke.

Landon watched them, as they tried to position themselves on either side of him, so they could double team him. The last guy was still on the fence, waffling.

Landon looked at him and said, "You're running out of time. Once that first punch is thrown, you'll be caught up in this, whether you want to be or not."

"I didn't do anything," he argued, almost desperately.

"No, but you're not doing anything to stop it either."

CHAPTER 9

I T WAS INSTINCT more than anything else that had Sabrina racing to her vehicle, now dodging in and out of traffic, driving to the spot where Landon had found Chica. At least that's what she told herself. As she pulled into the parking lot, she was surprised to find nobody there. And then she heard shouts farther down.

Driving down to the next parking lot, she saw Landon's vehicle and parked beside it, then peeked inside to see that all three of the little dogs were there, huddled together. She immediately smiled and whispered, "Hang on, guys." Then she bolted around to the side.

There she saw three young men with Landon, all down on the ground, punching the crap out of each other. She shouted and raced forward. The young men were punching Landon hard, but Landon wasn't suffering. He seemed to just roll over, pick one guy, and slam his fist into that guy's face, and that took care of one of them. Then two of them remained, one hanging off his back. As he slowly got to his feet, he was a bit wobbly, and she realized that his prosthetic was likely hindering him.

Still, he grabbed the kid on his back, bent over, and flipped him off onto the ground, and, with a big fist to the face, he was out cold. Then he turned to face the remaining guy, Jared. Landon stood up straight. "This is what you do for fun, *huh?*" He shook his head. "We'll see how much fun it'll be by the time I press charges."

"There won't be any charges pressed." Jared laughed, and now he had the BB gun in his hand. "All I see is you beating the crap out of my friends for no reason."

"You think so?" Landon asked.

"I know so." Jared smiled.

"You think they won't press charges against you?"

"They're welcome to try," Jared taunted him, smiling.

At that, Jared took a couple steps back. He had the BB gun in his hand, but, as soon as he saw Sabrina, he started swearing. "Who the fuck are you?" he asked, waving the gun around in her face.

She glared at him. "It doesn't matter who the hell I am. What the hell do you think you're doing with that thing here?"

He just spat on the ground in front of her and snapped, "Get the fuck away from me."

"Really? That's how you feel about this?"

"Absolutely. This guy just attacked me."

"Like hell," she said, with a laugh. "Your daddy ain't gonna save your ass this time, you sorry piece of shit."

He stared at her, his mouth dropping, then he lunged toward her, yelling, "No fucking woman talks to me that way."

She stepped back, waited for the right moment, then launched a practiced karate kick that hit him hard in the jaw. If she'd gone for the throat, she probably would have broken his neck, but, hey, she didn't want to risk maybe killing the guy. She just wanted to make sure that he didn't come back after Landon again. Or her for that matter. The kid stopped, dropped to his knees, stared at her with a funny look, and then crumpled beside her. She raced over to Landon. "Are you okay?"

He looked at her, then down at the punk on the ground and grinned. "Where did you learn to do that?"

"Karate," she said, smiling. "There'll always be assholes like him in the world, and being a female makes me a little more susceptible to their perverse brand of entertainment."

He nodded. "Isn't that the truth. And I'm fine. These guys, on the other hand? Not so much." He pointed to the young men sprawled on the ground, just as one of them started to moan and stir. "Is there any honest local law enforcement around here that would be of any help?"

She winced at that. "I'm not so sure there is."

He nodded. At that, he pulled his phone off the dash and soon was talking to Badger on the other end. When Landon hung up a moment later, he said, "Badger needs a minute."

"Okay," she said, frowning, then looked around. "Is Chica here?"

"Somewhere," he said, "but all that probably set us back quite a bit."

"Unless she saw you trying to help out."

"Yeah, the only thing that would help is the fact that we were clearly against the guy who beat the crap out of her." He stared down at Jared.

"Such a waste of a life," she noted calmly.

Just then his phone rang again, and he put it on Speakerphone. "You're in luck," Badger said. "I'm sending somebody over and don't be surprised when you see who it is." Badger laughed. "Tell him everything you know, and, if you've got any evidence, show it to him. We won't go with local law enforcement, since we already know there's a problem."

"You got that right," Landon stated. "I don't know what the sheriff's deal in all this is, but he hasn't done jack shit so far."

"We'll assume that he won't in this case either, so sit tight. Help is on the way."

And, with that, Landon put away his phone. "You heard him. Somebody is coming to help." Landon shrugged.

"And can you trust Badger?"

"Yep, I sure can."

When he reached up a hand to his shoulder, she bit her bottom lip and asked, "How's the arm?"

He shrugged. "It's been better." He looked down at the punk kids. "I tried to get the third one to walk away. He was really against doing this but kept saying they would make his life unbearable if he didn't stay and fight."

"They probably would too," she agreed. "A kid like that is screwed, just like the girlfriend. They get in with the wrong people, then there's just no way out, as far as they can see, because their so-called friends threaten them."

He nodded. "That's the sense I got. He's the one who jumped on my back, and I just flipped him over and dropped him."

She nodded at that. "I saw. Even missing a foot, you are hell on wheels."

"So are you as it turns out." He gave her a big grin.

She shrugged, pleased. "I'm kind of glad I had a chance to put it to good use. I must tell my karate instructor how well I did." Then she chuckled. "I guess this is the best answer that we could have hoped for. Three assholes out cold, and you and I are okay. Mostly okay," she noted, looking at him.

"I'd be better if I had Chica," he replied, as he looked around. He pointed to the trees and whispered, "I think that's probably her right there."

At that, Sabrina spun to take a look and ever-so-faintly could see a dark shadow in the trees. "Wow, she blends in really well," she noted.

He nodded. "She's had to. There's been an awful lot of danger in this world for her. It shouldn't be that way. She should have gotten the good care she deserves, but she didn't."

"In her case maybe the earlier traumas were just a calamity of mishaps, not deliberate like this one with Jared."

"I'll go on that assumption," Landon agreed, "because anything else just breaks my heart. You know when people want comfort for themselves, they go and get a rescue animal. Then, when they're done with it, or they figure out it requires more of them than they are willing to offer, they dump it off, as if it's of no value anymore." Landon shook his head. "People like that? ... I'd just as soon go out and shoot them myself."

She chuckled. "I get it. That's the same for any animal lover," she murmured.

He nodded, then looked at her and said, "I don't think this is quite how you wanted to end your day."

"It doesn't matter," she replied. "It sure beats the boring stuff."

At that, he laughed. "Maybe I could take you out for dinner then—if we get out of this anytime soon."

She winced at that. "I suppose we'll have to give statements and all that BS, won't we?"

"Maybe," he agreed, "or maybe it'll be a whole lot less of a headache than we're expecting."

"I doubt it," she replied, with an eye roll. "Anything this kid can do to get off, you know he'll try it."

"Maybe," Landon said, "but you never know. Maybe we'll get lucky this time."

At that, she laughed out loud, until she heard the sound of a vehicle. When she turned and looked, she saw the deputy coming toward them. "Don't look now," she said, "but, if this is your help, it's bad news."

He looked over, then frowned. "No, I don't think that's my help."

LANDON QUICKLY PULLED out his phone and called Badger. "Please tell me that you didn't send the deputy."

"Hell no, I sure didn't. Is he there?"

"He is, and he's about to find his son unconscious on the ground, and I'm likely to find myself in irons."

"I'll find out where your help is. Shouldn't be too far away."

"Oh, it will be far away enough," Landon replied, with resignation. "I'm rarely so lucky as to avoid this stage."

"They're five minutes out."

"Hopefully they'll be here right along with *Deputy Daddy*."

"That would be good because Deputy Daddy apparently has an awful lot of explaining to do."

At that, Landon added, "I'm not so sure about that. This punk-ass kid has skated so far."

"You and I both know," Badger added, his voice clear as it rang through the air, "that their day has to end sometime."

And, with that, Landon hung up and turned to face the

deputy striding toward them. When the deputy saw the three young men on the ground, he immediately pulled out his weapon and held it on Landon and Sabrina. "Freeze," he yelled. "Put your hands where I can see them." Both of them put up their hands, and the deputy noted, "Wow, you don't even have a weapon."

"If you're looking for a weapon, then maybe you should check out your pissant son here," Landon declared loudly.

At that, the deputy's face worked hard, as he tried to figure out what was going on. "What the hell happened here?" he asked, as he walked over and bent down to his son, placing fingers against his son's neck.

"Like you care," Sabrina retorted bitterly. "You've let this monster run roughshod over our town for years now, and you've never done a damn thing about it," she stated, with a sneer. "You think any of us give a shit anymore?"

He stared at her in shock. "I don't understand. What is this?"

"All three of them jumped Landon, and believe me. I saw it happen," she snapped. "He's an injured war vet with an ankle prosthetic, and your asshole of a son and his posse jumped him and tried to beat the crap out of him. Then Jared pulled out his trusty BB gun and tried to shoot him."

At that, the deputy's face flushed, and the muscles in his jaw went rigid. "No way, you're lying, and you've got no fucking proof otherwise."

"Oh, so the two of us need to show you proof, not these three losers?" she asked in disbelief. "You'll listen to these louts, *huh*?"

"Of course we will," the deputy said, bending down to check his son's pulse again. "He'd never do something like that." But something odd filled his voice.

She looked over at him. "I've got news for you. He would and he did. And you know it. You've seen it yourself. You've even tried to warn him, but he's not into warnings, is he?" she asked. She shook her head. "Your son is a waste of space, and you could have done something about it when he was still worth saving, but now? ... It's just too damn late."

He looked at her in shock. "Who the hell are you?"

"A local nurse," she replied, "and I also volunteer at one of the animal clinics, where we see the fruits of Jared's labor with his BB gun all the time in the injured animals. But you don't give a shit about that, do you?" she asked, her voice hard. "All you care about is that your precious little boy gets to come home and have a perfect life with absolutely no accountability for his actions."

The deputy shook his head. "No way I believe you. This is bullshit," he snapped.

His son woke up just then and slowly sat up, looked around, and made a quick assessment. "They attacked me, Dad. They attacked me out of the blue, with absolutely no warning," he yelled.

His father immediately replied, "Don't say a word, son. Just don't say a word."

"Yeah, don't say a word," Sabrina taunted Jared, staring at him. "I mean, absolutely don't tell your dad that a woman dropped with you a single kick from a standing position because you were attacking me," she stated, with a sneer.

"So, you're admitting to hurting my son, are you?" the deputy asked.

"Keep it up, Deputy," Landon warned calmly. "Your job and the next ten years of your son's life are on the line right now. Maybe ten years of your life too, if you've compromised your position to protect this piece of shit."

At that, the deputy's jaw worked some more. "My son would never do anything like that."

"Keep telling yourself that," Sabrina said. "You just keep telling yourself whatever you need to in order to let you sleep at night. But you already know the answer—you just don't care. I mean, you beat up your own wife all the time. So, what else is new, and why would Jared be any different, right? I mean, that's what people are for, right? Just punching bags for whenever you want an outlet for your temper, right?"

At that, she watched the deputy getting angry, a little bit more than she'd wanted. She looked over at Landon. "So, where was that assistance you were talking about?"

He nodded behind her and said, "Right there. I wouldn't worry about it now."

She turned, and there were two FBI agents in suits, holding up their badges.

The deputy looked at them, slack-jawed. "What the fuck are you doing here?" he asked. "This is my town, my jurisdiction."

At that, one of the FBI agents looked at him and huffed. "Apparently you are slightly out of your own jurisdiction," he stated, "and you aren't taking these prisoners. We are."

"No prisoners here," the deputy protested.

"Absolutely there are. Three, by my count." The agent turned toward Landon. "Landon Snowden, I presume?"

Landon nodded. "Give me just a minute, and hopefully we'll have double video evidence too," he shared, as he walked over to a tree and pulled the video camera he'd placed there earlier for tracking Chica. He passed it over to them, and they quickly reviewed it. Once they saw what they had, they set it to where the deputy could see for himself.

His face turned gray, as he watched his son's actions.

"Wow, really nice job of you raising your son, *Deputy*," Sabrina noted, studying the video behind them. "Really nice."

Then Landon pulled his cell phone from his pocket and brought up the video taken with his phone propped up on the dash. He brought it over to the agents. "Then this one is from a closer angle." There it had everything from the beginning to where the fight ended, right in front of the other camera.

The FBI agents nodded. "Very convenient."

"Nope, not at all," Landon disagreed. "I'm here in the area, trying to rescue a War Dog that's here. This loser kid here crossed me the other day and threatened me, when I stopped him from going after the dog. He was here earlier today with his girlfriend, with the intent to kill the dog with his BB gun, and I stopped him again and witnessed him assault the girl, Caitlin. ... So, when I saw these three, obviously coming with the intent to jump me," he explained, "I left my phone on the dash, with the video camera running. Beyond that, it's just coincidence that we happened to be right in front of the video camera I'd placed earlier for tracking the dog," he added. "I did tell them they were being recorded, which can be heard on the tapes. This should tell you everything you need to know, not only about these three losers but also Jared's father, the deputy here."

Landon added, "You might also want to take a really good look at what happened to the deputy's wife, who dropped off the face of the earth a couple years back. Very suspicious circumstances. He was a wifebeater, and his wife had a medical record at the hospital for all the abuse, but the local authorities didn't step in, and apparently nobody could convince her to leave. She was too terrified."

At that, both FBI agents turned to stare at the deputy, whose face had turned a chalky gray.

The deputy sputtered, "All bullshit, she hated this town. She just got up one day and left."

"Yeah, sure she did," the lead FBI agent said. "Don't worry. We'll be checking into all of it." He held out his hand. "Deputy, your badge and your weapon, please."

Deputy Smith stared at him. "You don't have any jurisdiction here," he sneered.

"Maybe it seems that way to you, but the sheriff is on his way. So, if you want to keep running off your mouth, have at it," he snapped, his voice hard.

When the deputy failed to comply, the agent continued. "When we get called in because local law enforcement is corrupt, then find evidence like this, you're not in much of a position to object to anything. All bets are off, and you would do well to not make things worse for you than they already are. Your badge and weapon, Deputy."

CHAPTER 10

SABRINA WALKED BACK to her car, still a little dazed at what had just happened. Landon walked at her side. "Now what?" she murmured, as she watched the sheriff, who had just arrived, reading his deputy the riot act. The FBI guys had stepped in to keep things calm, but she had backed away completely.

Landon stayed close to her side and said, "It's all right now, you know."

"Is it though?" She looked back at the group of men and then shook her head. "I don't even see how it ever came to this."

"It's a father's love for his son," Landon noted. "Sometimes it's misguided and goes in the wrong direction."

She nodded. "Do you really think they had something to do with the mother's disappearance?"

"I wouldn't be at all surprised. The girlfriend intimated as much, not by her words but by her own actions. She is so young but already so completely beaten down and trapped in that life. She was in rough shape when she left here earlier today, feeling like her life was over already, with absolutely no way to escape. The mother quite likely had that same sense of desperation and feeling of hopelessness that this would never change. Even if she did try to leave, would they have let her?" he murmured. "The girlfriend was afraid to have me give her a ride back and chose to walk for fear of Jared finding out. Even his friend chose all this trouble over crossing Jared, knowing his life in town would be miserable."

"I don't know," she said, wrapping her arms around her shoulders. "It just sucks, however it ends up."

"Absolutely it does," Landon agreed. He looked over at his dogs, then opened up the front of the cab and let them out again. They immediately greeted her like a long-lost friend.

She bent down and cuddled them. "They really are beautiful dogs."

"They are. They're also tiny and easy to deal with," he noted, chuckling. "Sure glad I taught them to be still on my hand signal. They would have totally ruined my video."

"That's an amazing feat in itself."

"I really needed them to behave in certain situations, especially with Joe as sick as he was. So, most of the time I indulge them, but, when I need them to be quiet, I can get it."

"A nice rottweiler might have come in handy back there. You never wanted a big dog?" she asked, looking up at him.

"It's not so much that I never wanted a big dog. I was off doing missions, away from home for months at a time. Then I got hurt and all. I hadn't planned for getting three Chihuahuas in particular, but, when this opportunity arrived, I just went with it."

"I can appreciate that." She tried to focus on him and the dogs to keep her mind off what was happening off to the side. "What do you really think they're waiting for?" she asked in frustration.

He looked at her and said, "An ambulance probably."

Her lips formed an O, as she hadn't considered that. "I

guess that makes sense. Did I really hurt Jared that badly?"

He shook his head. "I doubt it, but you were fully justified. They all look worse than they are."

She shuddered. "Honestly, I'm still kind of shaky about it all. I'd like to just go home."

Landon nodded and put an arm around her shoulders. "I would take you home in a heartbeat, if I thought we were allowed to go, but there'll be questions first."

She sighed loudly. "Why should we be questioned when Jared's the one tormenting us?"

"And that's what we'll tell them," he replied. "Thankfully we have the video evidence, which will go a long way, but we still must give statements."

At that, the sheriff walked over, reached out a hand, and shook Landon's, as he broke his hold on Sabrina. "Sorry for everything that's gone on here. I do have some questions I need to ask you."

She straightened up and looked over at him, shaking her head. "Now is not a good time. I need to go home and calm down first. ... I'm really still shaken up."

He looked at her, patted her awkwardly on her arm, and nodded. "I need to ask questions now. I'm sorry about that. It's not how our department operates."

Her eyebrows shot up at that. "Yes, it is," she agreed flatly, knowing the FBI agents were listening. "That deputy has been getting away with this shit and covering up for his son for a number of years, and you know it."

At that, Landon again put his arm around her shoulders and pulled her closer.

The sheriff just glared at her. "Not under my watch," the sheriff replied stiffly.

She nodded. "Absolutely under your watch. I've made

formal complaints myself because we've dealt with his abuse of animals down at the vet clinic."

He shook his head. "I don't know anything about that."

She snorted. "You must be dead not to know about that. You've been protecting him since day one. I remember you yourself telling me that you felt Jared would just grow out of it. Well, he didn't. As Landon here would say, Jared did the opposite and grew into it. He's bad news, and you know it. You've known it all along."

The FBI agents were busy taking notes about what she said, when she looked over at them, speaking to them directly. "I don't know how any of this pertains to you or whether you can help the local community get rid of bad law enforcement," she said, "but this is a real problem here. And it's been going on for a very long time."

At that, the sheriff got angry. It was also obvious that he'd been trying to keep things cool because he was trying to placate her, instead of getting into an all-out argument. "Look. Obviously you've had a lot of grievances in this community against my deputy's son, and I get it. Jared's been a troubled boy for a long time. There was only so much we could do, until he crossed the line."

She gave him a flat stare at that, and he had the good graces to look ashamed.

"Obviously we haven't done a great job, and that's something we'll look at moving forward."

"Yeah? What do you think you'll do moving forward?" Landon asked in a hard voice. "Jared attacked me. Jared attacked her, and he threatened to shoot both of us."

"It was just a BB gun," the sheriff protested.

At that, the FBI guys raised their heads, stared at him, and asked, "Seriously?"

The sheriff flushed. "Okay, fine. We'll deal with this, one way or another, and I promise Jared will pay for this."

"I, for one, don't believe you," she stated, facing the sheriff. "As a matter of fact, I think you should be pulled from duty too." She looked over at the FBI agents and asked, "Is this anything in your jurisdiction?"

"Not particularly," they replied cheerfully, "but you can bet we're on it. Especially after all we've seen and heard. This is not how law enforcement is allowed to operate. Doesn't matter what state you're in." He looked over at the sheriff and asked, "Do you not agree with that, Sheriff?"

"Obviously. I'll take a hard look at everyone in my department," he noted stiffly. "We'll need to make some changes in the way some things are done going forward."

But she wasn't having any of that. "That's not good enough," she stated flatly. "You didn't give a crap all this time, and the only reason you're giving a crap now is because the FBI guys are here, and it's all on video. If they weren't here, you would most certainly be breathing down my neck right now," she snapped.

At that, Landon leaned over and whispered, "It's okay. Take it easy."

But she was trembling now. "No, it's not okay," she declared. "Not only is it not okay, I'm completely stressed and overwhelmed at the altercation I had with that piece of shit Jared over there. I can't believe he's been allowed to roam the streets and terrorize everybody in town for all these years because *you* have let him, Sheriff. Now you're telling me it'll be a different story, but it won't. How can it be because you'll probably even keep your damn deputy. And I seriously doubt you'll even look into his wife's disappearance."

At that, the sheriff looked at her in surprise. "What

about his wife's disappearance?"

"Do you have any idea what happened to her?" she asked bluntly.

He shook his head. "I don't know anything about this. What are you talking about?"

"I suppose you have no idea that Deputy Smith battered and beat the crap out of his wife constantly for years, until one day she just disappeared, never to be heard from again?"

At that, the sheriff looked mystified. "No, I haven't heard anything about any of that."

"Then you haven't been listening," she snapped in exasperation. "But that's also very typical. For all I know you're a wifebeater too."

At that, he got angry again, and Landon immediately held him off and added, "Look. She's upset and witnessed all of this come down right in front of her. Involving her, which has been traumatic," he stated. "Now you're the one who wanted to ask questions, when she asked to do it later. Instead of later, now she'll tell you exactly what she feels and what she wants to say, without benefit of any filters because she's stressed, she's tired, and she's exhausted from everything that's just gone on. The fact of the matter is that your deputy's wife disappeared out of the blue a couple years back. Jared's not married, but he's got a good start as a wifebeater as his girlfriend has taken quite a bit of abuse already," Landon shared. "I got that from Caitlin directly, after I watched Jared throw her out of his truck to the pavement right over there, then drove off and left her. When I tried to help her or even give her a ride, she declined, stating she couldn't be seen accepting any help from me, or she would pay for it, and Jared would likely come after me. Not to mention the fact that she also thought her life was over and that nobody could help her because everybody protected him. Everybody has allowed Jared to get away with this kind of crap behavior for years, so Caitlin knew there was no way for her to get free. Probably just like Jared's mom."

The sheriff shook his head. "I don't know anything about that," he protested immediately. "No way I would condone that."

"Really?" Sabrina asked, staring hard at him. "I'm not sure I believe anything you say anymore."

He glared at her and then shrugged. "I can see why you might feel that way, but that's not the kind of behavior we allow here."

"And yet," she replied, exhausted, letting her voice fall away, "that's exactly what's been going on. Deputy Smith has been beating up his wife for a long time. Maybe you should talk to Jared about his mother. Hell," her voice got stronger, as she said, "maybe the FBI should talk to all three of you. For all we know, the sheriff here helped Deputy Smith and Jared beat up Mrs. Smith and possibly killed her too. Deputy Smith has got to have something on the sheriff in order for the sheriff to keep bailing Deputy Smith and that asshole Jared out of trouble after all this time."

Noting the FBI agents silently listening in, the sheriff's expression turned thoughtful. "You've certainly given me a lot to think about. … You can bet there'll be an investigation into it."

"Oh, there will be now," Landon promised. "If nothing else, these two FBI agents and I will be following up to make sure your entire department is completely cleaned up, and, if there's any wrongdoing on your part, I will move heaven and earth to make sure you're removed from office."

The sheriff winced. "There has to be cognizant wrong-doing," he noted, "and I can tell you that there hasn't been."

"How about willful blindness?" Sabrina snapped. She looked over at the two FBI agents. "I don't want you to leave without having a way to contact you." One of the men pulled out a business card and handed it to her. She looked down at it and nodded. "Thank you. Hopefully we can get this resolved relatively quickly."

"What is it you'd like to see happen?" one of the agents asked.

"I want the kid charged, and I want him stopped. I want the deputy charged, and I want him stopped, never to hold office again. And I want a full investigation into the sheriff's potential wrongdoing because willful blindness is not an excuse any more than ignorance is," she stated, glaring at him.

The sheriff flushed. "I get it. You're upset, and you've been through a lot." He looked over at Landon. "I presume you're taking her somewhere safe."

"I am," he confirmed, "but that doesn't change the fact that she lives here and that she's also afraid of reprisals, as is the girlfriend, Caitlin."

"I'll be talking to the girlfriend immediately," the sheriff stated. "I didn't know anything about that."

"That's because she didn't feel that she could come to you because your deputy has been covering that kid's ass for way too long," Sabrina snapped, glaring at the sheriff. "If you let that kid out on bail, her life will be in immediate danger."

He frowned at that. "I'm not exactly sure what the prosecutor will do with this. I'll be contacting them."

Landon looked over at the FBI agents, who were studying the sheriff. "There's no reason you can't put Jared in jail right now, for at least forty-eight hours?" he asked. "Even longer, as we'll be pressing charges."

The sheriff nodded to the agents. "We can get back to my office and discuss it."

"What's to discuss?" she asked immediately, afraid a coverup was happening. "Because that just sounds like you're trying to protect that idiot asshole again." The sheriff surreptitiously glared at her, and she shrugged. "If you think I'll go away now, then you're wrong," she declared. "You almost make me want to run for sheriff myself. Maybe it's time that we have somebody who's honest and law-abiding in this place."

He stared at her, then pushed his hat back and replied, "I guess you do feel strongly about this."

"Oh, I do," she stated, with a nod. "Any injustice is something I hate, but, when it comes back on animals, and the perpetrators are getting protection, you can bet I don't have a whole lot of compassion for those people."

The sheriff nodded. "We've never had a female sheriff before."

"Doesn't mean it can't happen," she snapped. "I've worked in hospice and long-term care for years. I deal with people who would love one day more, a sickness-free day, a chance to live the life they had hoped to live, and they die at the hospital, day in and day out, and here this crap-son of your deputy has thrown away every chance he's had, making this little thug life only for himself as a supposed *big man*, and you're all about covering it up and turning a blind eye." Sabrina shook her head. "You should be ashamed of yourself. How do you even look at yourself in the mirror?"

With that, she turned, looked back at Landon, and said, "I'm heading home."

"Let's go for coffee first," he suggested. "You need to calm down."

She shrugged. "In that case we'll go to my place for coffee. I sure as hell don't want to be in public if I break down when I think about all the hardship that kid has avoided, as he sits here and whines about his life, while Jared caused undue hardship to how many others?"

"Let's do that. Sure."

She raised her voice for the two FBI agents to hear. "A parent's job isn't just to raise a child but to prepare them for life in a world that needs a decent contributing member of society, not a piece of shit." She gave another hard look at the sheriff and the shitty deputy, standing nearby, and added for their benefit, "You can bet I'll be following up on this publicly, if I don't see some results."

And, with that, she walked over to her car and got in. She was shaking so much that she immediately realized she shouldn't be driving, but she still wanted to get out of here as fast as she could. She figured if she got down the road a bit, she could just hit the closest coffee shop, pull in, and let Landon know where she was. And that's what she did. The coffee shop was the same one where they'd had breakfast. She could even walk home from here, if she needed to.

She figured that, rather than going home and bursting into tears, then sit there and find life more than she could handle, she needed some distance from the scene of the attack, and Landon was right when he had suggested that they should just go for a coffee and calm down. After she had pulled into the parking lot, she sent him a quick text, then she walked inside.

She ordered coffee and went to the far back table and sat down. When the waitress came by with her coffee, she brought her a menu. "That's a good idea too."

"You okay? You look like you've had a rough day."

"Yeah, you could say that." Sabrina shook her head. "Who knew a day could be this bad."

"Sometimes they can be pretty ugly all right," the waitress agreed calmly. "Sometimes I think our job is just to survive the day. Sometimes it's all I can handle, and even that is iffy some days."

"I hear you there." Sabrina sat back in the booth, closed her eyes, and tried to let some of the stress slide away from her. But it was tough. She just wanted to know that it was all over with. She wanted to go home and cry. Yet, at the same time, that was the last thing she wanted to do.

She wasn't cut out for this, and she sure as hell wasn't cut out for arguing and trying to get bullheaded men to see the error of their ways. She had no intention of running for sheriff, but she sure wished that somebody honest and decent would. Hearing someone approach, she opened her eyes to see Landon sliding into the seat across from her.

He studied her carefully, then spoke calmly. "How are you doing now?"

"Rough," she replied. "It's been a hard and scary day."

"I'm sorry for that," he said. "You really surprised me when you showed up. But then you really shocked me when you dropped Jared."

She grinned at that. "Nothing quite like the sense of satisfaction you get from doing what you need to do to protect yourself," she murmured. "It's frustrating when you also know that he shouldn't have been out there on the loose in the first place."

"No, and, depending on what the charges are, he could easily make bail and get out."

"In which case, I'll be toast," she stated, with a defeated sigh. "I just don't understand how something like that could happen in a lawful society."

"We'll make a case to keep them locked up, with the danger they present as our justification."

"Yeah, I don't know about that." She groaned. "Jared seems to have a lot of pull."

"The deputy does, but that doesn't mean he will in this case."

She shrugged. "I don't know. Right now I just need to find a way to make this all go away. I definitely need to calm down, so it's not completely ruining my world."

"No, I hear you," he said, just as the waitress came by with coffee for him and a menu. He looked over at Sabrina and asked, "Did you order?"

She shook her head.

Landon looked at the waitress and said, "Give us a few minutes?"

Sabrina continued. "Honestly I think food's probably a good idea, but my throat is all choked up." She held up a hand, and he could see she was still trembling. "Now I'm even more worried that the little puke will come after me."

"I am too," he agreed. "I just don't know how big a problem it is."

"I don't know either," she muttered. She picked up the menu, then looked at it and decided, "I need to eat something." When the waitress came back a moment later, they both ordered burgers and fries.

He looked over at her and grinned. "I can appreciate a woman who orders a burger and fries."

"You mean, instead of being the one always on a diet and ordering a green salad?" She shook her head with half a laugh. "That doesn't work for me because I'm always at the hospital or the vet clinic. So it seems like I never quite get enough calories as it is."

He immediately sobered. "I know. We always ate well before a mission, but when we were on one? It was a whole different story. Sometimes there's nothing you can do to make something any easier."

She nodded at that. "It's so hard," she murmured. "Sometimes it just seems like there's so much going on at once, and you can handle it all quite well for a time. Then suddenly everything blows up, and you don't have any rhyme or reason why. Like right now with my supposed friend Angela," Sabrina noted. "I don't really need that right now. But on top of everything else, I *really* don't need it. She's the one I would normally seek out to commiserate over this nightmare." Sabrina sighed heavily. "Instead I don't even feel like I can go to her."

"Which is very sad," Landon replied. "And definitely bad timing in your world. It's up to you how to respond to Angela. Is it better for you mentally to stay away from her or is the separation itself a form of emotional stress?"

"I don't know," she admitted. "I mean, the whole reason we argued is pretty foolish, yet, at the same time, I feel like it shouldn't have gotten anywhere near where it has now ended up."

"Do you think you two could talk it out, maybe move on from it?"

She nodded. "That is something I'm considering. I'm not sure we do move on from this, as stupid as the instigating event was. I'm also reevaluating my off time, though I don't want the animals to suffer."

"No, of course not. However, you already have a job

with plenty of overtime. And it's not your clinic. That's their responsibility, isn't it?" he asked. "It would make sense that, if they're doing well enough to be that busy, they should have the funds to hire somebody permanently. If they're not doing really well financially, then maybe they need to have someone look at their financials and see where it is they are bleeding money. In the end, they may need to recruit far more volunteers—hopefully retired people with no daytime job either."

"Angela's boyfriend is a vet, and he's trying to buy into the clinic, I guess," she shared, with a shrug. "So I don't know how much of that is coming into play. The owner and existing vet is holding out for more money and control."

"I imagine that all could be a part of it, but I'm not sure if it's a good thing or a bad thing."

"What do you mean?" she asked.

"If you're trying to sell half a practice, you want to make it look like it's really, really good and solid financially, don't you? So, if you cut back on your staff, and you cut back on your expenses, you make the bottom line look better."

She winced at that. "That would suck. Surely the animals deserve better than that."

"It also shows that he would need somebody because he would be running his feet off, and that's not something anyone can do long-term."

"Right, but that wouldn't involve my friend. I don't think she would be involved in something like that. She would be on the other side of that, trying to help her boyfriend buy in, probably not even thinking that the short-staffing was intentional."

"And we don't even know that this is happening," he reminded her. "We're just brainstorming."

She nodded. "Right, but is everybody into lying and cheating?"

"I think right now your whole viewpoint is tainted by what's been happening to Chica and to the animals at the clinic," Landon suggested. "Your feelings were already hurt because you're on the outs with your friend. Then this fiasco with Jared and his posse was way over the top of anything you could have expected. This just isn't a good time for you to be labeling your fellow man in general."

"We're not supposed to be judging each other at all," she argued in a wry tone. "But somehow it doesn't seem to be quite that simple."

He grinned. "Nope, things are rarely as simple as it seems like they should be. And a scenario like we're dealing with right now just makes everything harder."

"That's for sure," she agreed, then she yawned. "Now I'm really feeling tired too," she murmured. "I think I'll just head home after this and crash."

"That sounds like a good idea."

She looked over at him. "What will you do?"

"Would you care to hazard a guess?" he teased, with a wry look.

She winced. "You're going right back to see if you can get Chica to come with you."

"Yep. Exactly. I'd like to at least regain the ground I no doubt lost with all that commotion."

She nodded glumly. "For a moment there, I forgot all about her. That makes me feel worse than anything else."

"It doesn't have to be something you feel guilty about," he stated immediately. "I'll do everything I can to bring her in. All that noise and drama won't have helped, so I want to go back and spend as much time as I can with her. ... I should probably see if they have sandwiches or something here that I could order to-go. Then I can grab some water and sit out there for a couple hours to see if I can get close enough to catch her."

"Do you think she's dangerous?" Sabrina asked suddenly.

"No, I don't. In fact, I think she's probably close to giving up—or she'll be even warier."

She stared at him, her eyes going round. "What do you mean?"

"She's pretty skinny. I'm feeding her, but I think she's been badly treated and is very wary of people. Once that happens, you must regain that trust, but it can take a long time. She won't be a fast project. But then I saw something in her gaze, and it was like she was … hopeless."

She gasped and put her hand to her mouth, then nodded. "And, when you do catch her, you'll take her home, I presume."

"I guess. That would make sense."

"So, will you keep her?"

"I don't know yet," he said. "I would need to see how she gets along with my dogs. Plus we don't yet know how badly hurt she is and whether I'm the person to give her the best care."

"You are," she declared immediately. "You care about her, and that's what she needs."

"Maybe."

"Where's home?" she asked.

"New Mexico."

Her eyebrows shot up at that. "Interesting. Gran lived there for a while, and I remember visiting her a lot."

"Yeah, how do you feel about it?"

"It's fine," she said. "The winters here are a bit much sometimes, but that's not anything to be terribly upset about—well, not until Angela started acting so weird and then Grandma has forgotten me."

He grimaced at her last words. "Sorry about that. ... I like it there. And, besides, the friend I looked after, Joe? He left me his house, and it sits on five acres."

"Oh, wow. Five acres and a home? I'm so jealous. I like Gran's little house, but the neighbors? Not so much."

"Move to New Mexico," he stated immediately.

She snorted. "Like that'll help. I don't have a home there."

"What is your financial situation like?" he asked. "Not that I'm trying to be nosy, but property prices are pretty reasonable there."

She frowned at that. "I guess they probably are, aren't they? They're reasonable everywhere but Florida and California apparently—and, of course, most of New York."

"New York's housing market is always tough, especially in New York City," he noted.

"Anybody who lives in New York City is nuts, in my opinion." She laughed. "I don't like traffic that much."

He grinned at her. "Me neither. Besides, if you moved to New Mexico, we could see each other."

She looked at him and then slowly nodded. "That would be nice, but I sure won't make a decision like that based on knowing you for a couple days."

"I wouldn't expect you to," he said. "But honestly I think we've already made impressions as to who we are inside. That tends to happen almost instantly, and then people spend weeks and months trying to justify it."

"You're saying that we make decisions very quickly, then

we must spend the next however long justifying it to ourselves and to those around us?"

"Exactly," he agreed. "I think we make snap decisions on people, just like animals do, and then spend time trying to back it up or trying to make it fit the parameters of how you want the person to be in your life." He reached across the table and gently laid his fingers on top of hers. "I'll confess to you that I've made a snap judgment."

"What's that?" she asked in a mocking tone, though inside she was intrigued. She had definitely felt drawn to him from the start, but to make a decision like that so quickly was not her style.

"I've decided that I like you," he stated and then chuckled. "Like you didn't know that already."

She smiled. "There's no doubt we hit it off," she agreed, "but that's a long way from moving to New Mexico."

"The weather is nice," he repeated with a big smile, "and there is five acres and a house."

"Yeah, that's your place though," she replied. "I don't know what it would cost to buy something like that myself."

"I don't know either, and it depends on whether you have a down payment."

"I work all the time and don't spend anything beyond basics, except on animals," she noted, with a wry tone. "So I'm doing okay."

"Good. So I guess the question is whether you really want to stay here or not. Maybe you were supposed to fight with Angela after all? That would make the move easier, correct?"

She stared at him. "You're not serious, right?"

"It is certainly something I would love to see you do because I'm selfish and want to have you nearby so we could spend more time together. ... I must admit that, if I end up getting Chica, I would probably immediately head home and spend some time there, trying to get Chica adjusted to life with me and the three little dogs."

"That would be a good idea for you and them," she agreed cautiously, "but I can't say it makes me very happy."

"Exactly. And, of course, you don't want to move blindly without coming for a visit first," he suggested, "so I would like to schedule that, so maybe you would feel free to come and see how we live and see how Chica is doing."

Sabrina gave a nervous laugh. "Why don't we pull that back a little bit. I have Grandma to think about too, and let's see if you get Chica first."

"Oh, I'll get her," he promised. "I just don't know what kind of shape she'll be in when I do manage it. But keeping her and my three dogs in a hotel won't be a good idea, and you have your own two dogs. Plus, you already told me how your neighbors had discouraged you from bringing any extra animals to your place."

She nodded. "Yeah, and a dog like Chica needs a lot more room. But then again, if she's injured or needs rehab in the beginning, it'll take time for her to heal. And, in that case, she could do well in a small space for now."

"She will for a little bit, but she'll also feel better if she has a space where she's free and yet secure."

"Agreed. And my place might work for a temporary spot to allow her to heal a bit, before you move back to New Mexico. My two dogs are sweethearts and would love Larry, Curly, and Moe. Plus, I think they'd love Chica, while not being rough on her, as she recuperates here, if needed."

Landon nodded. "Chica is used to the smell of my three by now. And Chica is said to have a sweet personality. So she might easily accept your dogs as well."

She groaned. "When you and Chica leave for New Mexico, I might consider a visit," she admitted, and then she shrugged. "But we'll have to see."

"We'll have to see what?" he asked curiously.

"I'm not trying to be difficult. I just want to know what you're thinking. I just feel like it's all too new. I had a bad relationship a few years back, which is why Angela is being overprotective, and I just don't want to jump into something this next time around."

He stared at her for a moment. "No pressure at all, but can you really tell me that you feel like I'm somebody you should be worried about? I guess I'm just wondering what your instincts are telling you right now."

"You're asking me that *now*? After today? They're all over the board at present," she said immediately. "There's absolutely nothing I can count on where my emotions are concerned. Everything has happened so fast. And sure, Chica is the reason it happened that way, but it's not exactly typical."

He nodded. "I've been out of the dating game myself for a couple years now, mostly because of the time I spent with Joe, though I can't say I was looking for anything like this— until I saw you. Then, of course, my mind immediately started trying to find a way to see you again. And now, even after only a couple days, I'm trying to figure out how to spend time with you, after I've gone."

"And, if you have four dogs, one needing special care, you won't necessarily travel with them easily."

"No, but, if that would be a deal breaker," Landon stated, "I would find a way. Especially if I decide to do something with my brother. And he'd always be there to help with the dogs. He's dog nuts himself."

She smiled at that. "That's nice." She sighed. "And it's nice to know that my instincts aren't terribly wrong when it comes to meeting new people. ... I trust you, and I enjoy who you are as a person, but I can't say that I truly know you."

He nodded. "I always thought that would be one of the best parts of a long-term relationship, you know? The spending time, getting to know each other. I've been fairly isolated for a while, so I'm definitely on the rusty side when it comes to the dating world."

She chuckled. "What you are is very forthright, and I appreciate that."

"I don't think most people do though," he quipped, once again sending her that engaging grin that made her heart melt. "You're supposed to say all kinds of flowery stuff to keep a girl interested," he noted, "but that's never been my style."

"I can't imagine it being anybody's style," she replied. "It always sounded insincere to me, which is probably why I've struggled a lot with relationships over this last while. Everything just came off as not being my style."

He nodded. "And that's good because that means you are still here and hopefully waiting for me."

"Waiting for you?" She snorted at that.

He flashed her a bright grin. "I get it, so not exactly waiting for me. But, hey, a guy could hope."

"If you leave, and we'll try to keep up some kind of a relationship afterward," she said, "then I'd be waiting for you. But don't hold your breath on that one just yet."

"Got it." Just then the waitress returned with their platters. Sabrina stared down at hers in surprise. "Oh, gosh, I forgot how big these meals are."

"That's okay too," Landon added. "I'm starving." When the waitress came back with extra ketchup, he quickly ordered a couple sandwiches to take with him, when they were finished.

Sabrina offered, "You can box up anything I don't eat here too."

"Are you kidding? I'll probably eat that here myself, before we even leave," Landon said.

She nodded. "I have a small-capacity stomach and just can't pull off something like that too easily."

"Maybe not, but you don't always know what you'll do regarding food, until you start in." And, with that, he picked up his burger and started munching.

She watched in amazement as he managed to get his jaw around the huge burger without any difficulty. She shook her head at that. "That'll be a lot harder for me."

"Yet I think you'll handle it just fine," he coaxed her.

She gave it try, but, when she got down to the last couple bites, she set down her burger. "Wow, I'm about stuffed." She had a few fries, then shook her head and said, "The rest is yours, if you want it."

He looked at her, then looked at her plate and asked, "Are you sure?"

She nodded. "Absolutely."

He reached across and picked up the last of her burger. He popped it into his mouth and a moment later was finished with it. Then he pulled over her plate and started working on her fries.

She chuckled. "You really were hungry."

"Yep, I'm hungry a lot these days."

"Often it's the opposite for me. Particularly with the

type of work I do. I come home more emotional than anything. Then I just want a bowl of soup or something light."

"Maybe it's time for a career change."

"Maybe, but I think I'm a better person for the kind of work I do."

LANDON THOUGHT ABOUT Sabrina's words and thought about what she'd mentioned earlier, about making the most of the life that you had, while you had it, and he nodded. "I think you're right. I hadn't really considered it that way. It's the same as me knowing that my world was much better for the time and effort I chose to spend with Joe, even if it wasn't easy," he added. "I am a much better person because of it."

She smiled. "It's hard to imagine that you weren't pretty terrific already."

"*Hah*, but maybe I wasn't back then," he said, with a smile. "When you think about it, a lot can happen in two years."

She nodded. "Yeah, that's true. I've only lived here since grade school. I have thought about moving a few times."

"We've at least come to an agreement on one thing," he noted suddenly.

She looked over at him. "What's that?"

"That we want to stay in touch." There was a question in his expression, as he looked over at her.

She smiled and nodded. "Yes, that would be lovely."

"Good. Now let's get you home."

She nodded and slowly stood up.

"You look like you're really tired," he said, studying her.

She nodded. "I'm not feeling all that great right now." She looked at him funny, and it was all he could do to reach out and grab her before she collapsed. He quickly propped her up on the bench seat, checking on her. She was conscious, just woozy.

"I don't feel so good," she whispered, and he quickly started digging money out of his pocket. The waitress came running and handed him the bag with the to-go sandwiches, as he handed her the money. Then he picked Sabrina up in his arms and carried her out to his truck.

He propped her up against the truck and said, "I'll take you to the hospital."

"No, no, no," she muttered. "Let's not." She yawned, and her head lagged to the side a bit. "I'm just tired."

"No," he declared. "You're not just tired." He opened the door to the back seat and laid her down awkwardly on the bench. "I'll buckle you in, and I want you to stay here," he said.

"Where will I go?" she asked, slurring her words a bit. She frowned at that.

"Your car is here. We'll leave it for now, until I get back here," he told her, but she was already out now. He hopped into the front of the truck and, using his GPS to navigate, raced to the hospital. He pulled up into the emergency bay and quickly carried her inside and set her down in a wheelchair that was empty and available. Then he pushed her over to the emergency reception area and explained what had happened. The woman looked at him, then over at her, and immediately said, "Wait just a moment."

He was called into a room within minutes. He wheeled her inside, then picked her up and got her settled on the hospital bed.

The doctor came in about ten minutes later. He looked at Landon and asked, "What happened?"

As Landon explained the scenario at the coffee shop, the doctor stared at him, an eyebrow raised. "Was she in any kind of altercation before that?"

At that, Landon nodded slowly. "I didn't see her get hit, but yes," he replied. "I had a problem down at the park with three guys who jumped me, and she pulled up in her car, just after the fight started. One of them went after her, when she was trying to get them to stay off of me," he explained. "Before I even knew what happened, she whirled around and karate kicked him. He dropped like a rock, but I didn't think he even touched her."

"That kick may have jarred something, I guess," the doc suggested. "We'll need to get some X-rays to see if we can find anything. She's breathing well, but her blood pressure is way up. We'll run some tests and see what we've got."

At that, Landon had to be satisfied. "I'll need to wait outside, I presume?"

"Yes, this will take a few hours."

Frowning at that, Landon stepped out of the room.

Back outside the hospital, he raced to his rental truck and hopped inside. He went back to the restaurant where he pulled her purse and anything personal from her car. He locked it up, then returned to the hospital, where he dropped off her purse and cell phone in her hospital room. At least they would have her medical card and anything else they might need. Then he stepped outside again, sat in the truck with his dogs, and called Badger.

"What the hell?" Badger asked, while Landon explained. "Did you see him touch her?"

"No, that's the confusing part."

"And you don't know of any underlying health condition?" That question came from Kat.

"Nothing I know of," he replied. "But, while you're on here, I think I'm ready for a better prosthetic," he stated bluntly. "Carrying her was a challenge."

"That would have been a challenge for anybody, as unconscious people are an enormous dead weight," she noted calmly. "But, yes, as soon as we can get you back here, we can get some measurements done."

"Much appreciated." Landon sighed in relief. "Now I just have to convince her to come back too." There was a moment of shocked silence from Badger and Kat, before Landon laughed. "Yeah, I know. It wasn't what I was expecting either."

"But you know what?" Badger added in a curious voice. "I should have expected it."

"Really? And how would you even have known she was there?" Landon asked.

"I wouldn't have," Badger admitted, "but it's been a pretty steady bet that most of the guys who have gone out to do welfare checks on these War Dogs have come back with a partner."

He stared down at his phone in shock. "Seriously?"

"Yeah, I'm serious. I know it sounds ludicrous, and I'm not trying to make a mockery of it, but it seems like most of the guys have come back with somebody special in their lives."

"She's definitely somebody I'm interested in having in my life, but we're a long way away from that," he noted.

"I'm pretty sure they all thought the same thing as well," Kat replied, laughing. "But it's amazing when you get down to it. People really need each other in these circumstances, and you quickly get to a level that would never have been possible in any other situation."

"What do you mean?" he asked, not quite understanding what she was saying.

"In times of trouble, you find out who shows up, the real person," she stated in a quiet voice. "In a normal situation, you date someone over time and may still never get to the core of who they really are. You see what they want you to see, but, once there's any stress or difficulty in life, that's when you really see who they are."

"*Huh*, I guess you're right. I hadn't considered that before."

"And it's not something you would normally have to consider even now," she noted. "But the fact of the matter is, you've got something strange going on that you're trying to get to the bottom of. I hate to get back to the point in question, but how is Chica?"

"Injured and struggling," he stated bluntly. "I'm working on her but fear I've lost ground after all the ruckus earlier. I want her to come in on her own, but trust is a hard-won thing."

"Have you seen her?"

"Yes, but not close enough to check on her condition. Unfortunately she was there, watching the fight," he murmured, "which wasn't exactly the best thing for her to see."

"I'm not so sure about that though," Badger said. "She would have seen you fighting for the side of right."

"Do you think it matters to her though?" Landon asked, with a note of humor. "I'm pretty sure she's as nonpolitical as they come."

"She might be," Badger agreed, "but she'll also have a good idea that you were against the guy who hurt her."

"Now that I can understand. It still pisses me off that this guy has been getting away with hurting animals for quite some time now."

"Hopefully not for much longer," Kat said. "That's not something any of us wants to have happen."

"And yet, if it hadn't been for the FBI showing up when they did," Landon noted, "I'm not sure we would even be having this conversation."

"That's the most worrisome part of it," Badger murmured. "Have you been in touch with the agents since?"

"No, not yet, but you're right. I need to tell them about what happened to Sabrina. And as much as I don't want to call the sheriff, I probably should."

"Talk to the FBI first," Badger stated. "They should have a much better idea of what's going on there and what to do next and whether to involve the sheriff."

"Okay." Landon hung up and quickly called the FBI agent. Landon explained what had happened and told them he'd just taken Sabrina to the hospital.

"Do you think it's related?" he asked.

"That's what I thought at first. I'm not sure. I don't know what's going on, but something happened."

"Keep in touch regarding her condition," he said, "and, as soon as she is conscious, I need to talk to her and see if she has any idea what happened."

"Okay, I just wanted to let you know that we're struggling with all this."

"No, I got it. Where are you going next?"

"I'll be here with Sabrina for a little bit, and then I'm heading back to the same park to try and find the War Dog that I came for," he replied. "Hopefully that will lead me to solving that part of our problem. I was wondering if I needed to phone the sheriff."

At that, the other man paused and then said, "I'll call him."

"Thanks. I didn't really want to talk to him anyway." And, with that, Landon hung up and headed back inside and took a seat beside her empty bed. The nurse told him that she'd be back from testing soon enough.

When she did come back, she was awake. "Hey."

But her voice sounded off. "You okay?" he asked, studying her, with a worried expression.

"Not sure what happened," she murmured. "I still don't feel so good."

He nodded, but something about the way her voice sounded caught his attention. When the doctor came to look at her again, Landon motioned him outside. Once they were both in the hallway, Landon asked, "Doc, can you run a tox screen on her?"

At that, the doctor looked at him. "You think she's been drugged?"

"I don't know what to say right now," he admitted, "but something is definitely wrong. She doesn't even sound like herself."

"Oh, I know. And we did send off a tox screen, but we were thinking she may have taken something."

He shook his head. "Not intentionally. She's been with me for the last few hours. We had the fracas at the park. Then we went to a coffee shop to settle down a bit and to get some food. However, I drank the same coffee and shared the same food. I'm not at all happy with the condition she's in right now."

"You and me both," the doctor agreed, with a nod. "We've already pulled the blood sample, and we're running tests."

"Good enough," Landon said, as he stepped back inside again. She was sound asleep. He frowned at that because he'd really hoped to talk to her.

She suddenly jumped and opened her eyes.

"Hey, take it easy," he murmured. "You're fine."

She looked up at him, then blinked several times and said, "I still don't know what happened."

"Nope, neither do I, but it's kind of scary."

"It just seemed like everything was fading away on me. I didn't like that one bit."

"Neither did I." He frowned, studying her face. "Any idea what it was? Do you have any underlying health conditions or anything?"

She shook her head. "Nope, I would have said that I was healthy as a horse. But whatever it was, it seems to have passed."

"What about the confrontation with Jared? Were you close enough for him to hit you?" Landon asked.

"I don't think so. No, I kicked him. I don't think he touched me," she replied, staring at Landon. "Really I wouldn't have thought I would pass out like this."

He nodded. "We'll take it from here and see what the doctor comes up with. They are running a bunch of tests, so we'll see what comes back."

She nodded. "What will you do?" When he hesitated, she smiled. "It's fine. You need to go get Chica, if you can. At least reassure her that everything's okay."

He looked at her, then smiled and asked, "Is everything about animals with you?"

"Nope, not everything, but, in this case, we don't know who all might go back to try and hurt her. Or whether she is even still a part of the equation."

He winced at that. "I hope she's no longer part of their equation, but you're right. We can't count on it."

She smiled and said, "So go. I'll let you know if they release me."

He gently picked up her hand, lacing his fingers with hers. "You promise?"

She looked at him, then gave him a smile. "Yes," she replied, her voice low. "I promise. I don't have a death wish."

"I'm glad to hear that, but I'm also not terribly impressed that you're even down like this right now," he admitted. "I sure wish I knew why."

"Me too. You go take care of Chica, and I'll stay here and see what the doctor comes up with." When he hesitated again, she pushed him. "Go on. I don't like to think about Chica running into trouble."

"No, I don't either," he agreed, "and if you're sure you're okay—"

"I promise."

And, with that, he nodded. As he started to walk away, he stopped, then returned to her bed, leaned over, and kissed her gently on the cheek. "Stay safe," he murmured.

And, with that, he was gone.

CHAPTER 11

S ABRINA LAID IN the hospital bed, wondering what had happened to her. It was hard to think that this was from natural causes, but, hey, she was exhausted and had been wearing herself down with worry and too much work. But still, to even think that this could be the result of normal life stresses was a little far-fetched for her. When the doctor walked in several hours later, she looked over at him. "Well? What did you find?"

"You were drugged," he stated.

Her jaw dropped. "Seriously?"

"Yes, so we have a couple questions for you, and I'll need to phone the sheriff."

She winced at that. "Please hold off on that part," she said.

He looked at her, his expression serious. "Why is that?"

She quickly explained what had happened with Landon, the dog, the three punks, the two FBI agents, and, of course, the sheriff and his deputy.

He stared at her. "Wow, so you did manage to get into some trouble."

"Yes, but I didn't think I ever got close enough for any-body to drug me. I mean, I kicked Jared hard, and he went down pretty fast."

At that, the doctor nodded. "Well then"—he hesitated—"the man who brought you in ..."

"Yeah, what about him?"

"Is there any reason to suspect that he might have done this?"

She stared at him, feeling her heart chill at the prospect. "I would say definitely not," she replied, "but I don't know that for sure."

"So, you haven't known him very long?"

"No, I haven't," she said, not wanting to go into details.

"Think about it," he said. "Somebody got close enough to drug you."

"Do you know how it was administered?"

He frowned. "We're still checking into that. I should have checked your arms for an injection site."

"You may as well do that now, while I'm sitting here, trying to figure out what happened. You know what? My arm is sore," she admitted.

"Show me where."

Sabrina lifted her right sleeve. "Right here in this area. I just figured I'd wrenched it."

He checked it out and said, "Nope, there's definitely an injection site there."

"Wow, that doesn't make me feel very good."

"No, of course not."

"So, is it safe for me to go home?" she asked.

"Nope, not yet," the doc replied. "I want to make sure that the drugs run their course first."

"And what will the drugs do?"

"Normally these could theoretically knock you out cold and cause a lot of trouble."

"You mean, like a date rape drug?"

He nodded slowly. "That's exactly what it is. I'm just

not sure that's the reason it was given to you in this case."

"I don't know," she murmured. "I don't know anything about it."

"Good enough, but I still must report it."

"Can you report it to the FBI instead, please?"

He nodded. "Will do. Do you have a specific number?"

She winced at that and asked, "If you can give me my phone, I'll get it for you." She quickly texted Landon, asking for the FBI contact number. When he sent it back, she handed it over to the doc. "This is what he just gave me."

"Is this the guy who brought you in?"

She nodded. "Yes." And, in her heart of hearts, she knew there was no way Landon would have done this, but, at the same time, she also knew she would never convince anybody else at the moment, not when so much was going on around her. As she laid here, after the doctor had left, she had to wonder just who'd gotten close enough to her.

The sheriff had, but would he have done something like that, within such close proximity to the FBI? For that matter, the FBI could have done it as well, but ... that thought was like grasping at straws, trying to find something that made sense.

Shortly a nurse came in to give her some charcoal pills and to remind her to keep drinking water throughout the day, all to help flush out her system.

When Sabrina was finally alone, she managed to grab her purse and pulled out the card that Landon had given her. She dialed the number. When it was answered, she hesitated.

"Hello? May I help you?" a woman asked.

"I'm calling about Landon," she began, wondering if the woman would even know who she was talking about.

"*Uh-oh*, is he hurt? What's the situation?" she asked, very businesslike.

"As far as I know, he's fine," she replied. "I'm Sabrina. I just—"

"Oh my gosh, are you all right? He contacted us—Badger and I, I'm Kat—to say that you were in the hospital, and that you'd collapsed."

"Yes," she confirmed, relieved that Landon had contacted them. Surely an innocent man wouldn't have done that? She added, "It's kind of a weird thing to be calling you right now."

"Then better to spit it out," suggested the woman cheerfully. "Sometimes that's just the best way."

"Apparently I was drugged," she stated, the words bolting from her mouth.

"You were drugged? Do you know how or when?"

"There's a sore spot on my arm," she replied, "and the doctor keeps asking me questions about Landon, since he's the one who was close enough to have access. Of course I don't have any answers, but ..." Then Sabrina fell silent again.

"So what you're really looking to see is whether he's legit? And whether he's the kind of guy who would do that?"

"Yeah, I guess that's kind of what I'm asking. Of course, if it ever gets back to him, that will make me feel even worse."

"Better safe than sorry," she replied. "So, even if it does get back to him, you were still wise to contact us."

"The thing is, I don't know when he even would have done it. I drove myself to the restaurant and was there waiting for him."

"Now, did you tell anyone you were going to the restaurant?"

"No, I told everybody I was going home," she stated.

"Right, so going to the restaurant and collapsing there would possibly not have been part of the plan."

"What do you mean?"

"What if somebody had drugged you, thinking that you would go home and that you would then be home alone and unprotected, so they could come and ..." Kat let her voice fall silent.

"They could come and what?" Sabrina asked. "Because that sounds absolutely terrible."

"I know, and we won't jump to conclusions," Kat stated. "This is something that my husband does all the time. He runs ops and security for multiple companies. So the fact that you've even been drugged is already a huge issue. The fact that you weren't supposed to go to the restaurant, but you did, also says that this drug wasn't intended to take effect until you were home because there is a delay on these things."

"I guess," Sabrina murmured, "and instead I went to the coffee shop and texted Landon to meet me. I had coffee. Then so did he. And, when he got there, we ordered hamburgers. I was surprised I ate as much as I did. I hadn't thought I was that hungry."

"So you may have already been feeling the effects of the drug," Kat noted calmly. "So take a moment and think back to the scene where the trouble happened. Who touched you? Who had an arm around you or was otherwise close enough to have injected you?"

In a voice that revealed she hated to even acknowledge it, she replied in a ghostly whisper, "Landon. He had his arm around me part of the time."

"Okay, so obviously that's why you're calling, and that's

good," Kat reassured her. "Now keep thinking about it. Who else was there? Did anybody else get close enough to touch you? Did you stumble? Did somebody reach for you? Did somebody push you or smack you on the arm? Was there any contact like that?"

"You know, I was so upset over everything that was going on that I don't really remember."

"Okay, that's fine too," she said. "I do believe there are videos of the altercation with Landon, so maybe I need to take a look at those."

"Could you?" she asked. "Let me know … afterward. Please."

"Yeah, will do," Kat promised. "Where are you now?"

"I'm still at the hospital. The doc wants me to get the drugs out of my system first, but I was hoping to check myself out early, but now I don't know what to do."

"Of course you don't," Kat murmured, her voice sympathetic and compassionate. "And because you're not sure if you can trust Landon, you can't contact him for help."

"No, and that's kind of the next step that I would have done. I really like him," she said, her voice fading quickly. "But now I'm terrified."

"No, I understand fully," Kat replied. "I have the video here so just give me a few minutes." And, with that, Kat rang off.

Sabrina had to wonder if she could even trust this other woman and if she called her back again, was that an answer or was that just asking for more trouble?

She knew if she contacted Angela, she would be all over Sabrina with her *I told you so* accusations. That was definitely not what Sabrina needed to hear right now. But she also didn't quite know what to do or whether it was safe to go anywhere. She didn't even have her vehicle here, for crying out loud. She could probably catch an Uber and get down to where her car was. Plus, she knew that if Landon had nothing to do with any of this, he'd be pissed that she hadn't called him.

She went over every conversation she'd had with him, but there was absolutely no sign that this guy was a serial killer, rapist, or anything like that. But then how would she know? She had a terrible record when it came to judging men. *No, Sabrina, stop with generalizing,* she told herself. Okay, truth be told, she chose badly last time. The other guys she had dated were not for her, but they weren't abusive, like her last ex-boyfriend. But that last one was why she'd already called to check out Landon. Too bad she hadn't done that first. But then again, better late than never.

She was safe in the hospital, and, maybe for now, it was best that she just stay here. She had planned to try and coax them into letting her leave, but maybe it was best to be prudent and to wait. And, with that, she sagged back into the bed, feeling tremors starting to wrack through her system.

When a nurse came to check on her not too much later, she was literally shivering, her teeth chattering. Startled, the nurse said, "Hang on," and she bolted from the room, only to return with a warm blanket that she wrapped around Sabrina.

She sank into the warmth of the blanket, feeling tears in her eyes.

"It's okay," the nurse replied. "Sometimes it happens like this. Sometimes, as a reaction to the drugs, you can get into these shivering, chilled moments," she explained. "It's all right. You'll be just fine. Now close your eyes and just rest, if you can."

Sabrina didn't think there was any way in hell that would happen. But she surprised herself, and, a few minutes later, she drifted off to sleep. As she finally started to calm down under the heat of the blanket, she fell back asleep again. Then she woke up, crying out, startled and scared.

As she lay here in bed, huddled up under the blanket, her phone rang. "Hello," she said, her voice still weak.

"Are you all right? It's Kat," she said. "We spoke earlier."

"I'm okay. … I had to get a hot blanket because I was shivering, and I think I fell asleep again. I'm feeling kind of groggy."

"That's quite normal with that kind of drug," Kat noted. "I'm really sorry you're going through this."

"Me too," Sabrina said, choking up, almost in tears. "Did you look at the videos?"

"I did, and I saw where Landon had his arm around your shoulders, almost protectively," she noted. "I also saw where the sheriff tapped you gently on the shoulder."

"He did?" Sabrina asked in confusion.

"He did. Like a pat on the shoulder, yet it raised my suspicions."

"Jesus! The sheriff?"

"Yes," Kat confirmed. "So I don't know if you want me to contact Landon or not, but I really don't want you to be alone right now."

"Do I even have a choice?" she asked, the tears collecting in her throat. "I've got no place to go. Not with anybody there."

"What do you mean?"

"I live alone," she said. "I have for a very long time. It's one of the reasons why I picked up some self-defense courses.

And, although that worked earlier at the park, I didn't have any clue that something else was going on."

"No, and it's obvious that the sheriff makes it look like he's trying to get you to calm down, but there's no doubt that he had an opportunity to do something."

"What kind of a world is this where the deputy hides his son's crimes, and the sheriff aids and abets him, even after it's pointed out in front of the FBI?"

"And we don't know what that's all about yet," Kat added, "but I know that Landon, at no point in time, had anything in his hand to do that."

"But did the sheriff?"

"No," Kat admitted reluctantly. "At least not that I could see. It doesn't mean it wasn't there though."

"But then that could also go for Landon, right?"

"Yes," she confirmed, "it could. But Landon is still there looking after you, even now."

"I know. I get that, but I'm also the one who texted him where I was."

"Of course you did, but remember this too. If he wanted to drug you, why would he immediately take you to the hospital?" Kat paused, waiting on Sabrina to say something, but she remained quiet. "I don't know how to make you feel any better about Landon, but, at this point in time, I highly suspect the sheriff is the one behind it."

"Oh, God, I can't even think straight."

"I know. It's the drugs," Kat said, "and that just adds to the confusion for you."

"You're not kidding. ... Thanks for finding out."

"I've already contacted the FBI, and they're coming over to the hospital, so expect them in a few minutes to talk to you."

"Okay," she murmured, the tears falling now. "I sure wish I knew if I could trust Landon."

"Maybe you need to have a heart to heart with your own heart and see which way you're leaning," Kat suggested. "If Landon has done nothing at all to deserve this, then, of course, it'll hurt him to think that you don't trust him. *But*," Kat added, "you're also the one who has to look after yourself. So, if he's not the man for you, then that's just the way it is."

"I don't know," Sabrina moaned. "I hardly know him, but everything I've seen I've really liked. We were talking about staying in touch after he managed to rescue Chica because he's better off not keeping the dog here."

"No, I hear you," Kat agreed, "and you're right. It would be better for Chica if she had a permanent place to decompress, rest, and recuperate. It depends on what kind of shape she's in and whether she'll need hospitalization or not."

"Oh God, that poor dog." At that, she sighed. "I'll talk to Landon as soon as I talk to the FBI. Any chance I could see the videotapes myself?"

"No problem," Kat replied. "I can send them to your phone."

"Can you?" she asked. "I'd really like to do that. I really don't want to have this suspicion in my heart. The best way to deal with it is to find out for sure."

"Absolutely," Kat declared. "And just remember. He already told us all about you. I can't see someone doing that who would put you in danger or who would take advantage of you in that way."

"No, I don't think he would. It's just a terrible thing to even contemplate."

"It is, absolutely it is," Kat said. "I'll send the videos to you right now." And, with that, Kat got off the phone.

It struck Sabrina that at no point in time did Kat try to push what a good guy Landon was. She didn't try to do anything even remotely like that. She made it clear that it was entirely up to Sabrina to make a decision on her own.

Just the idea had given her a terrible mind-set. At the moment it was really hard for her to even figure it out. And yet it shouldn't be that hard. Kat had suggested that Sabrina look inside herself, but how do you do that, after one bad breakup already from a guy who was abusive, then seeing Jared and the deputy and everybody else so committed to being assholes? How did she make a rational decision after that?

Yet it didn't seem to be hard for so many people. She sighed, as she lay in bed, still under the warm blanket. When a knock came on her door, she turned slightly to look at the doorway, and there was the FBI. "It didn't take you guys long."

"Nope, not at all." They stepped forward. "How are you feeling?"

"Rough," she said immediately. "Like I've been drugged, and now I'm terrified."

He nodded. "With good reason apparently."

She gave him a sober smile. "I don't even know if I can trust you guys."

They contemplated her for a long moment. "You know, at the moment, I wouldn't trust anybody," the lead agent said, with a dipped nod. "Once you have a sample of corrupt law enforcement, like what you're dealing with here, it makes you very leery about trusting anybody in that field."

"I know," she agreed, "yet I was raised to be very law-abiding, and now it feels like everything was a lie."

"It wasn't," he stated. "It's just that, right now, it's a little hard for us to convince you of that."

She added, "I wanted the videotapes sent to me so I could see for myself what's going on in them."

"That's a good idea," he agreed.

Her phone buzzed. "And that'll be the tapes." She looked over at him. "What do you know about Kat and Badger?"

He smiled. "We've dealt with them for decades, in one capacity or another," he replied. "They're both honest and trustworthy. They are good people, and they run a tight ship."

Her heart sighed heavily in relief. "I'm really glad to hear that because it feels like I'm putting a lot of trust in them right now."

He nodded. "We understand that, and we know this isn't an easy time for you. It was tough enough before we found out you were drugged, but now? Well ..."

"Now it's completely unacceptable," she declared. "I just don't know what I'm supposed to do about it."

"You get better for a start," he suggested. "You couldn't have gotten too hefty of a dose because you're awake and cognizant."

"Yeah, but my brain is still quite fuzzy," she murmured.

"That's to be expected. Fuzzy is kind of normal."

She winced at that. "Still doesn't feel good though."

"No, I'm sure it doesn't," he said.

"What about Landon?" she asked. "Have you ever worked with him before?"

He shook his head. "No, I haven't, but honestly, if he's one of their men, he's been completely vetted. They are as trustworthy as the day is long," he added. "There are quite a few groups that we do work with. Obviously I can't turn around and tell you for sure specifically that Landon's solid and a stand-up good guy. However, if I had to bet on who the good guy was among any of those people out at that park today, he would be my only pick."

"And yet somebody out there drugged me."

"Which is why you need to look at the videotapes."

She nodded. "Is it clear who it is?"

"It is to us," the agent stated.

She reached for her phone, pulled up the first video, and watched. Even she recognized the moment in time when the sheriff stepped forward in kind of an awkward *Hey, let me help you out* kind of moment. Like, *It's all right. You'll be fine. Don't get hysterical,* then gave her a slap on the shoulder. "So that's why I didn't get a very strong dose," she murmured.

"That's what we think too." He nodded. "Just one more thing that we must look at."

She shook her head. "None of this makes any sense." She looked over at him. "Unless ..."

The one guy's eyebrow shot up. "Unless what?"

"Is there a relationship between the sheriff and the deputy?"

"You mean like a *relationship*, relationship?"

"God, no. I meant, are they uncles, brothers, related somehow, anything like that?" she asked.

"No, nothing obvious," he replied, "but that doesn't mean that the sheriff may not have another reason for keeping the deputy around."

"He must have some reason, even many reasons," she replied. "There is no possible way he didn't know all that stuff he denied knowledge of. And now he has certainly violated my trust. I get that, for him, that doesn't even register on his clock as being important, but there's definitely something fishy going on."

"We'll get to the bottom of it."

She looked at him and said, "It's not even your jurisdiction, your case, or anything."

"That doesn't matter," he explained. "We were here at the time, and we have cause to believe the sheriff and the deputy are both corrupt, so we've got permission to investigate."

She sagged into the bed. "Seriously?"

They nodded. "So, don't worry. We'll get to the bottom of it. You stay here and try to recover as much as you can from the drugs."

She nodded. "I'm not planning on going anywhere. I still feel pretty odd."

"Of course you do, but that's also the drugs. So don't make any quick decisions, and stay here." And, with that, the two FBI agents were gone.

"THERE YOU ARE, sweetheart," Landon murmured, his voice calm and steady. Sure enough, Chica was at the edge of the woods, staring at him. But terror still filled her gaze. It broke his heart to see her in such dire straits. "Hey, at least you're getting food this way," he murmured. "Now we just need to get you a little bit more trusting, so I can get a leash on you and get you into the truck," he explained. "I'm sure my little dog pack will help calm you down, but they'll be all over you. They've never met a stranger they didn't love," he said, with a wry tone.

He kept his voice calm and steady, waiting for her to

decide whether or not food was something she could come forward and grab. He hoped so; she was looking far too skinny, and that's not what he wanted for her. He waited, patiently letting his voice do the talking. The three little Chihuahuas were at his feet. He had them leashed, and they were just chilling in front of him.

Even Larry, his skittish one, appeared to be completely calm. Sometimes they got pretty rambunctious and crazy, but right now it was almost as if they understood that they needed to be here and to be steady and cooperative. As soon as protective Curly saw the new arrival, even though Chica was quite a distance away, Curly's tail immediately started moving in greeting.

"See? They want to meet you too," he told Chica. "They just want to know that you're okay, and so do I. Of course I want to take you where I know that I can look after you and make sure you have a good life," he shared, his voice gentle.

As he studied her, he watched her limp, but it looked like she was limping on two legs now. But who knew what these assholes may have done to her? Maybe it was just a case of bad timing; Landon didn't know. She'd had a pretty rough couple months, and that was something he was hoping to make up for, if he could just get close enough to her.

He knew that a wrong move would set her back weeks. He had a lead and rope beside him. But he needed to get her close enough to get it over her head.

He was pretty sure that, by the time he got it over her head, she'd be fine. She might fight it for a while, but, once he could get her a little bit calmer, he knew she would be okay. Those first few delicate moments would be tough. They were always tough. Training animals was like that though. It took patience, but it was a labor of love, and you just allowed the animal to do what it needed to do, until it could find that sense of trust somewhere deep inside.

And, even at that, Landon wasn't so sure how long it would take. He didn't want to push her and didn't want Chica to feel like she was out of time. He would be here in town for as long as it took. Hell, he didn't really want to leave at all, considering that Sabrina was here.

He looked down at his phone, wondering whether he should call the hospital, but he didn't want any sound to intrude right now. He sent a text to her. **Hey, just thinking of you. Hope you're feeling better.** Then he put away his phone. When no immediate answer came, he hoped that she was sleeping.

He didn't know what the hell had happened to Chica or to Sabrina, but, at some point in time, all these nasty little details would come out. He just hoped there wasn't anything even worse than what he was expecting.

Just then Chica took another step forward. "It's all right, girl," Landon coaxed her gently. "Keep coming. It's okay." He put out a few pieces of dog food and then had several more placed even closer to him. It was the only way to get her to keep coming closer. As she picked up those pieces, she looked at him warily.

"Do you want some more?" he asked. "I've got plenty."

When he opened the bag, Curly lifted her head and sniffed. "No, you're just fine, Curly," he said. But he tossed out another handful of dog food for Chica. She approached gently and warily took one more step, grabbed a few bites, then immediately retreated. "You know, if we could just get you a few solid meals, you wouldn't feel so bad," Landon stated.

At the moment, the area was empty, and there was no traffic to speak of. When he'd first arrived, it was somewhat bustling, but everyone had left. That was good and exactly what he needed. He just needed peace and quiet for Chica. A chance to get to know each other, a chance to sit here and become friends. She'd had an awful lot of the wrong kind of attention, and Landon was trying to make up for it.

He also didn't know what was happening with the sheriff or the FBI, but he wanted to make sure that nobody came back and hurt this dog. She was looking worse for wear in so many ways. He wanted to get her safe and checked over by a vet. There was a chance that she'd already been hit by the pellet gun, and, if that were the case, those pellets would be festering inside, something she did not need at all.

But first, he had to win her trust, and, for that, he had to get her to come a little closer.

"Come on, girl," he said calmly. "Come on. Just a little bit more." Whether it was his own dogs or something else, he didn't know, but she took one look, then got spooked and took off. His shoulders sagged.

"I tried," he muttered to the little dogs, all looking at him reproachfully. "Hey, it wasn't me." As it was, a vehicle came up and parked in the parking lot. He said, "So that's what disturbed Chica. See? Definitely not me." But the dogs didn't look terribly convinced. He sat here, waiting to see who it was, but it appeared to be a young couple walking their dog, as they headed over to an open grassy area.

He realized that would be the end of it for now. He got up and decided to drop another pile of food for Chica, and he would be back, hopefully within a few hours. Just as he left the dog food on the ground, his phone rang. He looked down to see it was Kat. "Hey, Kat. What's up?"

"Lots," Kat said, her voice determined. "So, first off, I got a phone call from your girlfriend."

He straightened. "Sabrina called you? Why?"

"Partly to do her due diligence and to check that you were a real legit human being who was trustworthy," she stated.

"I guess that's good," he replied, frowning.

"It's very good," she declared in a crisp tone. "Particularly considering two things. One, did you know that she had a previous relationship that went badly? Let me just put it this way, the bottom line is that she doesn't trust her own judgment with men, and perhaps with people in general."

"She did mention something about that, and she's currently on the outs with a female friend here in town and feeling taken advantage of," he shared. "So, I guess, given all that, it makes sense that she would make a phone call to see that I am who I am. And, of course, you gave me a glowing reference. ... I hope," he added, with a note of humor.

"I would have, except for the second point."

"What's that?" he asked, as he walked back to the truck. He opened up the driver's door, and the dogs all scrambled up and into the floorboard, then up onto the seat and into their bed.

"The hospital ran a bunch of tests."

"Yeah, and?"

"She was drugged."

He felt everything inside him slowly coalesce in horror. "I wondered because of the way she was acting. I knew something wasn't right," he said.

"It took them a little bit to find it, but she has a puncture mark in her arm."

"Wow." His mind was still trying to sort through that

information. "Oh, shit! Does she think it was me?" he cried out.

"It wasn't so much that she thought it was you, but that you were the only one close enough to have done it. You were the one with your arm around her."

"Yes, of course I put my arm around her. She wasn't looking very good. She was really upset and shell-shocked by the fight and the lack of accountability by anyone, and she was ..." His voice petered out. "Good God," he said, and now he started to get angry. "Who the hell drugged her and how?"

"Thankfully you had the two video files, so I took a closer look, and the only other person who got that close to her was the sheriff. At one point he reached out with his hands to pat her shoulders, as if to try to get her to calm down."

"Yeah, she got quite angry over that and kind of shrugged him off."

"It's a good thing she did because I suspect that was when the drugs were administered."

He froze. "Are we saying the sheriff did this?"

"I think so, yes," she stated. "You need to take a closer look at the videos yourself to understand why she contacted me. I sent her the videos, and I know that she has looked at them. I also sent the FBI to the hospital."

"Jesus, you know I would never do something like that."

"I know that," Kat stated reassuringly. "And I'm pretty sure she knows it too. But, on top of everything else, she did the right thing in calling me."

"She really did, didn't she?" he agreed, a note of relief in his voice. "It would have been way worse if she had just let that fester."

"Exactly. What we need to do is get to the bottom of

this, and fast, because someone could still be gunning for her."

"On that note," he growled, "I'm heading back to the hospital. I've been sitting here trying to get close enough to Chica to get a rope around her."

"Have you ... You've seen her?" she asked in a sharp voice.

"Seen her and been close enough to almost reach out and touch her, but I know that if I make a lunge, she'll just run, so I've been trying to give her some time. I've left her more food, and now I'm pulling out of the parking lot and heading to the hospital."

"Just be aware that Sabrina might be a little off."

"She has full reason to be off," he declared, his own fury mounting again. "Jesus, Kat. What the hell's going on here?"

"I'm not sure. She also asked me a couple questions that I didn't have any answers for, but I have thought about them at least."

"Like what?"

"She asked, if the deputy and the sheriff were related in any way."

"And?"

"I don't find any family relationship, but I'm not sure if there isn't some other reason why the deputy might be getting some kind of protection from the sheriff."

"Jesus. Especially now that the FBI is involved."

"They had to pull some strings in order to assume control of this, but, with the date rape drug confirmed, they are now."

"Thank God for that," Landon said. "They generally have to ask permission, don't they?"

"They went above the local authorities and got themselves invited," Kat replied, with a chuckle in her voice.

"Well, good. Something is working in our favor at least. That's shitty timing though. I spent a lot of time just trying to make her feel better, and now I'm the one with an arm around her."

"Exactly, and maybe the sheriff knew that. But then he also had to have brought it with him to the scene. But you don't know if that was intentionally meant for Sabrina either. Was it something that he was expecting to use on the kid to knock him out—or on you?"

"Right," he muttered. "Damn it."

Kat added, "I found it very interesting that, at the scene, Sabrina says she's going home, then rerouted to the coffee shop. It made me wonder if perhaps the sheriff figured he'd follow up afterward at her place."

"Jesus fucking Christ, he might have killed her."

"Yes, or framed you. Just stay calm and realize what's going on. Now you have the information I have, and so does she."

"Okay," he said, taking deep breaths. "And, Kat? … Thanks for the heads-up."

As she went to ring off, she added, "Remember. Sabrina's already been traumatized a couple times now. What you need to do now is keep her safe."

"Oh, don't worry," he stated, "that's at the top of the priority list right now."

"And so is Chica," she added, with a note of rebuke in her voice.

"Absolutely. And don't worry. Chica and I are fast becoming friends." He hesitated.

"What?"

"Is there money in the budget for a vet?"

"Does she need one?"

"Yeah, not only has she been starved for a long time, but I wouldn't be at all surprised if she doesn't have a couple BB pellets in her that need to be removed, plus antibiotics afterward. For all I know, it could be way worse than that. She's limping more than she was before, I think."

"Shit, I absolutely hate assholes who would hurt a dog."

"You and me both," he agreed. "So, yes or no?"

"I have no idea what Badger would say about the actual budget, but, as a human being, I would say that, if the program can't afford it, we'll figure it out."

"Well," Landon suggested, "how about I take care of it for now, and, if Badger doesn't, we'll just work some credit into my prosthetic bill."

She burst out laughing. "Still angling on that new prosthetic, *huh?*"

"You know it," he admitted. Still grinning, he hung up the phone, but the smile fell from his face almost immediately, as he turned the truck in the direction of the hospital. He needed to talk to Sabrina and fast. And the last thing he wanted was for her to be alone for any length of time.

Particularly if the damn sheriff was involved. This town sucked, and he would do his best to convince her to move to New Mexico. Maybe even talk his brother into a move down south too. At least Kat and Badger were good people.

CHAPTER 12

S ABRINA WOKE UP once again, still groggy and trying hard to get her head back together, only to realize she had a visitor. She bolted to the side in fear. When she realized it was Landon, she sat back in relief. "God, you startled me."

He smiled as he got up, then walked over and reached for her hand. "Hey, I got an update on what happened."

"Yeah, that's great, isn't it? Now at least we know why I collapsed."

He nodded. "And it's not your fault. Remember that."

She looked over at him. "But how the hell does somebody do that to me, when I'm right there?" she asked. "That's the part I don't like."

"Neither do I," he agreed, "because I was right there too."

She stared at him and slowly nodded. "I guess that's a good point. It's a little disturbing to think that somebody can do something like that without it being obvious or at least noticeable."

"I presume it was a pressure syringe, and he just did it really fast."

"So what does that mean? He's had practice?"

"That's possible too." He frowned at that, staring at her. "You know what? We might have to take a much closer look at this sheriff."

"Oh, we definitely do," she declared. Then she hesitated and added, "I phoned the people on your business card."

"Yeah?" he said.

"Kat is a really nice person," she noted calmly.

He chuckled. "Kat is a sweetheart, and she's also the one that I'm desperately trying to make me a new prosthetic. She's a genius at designing those."

"You do realize that the sheriff will deny it and will say that you gave me that drugs?"

"I know, but as long as you don't believe it, I'm good with that."

"No, I don't believe it, but, in the spirit of a full declaration, I did phone Kat to confirm it."

"She could only confirm what she knows," he replied. "And that isn't necessarily a whole lot. Be prepared that they'll no doubt say that I use those drugs because clearly I couldn't get a woman any other way."

She frowned at that. "I never thought that, but all I could think of was that you had your arm around me at the time."

He nodded. "And I presume that you saw the videos, and you're satisfied that it wasn't me."

She smiled up at him. "Yes, and I'm sorry for doubting you."

"You shouldn't be. We don't know each other well enough for that. Obviously I would have loved to have inspired blind faith, but I would probably be the first to tell you to not be stupid and to make your checks and balances so that everything in your life works. Never feel bad about being smart enough to check something out."

She sagged into bed. "I figured you'd be really angry

with me."

He stared at her in astonishment. "Never. And besides, you've had some hard days, and it was your own judgment you were probably doubting as much as me, but that's all water under the bridge, right? Honestly, I'm wondering if the whole drugging thing wasn't a setup, so they could throw out my testimony and yours, since obviously I'm somebody who would do something like that or you took drugs anyway," he mimicked, with a note of bitterness.

"Oh my. That's quite possible, isn't it? We all have our own filters that taint the way we look at things, don't we?"

He shrugged. "They'll say that the drugs just make it easy for me."

"Right, well, that's just bullshit."

At that, he burst out laughing. "Thanks for that vote of confidence."

"It was a vote of confidence right from the beginning, only Angela had me questioning my gut reaction," she confessed. "I'm sorry that I checked."

"No, don't be sorry about that, and I gave you the business card for that very reason."

"And a serial killer could have been on the other end," she said, laughing.

"Kat would probably take offense to that. She goes to great lengths to preserve that reputation of hers and to help us all out," he stated.

"I'm just kidding," she said. "Trying to lighten the mood. It's been a pretty rough day."

"I would suggest I take you home, but I'm not sure you're cleared to leave."

"Everybody keeps telling me to stay here and rest. But it's kind of a weird feeling. It's not where I want to be, and

I'm feeling ... well enough, I guess. I kind of think I should go home, but going home also sounds scary. ... If I hadn't pulled into the coffee shop instead and texted you, I would have been at home. Alone."

"And somebody could have gone to your place, expecting the drugs to have taken effect."

"Exactly. It wasn't very far away, and anybody in law enforcement could easily get my address."

"Do you have any security cameras at your place?"

"I do," she said, perking up, a note of excitement returning to her voice as she stared at him. "Do you think they actually went to my place?"

"Can you access the security cam video from your phone?" Landon asked her.

She stared at him. "What? I don't know. ... Maybe? Why is my brain not working?" she asked, as she immediately grabbed her phone. "I've never done this before."

"It's not hard in most cases," Landon suggested. "Everything is set up for that these days."

"I know, but that doesn't mean I'm any good at it. I tend to forget that I even have it on."

He didn't say anything and just waited, trying not to distract her. Finally she brought it up on her phone. "Here's the video now," she said. Landon moved to stand beside her, so he could look too. Sure enough, a vehicle pulled up at her house, an unmarked car at that.

As she watched, a man got out, walked to the door, and knocked. When there was no answer, he reached for the doorknob, and, looking around, quickly tried to open it, finding it locked.

"Do you always set the alarm?"

She nodded. "Yeah, I do. ... It goes back to that bad

relationship before."

"We'll talk about that at some point, right?" he asked.

"Yeah, one day," she muttered. "When I'm old and gray and when it won't matter."

"It had to be bad enough that you took up self-defense and that you always set your security," he noted, "so that's a good thing. And we've got his face right there—or will have once the film has been enhanced," he said. At that point, the guy went around to the back and appeared to be checking windows on the way.

"How many cameras at the back?"

"None."

"That's pretty common, but really we should set you up with full cameras."

"If I'd realized I was running into this kind of a trouble, I might have. I thought I was being paranoid by having the system at all. I had to do a budget-friendly system, so not too many cameras and the alarm just scares them away. It doesn't call anyone."

"I know, right? Nobody ever has all the stuff that they need at the time of trouble."

On her screen, they watched as the man at her place darted back to his vehicle and took off again. "Can you forward that to me?" She did, as he asked. "Now forward it on to the FBI."

"Oh, right." She shook her head. "I feel like an idiot."

Landon asked her, "Do you really want to stay in this town? Is New Mexico sounding better?"

"You're really strong on that whole New Mexico thing, aren't you?" She winced at that. "I don't really want to go back to my house, now that I know somebody has been there. My poor dogs."

"Yet they didn't do any damage on that trip—or they've disconnected your security system."

"I don't know about that either," she said.

"How long was he there for?"

"Well, it kind of blinked at one point in time, so I'm not sure."

"The camera would have continued to roll regardless. So maybe I should go take a look." He frowned.

"Look at what though? If he'd gotten in, the question would have been, *Where was Sabrina?* That's what he would have been looking for. So, if I wasn't there, it kind of makes sense that he would have come running out and off to whoever is involved in this."

"You mean, the sheriff?" Landon asked in a steady tone.

She winced. "Yeah. I was trying to avoid saying it out loud."

"I hear you, but you do know that sticking your head in the sand won't help in this case."

"Are you sure?" She laughed. "I was kind of thinking that might be a nice way to avoid everything."

"Nope. Won't work."

"No, probably not." She stared down at her phone. "It really sucks, you know? I thought I was safe and didn't have any troubles in town. Now it seems like everything has blown up in my face."

"Maybe not with your friend though. That kind of stuff may pass with time."

"Maybe," she said, then she shrugged. "Yet I haven't called her, even though I'm the one who's in the hospital and could use a friend."

He stared at her for a long moment. "Do you want me to?"

She shook her head. "No, God no. That would just make her even worse."

"So, I gather it was over me."

"It wasn't, … not really. That's what started it, but then it all spiraled into … something else completely. She has just been different since she got involved with this boyfriend, and I've been spending a lot of time there at the clinic, more about the animals than her. Now I'm wondering if maybe I'm better off not spending quite so much time there. And they can't use the excuse of the *impact on the animals* to snooker me into giving them free labor. They should be hiring more staff," she stated, with spirit.

He looked at her and then nodded. "Absolutely. And maybe that's a discussion that you need to have with them."

She snorted. "They may happily take my free time, but they won't listen to me," she snapped. "I don't know. At the moment I just have so many other things on my mind."

"At the moment, you don't need any of that Angela drama," he said. "That's for sure. But we'll get to the bottom of this other mess fairly quickly."

"You think so?" she asked in a wry tone. "Doesn't feel like things are moving very quickly."

"It's actually very fast," he said, chuckling. "Remember? The law works very slowly."

"Maybe, but you haven't convinced me that this is anything but slow yet."

He just grinned at her. A moment later his phone rang. "Hi, Kat. You're on Speakerphone."

"That face on the home security video that you sent," she said, getting right to the meat of the matter, "that guy is another deputy at the sheriff's office."

"Jesus Christ," Landon said. "Is the whole station corrupt? And you know they'll just say that he was concerned and went to check up on her."

"Right, but what we don't know is whether the home security system is even operable now. If they're smart, they didn't touch it," Kat noted. "But, if he did, then that's a whole different story."

"I get that," Landon said, "but it's still not anything conclusive at this point."

"Nope. Did you send that to our friends at the FBI?"

"We did," he confirmed, "so hopefully somebody there is checking it out."

"Yeah, hopefully," she replied, her voice distracted. "Okay, I'll let you go. Badger's not up-to-date on the current intel and is giving me the stink eye, so I better go fill him in." With that, she hung up.

"She seems like a really nice person," Sabrina repeated, "and quite likable."

"She is. She's the best. And the both of them are very talented. And live in New Mexico too."

She smiled. "And it's always nice when people are able to work in a field that they enjoy. Helping people must give her pleasure."

"Pleasure and passion in her case. According to my brother, she's also missing a leg, she and her husband Badger both," he shared, "and that's what started her down the prosthetic pathway. She couldn't find anything that was decent for herself either."

"Wow. How did she lose her leg?"

"She was born with some kind of a problem. Her leg just never grew right, and it didn't develop properly, so, at some point in time as it was holding her back, she made the decision to have it removed. She struggled with the prosthetics that were available from the start and eventually figured she could do better. Now she's ahead in her field, like you wouldn't believe."

"I'd really love to meet her. It's so great to know she's doing something that really matters to her."

"Yeah, it mattered to her personally to begin with, and now it matters even more, since that's what she does to help us all. She designs Badger's prosthetics as well."

She stared at him. "Seriously?"

He nodded. "She works particularly with war vets, who are coming out of traumatic injuries. Not exclusively but a lot of her clients are war veterans."

"Wow," she said softly. "I'm really glad she's there to help them."

"Oh, me too, believe me," he replied, with a chuckle. "I'm just hoping that, when I get back, we can find something that'll work for me."

"This doesn't work for you?" she asked, motioning at his ankle.

"It does, to a certain extent, but there's got to be something better," he noted.

"Yet it doesn't seem to hinder your ability to do anything."

"Nope," he said. "Why would it?"

"I know a lot of people who would consider that something of a handicap. And there is my word choice again. Not that I think that way."

"Yeah, people make that mistake," he agreed, "but, as we saw at the park, they generally don't make it twice."

She smiled at him. "I really like hearing that. I like hearing the self-confidence in your voice and that whole attitude that says, *You are just fine.*"

"I *am* just fine," he declared, looking at her. "It took me a long time to get here, but I did." His gaze was steady as he stared at her. "What I'm not so sure of is how other people react to it."

She paused for a long moment and then asked, "Do you mean me?"

He shrugged. "Sure. Just because I want you to move to New Mexico so we can see each other doesn't mean that you've actually thought about what life would entail with someone in your life who wears a prosthetic."

She stared at him, frowning. "Remember that part about me working in hospice and long-term care? I work with people with broken bodies or bodies giving out at the end of life," she stated, "and there's nothing pretty about that at all. Colostomy bags, IVs, catheters, urine bags, bed sores, gangrene, and plenty more. Basically I'm used to it all, and it doesn't bother me a bit," she stated firmly.

He seemed to search her face, and then he smiled. "Good," he said cheerfully. "I'm really glad to hear that."

She laughed. "And that's it?"

"It is for me," he replied. "You might need to revisit that down the road, but, for me, I'm good."

"I'm glad to hear that. Although I can't say that I ever felt like I was interviewed for a dating position before."

He burst out laughing again. "Oh, I do like your sense of humor."

She smiled at him. "I guess it's what keeps us real, isn't it?"

"It absolutely is. So what do you want to do?"

She shifted at the sudden change in the conversation. "Meaning?"

"Do you want to stay here? Do you want to try leaving?

What would you like to do?"

"I'd like to leave, but I'm not sure about staying alone at my place."

"You won't be staying alone," he stated. "You're about to have four houseguests."

She winced at that. "Four?" she repeated. "Are you telling me that the FBI guys are staying with me too?"

His laughter rang out, free and clear. "No, just me, along with Larry, Curly, and Moe."

"Oh my." And then she giggled. "Yeah, I'm sure they'll be a hardship to handle."

He gave her that smile of his and whispered, "They can be. They absolutely can be."

"No, I don't believe that for a minute. And I don't even care. They are absolutely welcome. ... And thank you. I will feel better if you stay."

"Are you sure though?" he asked, looking at her. "I mean, really sure?"

"Yes." She smiled. "Really sure."

"Okay, that's settled then." He hopped to his feet. "Let me go see if I can find somebody to get your release papers."

"I can always just walk out of here," she suggested. "They're all so busy that I don't think they'd give a crap if I left or not."

"I don't know about that," he said. "You do know that you're a walking, talking crime scene."

"The hospital took everything they decently could from me," she noted, with a wince. "So I highly doubt that anybody will care. But go ahead and ask, if it will make you feel better."

He nodded. "It will." And, with that, he disappeared.

She laid back into the bed and thought about what she

had just agreed to, but there was absolutely nothing inside her that felt bad about it. But she also knew that Angela would be screaming at her to run, but Sabrina didn't feel that way at all. Maybe she was making a mistake, but she didn't think so. And just when she was ready to get out of bed and to find some clothing, her phone rang. It was Angela.

Sabrina stared down at the screen, wondering if she even wanted to answer, but knew ignoring it would only make things worse. Finally, she answered. "Yeah, what's up?"

"Are you okay?" Angela asked. "Somebody said something about you being in the hospital."

"Wow, small town," she replied.

"Yeah, I guess. What happened?"

"I got into a bit of an altercation, and then I collapsed at lunch, but it's nothing. The doc has already taken care of it, and I've just been released. I'm going home now."

"Do you want me to come over?" she asked instantly.

"No, I don't. I want to just go home and have an early night."

"Are you sure? Are you really okay?" Angela demanded. "I don't know what's going on between us, but it seems like everything is wrong."

"Maybe it is," Sabrina said. "I don't know. I guess we got off on the wrong track, and we just haven't managed to get it straightened out."

"I've spent a lot of time with Jason," she admitted.

"Did he ever get the deal hammered out with the vet clinic?"

"I think so," she said, "and that's taken a lot of stress off me. I've probably been pretty short-tempered with you recently. But just knowing that we were moving forward with buying the vet clinic, ... that's been, ... that's been huge."

"*We?*"

Angela hesitated. "Yeah, we, ... uh, ... we're getting married." And there was kind of a squeal of delight in her voice.

"Wow." Sabrina stared at her phone. "When did he ask you to marry him?"

Angela hesitated again. "A couple weeks ago."

"You got engaged a couple weeks ago and didn't tell me?"

"No, I didn't. Jason just wanted to keep it quiet for the two of us."

"Oh." At that, there was just no stopping the hurt. "We've literally known each other since second grade, and you didn't tell me the biggest news of your life? That'll take a little getting used to." Maybe it was just not having seen the truth of how distant they'd become over the last little while, but this might be the wake-up call she needed.

"I wanted to tell you," Angela explained, "but I didn't know how to go against him. I mean, he felt so strongly about it."

"Why is that?"

"At least until the deal was worked out for the vet clinic, he didn't want anyone to know. He didn't want it to impact the deal or anything."

"*Right,*" she replied, not sure how that would make a damn bit of difference. "Well, congratulations."

"Thanks. I'm really sorry I didn't tell you."

"Yeah, well, it's your news. You get to tell whoever you want," she stated. "Look. I've got to get moving." Not giving Angela a chance to say any more, she hung up. She had to admit she was more than stunned, and that too was an understatement.

As she sat here, trying to digest the news, Landon came back in.

He took one look at her face and frowned. "What's wrong?"

She stared up at him, blinked several times. "Angela just called." Sabrina shrugged. "Apparently she got engaged a couple weeks back and never told me."

He stared at her. "This is your 'best friend' Angela?" he asked cautiously, with air quotes and all.

She gave a burble of laughter. "Yeah, you know, *that* best friend. She just told me now, after calling because she'd heard I was in the hospital."

"Did she give a reason why she didn't tell you?"

"Something to do with her boyfriend not wanting the news to get out in case it affected the deal with the vet clinic somehow."

"Wow. That's very strange."

"Believe me. I'm sitting here in shock myself. But it's just reinforcing the idea that maybe it's time to back away from that friendship. After all, Angela already chose to do that."

"Or, just playing devil's advocate here, you realize that she was in a tough spot, if her partner wanted her to not tell anyone."

Sabrina shook her head, thinking how Angela would have never accepted Landon. So, in a way, their decades old relationship had just bit the dust. "Sure, but she also could have told me and asked me to keep it between us."

He nodded. "I don't know what to tell you about that one."

"Yeah, me neither." She gave a wave of her hand. "Obviously it's not today's issue." It might not be an issue ever again. It sure felt like it was yesterday's problem that had now become something much bigger than it needed to be. She didn't even know what to think about who Angela was now.

"By the way, I saw the doctor, and he's signing you out."

"Just like that?"

Landon nodded. "Just like that." Then he grinned at her. "Of course I did promise to bring you back to the hospital if anything happened and about ten other provisions."

"Sure, that's pretty standard around here. But I am more than ready to go. Trust me." With that, she pulled back the blankets, slowly stood up, and sank down immediately. "Whoa, still a little woozy."

"Yeah, but we've got a magical way to get you out of here." Smiling, he produced the wheelchair from behind his back.

She groaned. "Seriously?"

"Yeah, absolutely seriously." He chuckled. "Somehow I figured you would not be a great patient."

She glared at him. "That's not fair. I would have said that I would make a model patient. But nobody ever really knows what kind of patient they'll be until they're in the hospital."

Just then a nurse popped in. "Thought you might need a hand getting dressed."

"That would be great, thank you. I'm a little wobbly still, more than I expected," she admitted.

"Yes, that's pretty common," she confirmed.

"I'll go move my truck closer," Landon said, as he

slipped out the door. "Be right back."

With the help of the nurse, Sabrina quickly got dressed and was sitting up on the bed, when Landon returned.

"Perfect," he said, with a smile, when he poked his head in the partially open door. "Let's get you home." And very slowly he helped her to stand, then sit down in the wheelchair. "You're really feeling rough, aren't you?"

"Yeah, I am. They ended up pumping my stomach, and now it hurts."

"Of course it does. Oh, man, they wasted that great burger."

She burst out laughing. "I didn't even think of it that way, but you have those sandwiches still, so it's not like you need me to cook."

"They didn't pump my stomach, silly. I wouldn't need you to cook anyway," he added cheerfully. "I'm pretty capable of doing what I need to do."

She smiled. "I have no doubt about that," she murmured.

He carefully wheeled her down the hall and out of the hospital. When he got her up to the truck, she saw his three dogs, excitedly waiting for his return, yet not barking.

"They're really good at being left alone, aren't they?"

"We did a fair bit of traveling for doctor appointments and treatments over the past couple years with Joe," Landon mentioned. "So that became something they adjusted to."

"Sad that they had to become adjusted to something like that though," she noted.

"As it turned out, these dogs were good for Joe, and Joe was good for them," Landon stated, with that same cheerfulness. "Let's just make this happen." And, with that, he helped her into the back seat. "Are you sure you're okay? I could easily move them to the back seat," he offered.

"No, don't worry about it," she said. "I'm happy to sit here, and it's not very far to my house anyway."

He carefully began the drive to her home, checking on her in the rearview mirror. "I would really like to bring your vehicle back home, but you're not up for driving just yet."

"No, definitely not, but maybe tomorrow. It should be okay at the restaurant overnight, shouldn't it?"

"I would think so," he replied, "but, if you're worried about it, we could give them a quick call and explain."

"Oh, that's a good idea." She pulled out her phone, looked up the phone number, then quickly called and explained it to the manager. Ending the call, she shared the details with Landon. "He's okay with leaving it overnight and was wondering whose it was already."

"Of course he was. I mean, it's his place of business, so they always keep track of cars coming and going, for a variety of reasons these days," he noted. "So that's all good."

She smiled at that. "This is definitely not quite the way I thought my day would go."

"No kidding," he agreed. "Did you talk to your supervisor about taking tomorrow off?"

"No, but I'm off tomorrow anyway," she stated. "The question is whether I'll be ready for work on the day after that. Right now, I'm not so sure. The doctor told me to give it a couple days."

"Sounds like common sense to me."

She nodded. "I never have used much sick leave in the past."

"And you certainly don't need to feel guilty about using it now," he said. "This is one time you really need to look after yourself."

She sighed. "Yeah, I'll just wait and see how I feel tomorrow."

"Good enough. I won't badger you."

"Really?" she teased. "I got the distinct impression that you would."

He burst out laughing again, and she smiled, loving the way it just felt so right, so natural to be with him. As soon as he pulled into her driveway, he said, "Just hang on a second, and I'll come around to your side."

"I'm fine, you know?" she replied.

"Maybe you are. Maybe you aren't. But I promised the doc that I'd look after you."

She stared at him. "Seriously? So now you'll force me to wait until you get here to help me?"

"I've got to get the leashes on the dogs too," he pointed out.

At that, she immediately winced. "No, you're right. Pull them out before they destroy your rental."

He chuckled. "The chances of them destroying anything is practically zero, but we don't want them having an accident in here. With three dogs, it's just triple the threat." And, with that, he clipped on their leashes and pulled the dogs out, then opened the back door and helped her down.

"Now let me know how you're feeling," he said. "I don't want you overdoing it."

She rolled her eyes at him. "You do remember I'm a nurse, right?"

"Yep." He smiled. "And, just in case you didn't know, I've got quite the first aid credentials as well. I did an awful lot of medic work in the military," he noted. "So between us, we'll make sure that you're just fine."

She groaned. "Somehow it sounds like I'll be coddled

the whole time."

"Hey, it could be worse." He raised an eyebrow at her.

She nodded. "No, you're right. It could be much worse. The fact of the matter is, I'm free and clear after whatever the hell that nightmare was, and, with any luck," she added, "it won't happen again."

"No, not on my watch," he declared, "and I'm really sorry it happened in the first place."

She shrugged. "It wasn't your fault, and you didn't do it. If anything, I provoked them, especially the sheriff. So, what we need to do is make sure we catch that asshole, so he can't do that to me or anyone else again."

LATER ON, WHEN Sabrina was tucked into bed, with all five dogs curled up beside her, much to her joy and his disgust—*traitors*—he walked downstairs to double-check again that everything was secure for the night. He'd already phoned Badger to give him an update, and he hadn't heard anything from the FBI yet.

The windows and doors were all locked, and she'd already set the security alarm. He would stay in the spare room, but he had no doubt that the dogs would stay with her. His three had taken to her like he'd never seen them with anyone before, including Joe. Of course that was a good choice on their part, and Landon was glad to see it. As he wandered back upstairs, he heard her whimper in her sleep. He walked in and checked on her, but she seemed to be doing fine.

As he stepped away, she called out, "Is there a problem?"

"No, I was just checking on you. I heard you cry out,

but I guess you were asleep."

"Yeah, sorry. I do that sometimes," she noted.

"So I gather whatever happened before in your prior relationship was fairly traumatic."

"Yeah, but it was also years ago, and it too could have been much worse. It just feels like everything in my world's kind of disconnected."

"And that's also because of the drugs and the fight at the park, plus, you know, the problems with your *friend*."

"I know, … and it feels like I'm grieving, which seems stupid."

"No, it's not stupid. You just have to decide if that relationship is something you want to keep in your life. I realize it's been one long friendship, spanning decades. So the grief is understandable. Still, the length alone of any relationship doesn't deem it as being good for you or your mental health."

"And here I thought that relationship countered the stress in my job."

Landon nodded. "And it did, for a while. It's just that friendships, if they'll endure over time, need a lot of give and take," he suggested. "It depends on whether the two of you have the same level of interest in giving and taking, now that she has a partner."

"I always thought that our friendship would be something the two of us shared forever, like getting married somewhere around the same time, having kids somewhere around the same time. We always talked about our kids growing up as friends," she muttered.

"Maybe it will still happen. … You don't know what the future holds. Right now the friendship has taken a decided turn, but, with time, you can reconsider if it's major or minor in the scheme of things."

"I guess you've had friends for a long time, haven't you?" she asked.

"Like you, I had friends for a long time," he began. "Some of them have been the best of friends, and some of them haven't. Sometimes we part ways for a long time with someone, and then, when we do get back together again, it's like we'd never been apart. And, with others, it seems like we're completely different people now and have absolutely nothing in common."

"Yeah, I wonder if that's what's happening to us," she said.

"Give yourself time to digest all the upheavals in your life right now. Give Angela time. She has a partner now, and I don't know how you've found it to be, but it always seems to me that, when somebody adds a new partner in the mix, the friendships and relationship dynamics all change."

"I think that's sad," she replied. "It's not supposed to be like that. You're supposed to add to your family, not exchange them."

He didn't say anything to that, but, as he walked back into the hallway, he whispered, "Sleep well."

"Did you check downstairs?" she asked anxiously.

"I did. It's fine." He lifted his chin, smiling. "Reach out your right hand."

She immediately did and laughed. "Are they all here?"

"All five of them," he confirmed. "Believe me. Nobody is getting anywhere near you."

"That would be nice," she murmured. "It's such a weird feeling, knowing somebody drugged me."

"I'm right here, and nobody will get through me to get to you," he declared.

"I wouldn't even want to put that on you," she muttered. "That's not fair."

"Doesn't matter if it's fair or not," he noted cheerfully. "I wasn't at all happy that you had to take any crap off that punk before you took him down, and I'm especially pissed that you got drugged right in front of me."

"That's just BS. *I* didn't even know it. The fact is, you're the one who got me to the hospital and who saved me." She shook her head. "If I'd gone straight home—"

"But you didn't," he pointed out, "so let's get you through this first night. Then every other night after that will get easier."

She thought about his words and murmured, "If you say so."

"Look. If you get worried or you get scared, you just give me a call." He pointed down the hall. "I'll be right in your spare room, after all."

She chuckled. "That doesn't mean that you must stay up and babysit me."

"No, I won't. I'll get some sleep too." And, with that, he walked away. He headed to his room and laid down to crash, after leaving the door wide open, so he could hear if she struggled in the night.

Something woke him in the wee hours of the morning. He checked his phone and noted it was two in the morning. He frowned at that, got up, and looked out the window. Something was bothering him, but he had no idea what. As he continued to search outside, he thought he saw a shadow.

He had taken a few minutes to get on his prosthetic, then made his way downstairs. No way he wouldn't check this out. As he got to the first floor, he went straight to the alarm and realized the light was off. Swearing to himself, he quickly sent an alert to Badger, and then checked the front door and then the back door, wishing he had a weapon with him.

He was pretty damn decent without one, but it was a whole different story if the intruder came with a gun himself. And, if it was some corrupt member of local law enforcement, that was a vastly different story, since they had all kinds of weapons available. As he watched, the shadow came up to the back door. Swearing at that, he pulled out his phone and sent her a text. **Intruder downstairs. Stay in your room.**

He didn't know if she saw it or not, but the guy was now picking open the back door, before Landon had a chance to warn Sabrina further. As the masked intruder stepped in silently, Landon waited to see if it was just the one man or if there was a second one. As the guy moved a step deeper into the room, he looked around and slowly closed the door carefully, so it didn't make a sound.

At that point, Landon was on him.

CHAPTER 13

S ABRINA BOLTED AWAKE, with that inner sense that
something was wrong. Almost immediately, her phone
buzzed. She snatched it off the nightstand charger and took a
look at the message from Landon. Her heart froze. She
bolted out of bed, pulled on a sweatshirt, and with the dogs
ahead of her, she crept to the stairs. Hearing the sounds of a
fight going on downstairs, she raced down to try and help.

She knew Landon would have a fit at that, but she
hadn't taken self-defense courses for nothing. She'd already
proved herself capable once. And she also knew that, for all
his strengths, he also had one glaring weakness that others
would exploit. But she'd never mention that to him. As she
stepped into the living room, she turned on the light. Almost
immediately Landon called out, "Call the FBI."

"I already did," she replied.

As Landon gave another hard right to the intruder, who
was already down, the man stopped struggling, lying flat,
now unconscious.

"Wow." She looked at Landon and grinned. "You look
totally badass like that."

He frowned at her, then looking down at his undershirt
and shorts, he asked, "You mean, with a missing foot and
shrapnel scars everywhere?" He shook his head. "I look like a
bionic mess."

"Yeah, like I said, *badass*." She grinned.

He looked over at her, heard the sincerity in her voice, and smiled. "You just like cyborgs."

"Hey, I'm totally okay if you're a cyborg," she agreed. "That'd be pretty cool too." She walked closer, looked down at the masked man on the ground. "You want to take that off?" She pointed. "I really want to know who the hell is tormenting me."

Landon pulled off the mask, and, sure enough, it was Deputy Smith.

"Wow," she said. "He really doesn't want to give up on this, does he?"

"Nope."

Almost immediately knocking came at the back door, and the FBI called out to identify themselves.

Landon turned to her. "Better let them in."

She nodded and raced to the door. As soon as she opened it, the two men stepped in, and she pointed and told them, "In the living room."

They stepped into the living room and took one look at the scenario. One agent whistled, and the other shook his head. "So he's out cold, and look at you." He pointed at Landon's prosthetic in surprise.

"Yeah, look at me. A bit of a mess, not quite as functional as I would like to be," Landon admitted as he cuddled the dogs now crowding around him, "but I'll be damned if a punk like this will break in here and—"

"He did great," Sabrina stated, with pride in her voice. Then she stepped closer to Landon and put an arm around him.

"I can see that," the agent confirmed, still looking at him. "What happened to you?"

Landon shrugged. "The vehicle I was in drove over an IED."

At that, both agents winced. "Jesus. ... Is that one of Kat's?"

"Nope. We're working on a new one with Kat," Landon replied. "This foot and ankle are all right, and I get by, but they are not nearly as good as hers would be."

"They sure as hell did the job here though," the lead agent stated. "You got nothing to be ashamed of over this."

"I wasn't ashamed to begin with," he replied, his voice hard. "But I am beyond pissed that this guy is even free to come and attack her."

"Don't worry. We've already picked up the sheriff, and now we've got this guy. Jared was released earlier this evening. On bail supposedly."

"*Sure*," Landon remarked. "I wonder who was behind that."

"No worries. We got a tail on him. He can't go long without us arresting him for something. However, what we still don't know," the second agent added, "is why the sheriff is heavily involved in this."

"But," the lead agent noted, "we'll get to the bottom of it." At that, another vehicle pulled up, and they looked out and said, "This is one of our guys, and we'll take Deputy Smith off your hands."

"And what if he gets loose again?" Sabrina started to tremble.

At that, Landon wrapped her uptight and said, "It's okay. Believe me. He won't get out on bail."

She looked up at him and shook her head. "But you don't know that, and obviously the whole system in this town is completely corrupt."

"Yeah," Landon agreed, "but you're not staying in town anyway, so whatever."

She looked up at him and started to giggle. "Are you using this as a means to get me to move?"

"Absolutely." Then he looked over at the agents and grinned. "I'm trying to convince her to move closer to me."

"If this doesn't do it"—the agent nodded at the deputy out cold on the floor—"I'm not sure what will. This is just BS."

"I'm glad to hear that," Sabrina said, "because I was starting to wonder what the hell was going on with our world."

"It's garbage, that's what it is," the agent added, "but don't worry. We'll fix it."

She nodded but didn't say anything. And she knew that Landon understood her reticence. By the time the agents and Deputy Smith were all gone from her home, she looked at Landon and sighed. "You know that there's not a chance in hell of getting any sleep now."

"I know," he agreed, yawning, "but we need to try. After the day you've had, plus the way the night is going, you'll need more than tomorrow to catch up. So you might as well let your supervisor know."

"We'll see," she temporized. "Maybe not."

"Might as well turn in your notice at the same time too," he added, with yet another yawn.

She stared at him and shook her head. "Oh, no you don't. You're not springing that on me right now. Besides, I can't leave Grandma."

"We can move her too, and you both can move in with me at that point, with both of us caring for Grandma. With five acres, we can take in all kinds of animals—maybe start a bit of a rescue."

"Yeah, you know what the problem with that is," she admitted, "we'd keep them all forever."

He grinned at her. "Perfect. You could always get a nursing job anywhere in the States and in whatever specialty you wanted to work in," he explained. "However, if that's not what you want to do anymore, maybe it's time for a complete break. Change careers. Your choice."

"The idea of moving is appealing," she admitted, "but I'm sure as hell not making a decision like that lightly, especially not tonight, with these drugs still clouding my system."

"No, of course not," he agreed, "and you'd have things to sort out that take time, like dealing with the house and all."

She nodded, and then he yawned again, and she could see the fatigue on his face. "Look at us. What a pair we are right now," she said. "Come on. Let's get you to bed too."

"I'm coming, but, man, I forgot how intense physical exertion at this level, with all that adrenaline, can wipe you out afterward."

"What? How very ridiculous that you forgot something?" she teased, gasping in mock horror.

He just rolled his eyes at her. "Now you're just making fun of me."

"Of course I am. There was absolutely nothing lacking about your performance tonight. Believe me. Nobody could possibly be upset at how well you handled this."

"Maybe so, but I might have to work on some of those self-defense moves."

"Oh, that's not a problem," she said, perking up, grinning. "I can help you with that."

He burst out laughing. "See? That's another thing that we can both do together."

"What's that?" she asked.

"Train together."

She chuckled, as they made their way up the stairs. All five of the dogs immediately raced toward her bedroom. "I kind of feel bad because they're trying to finagle their way into my bed."

"What do you mean, *trying?*" he asked, with a laugh. "They already did."

"No, I know," she said, "but maybe you need them tonight."

"No, I just need sleep."

And then she noticed he was limping. "Do you need help with that?"

He shook his head, his voice a little stiff. "No, I'm fine."

She stopped, stared, and asked, "Seriously?"

"What?"

"I can't believe you'll get all prideful right now. Especially after helping me after I got hurt, and now that you're not feeling so well, you'll try and be difficult?"

He stopped and stared. "Was that being difficult? … I'm not used to people seeing me without my prosthetic."

"No time like the present," she declared immediately. "Come on. Let's get you into bed." Then she stopped. "You know something? Screw it. Let's just all pile in together, so we can get some sleep." And she directed him to her bedroom.

"You're inviting me to sleep in your bed?" he asked. "I get that I have a prosthetic, but I am still very much a man."

She chuckled. "I'm really glad to hear that." She smirked. "Like *super* glad to hear it because that cyborg demonstration was pretty damn awesome." And, with that, she pushed him to her bed, helped him unbuckle the ankle strap, the gel sock snapping out with a push of a button.

She took a quick look at it. "This doesn't seem too badly inflamed."

"It's gotten better," he noted, "after multiple surgeries."

She nodded. "Good. Now off to bed."

"Do you mind if I take off my shirt at least?"

"That's fine," she said. She pulled off her sweatshirt that she had thrown over her pajama shorts and tank top, before investigating the fight downstairs. She sighed. "I need to crash for like twelve hours."

"You might get a couple," he suggested, "though you may want to turn off your phone too."

"Oh, good idea." She quickly turned off her phone, turned out her night light, and curled up in bed. "Good night." She listened as he settled on the bed beside her and heard a whispered, "Good night." With a soft chuckle, she closed her eyes and slept.

Sabrina woke up the next time because a furnace was wrapped around her. She realized that, at some point in the night, they'd come together spoon style, and his arm was wrapped around her, just across her ribs. She was tucked up against him, thinking nothing felt as right or as natural.

He murmured, "You're thinking too loud."

"I just woke up," she protested softly. "I'm hardly thinking at all."

"You should start then," he added, "especially about New Mexico."

At that, she chuckled. "You won't make it easy on me, will you?"

"No. Come on. You know you want to."

"I might want to, but that doesn't mean it's the best answer right now."

"But it's not a bad answer either," he argued gently. Then he kissed the back of her neck. "Personally, I think it's a great answer."

She smiled. "I don't even want to see what time it is."

"It's about eight o'clock," he said.

"That's not terrible," she murmured, "at least yesterday's over, and our day gets to just be our day."

"That's the plan, except I need to go back and deal with Chica."

"Do you think you might get her this time?"

"I was pretty close last time," he noted. "So I'm really hoping this will be it."

"And then what?"

"The vet would be the next stop," he said, "for a full checkup and possibly some IV fluids. More if she's got embedded pellets, infection, or even a broken bone. I just don't know."

"I'll come with you then," she offered.

"I don't have a problem with that," he replied. "In fact, the way things have been going, it's a damn good idea. You'll need to be really quiet though out there. Chica's definitely jumpy and has a way to go yet."

"I understand," she murmured. "The whole thing still breaks my heart though."

"I know, and that's another reason to go get her before anybody else gets involved in this."

"That would be nice," she agreed. As she lay here, she added, "I really should get up."

"The more you say it, that just means you don't want to leave the bed."

"Oh, I don't want to at all," she agreed. "This is way too comfy."

"Did you have something better to do?" he asked.

"If I stay here, I'll think of something better to do." There was silence, and then she chuckled. "Remember that whole cyborg thing? I'm not kidding. That was really awesome."

He nudged his forehead gently against hers. "Care to be a little more specific?"

She shifted so that she was looking up at him and smiled. "I don't know. I just found it to be damn sexy." He stared at her in surprise, and she laughed out loud. "Did you honestly think that I would see you as some kind of a freak?"

"I am a bit of a freak to many people," he noted.

"Not to me," she said. "That was beautiful. And I would not be at all averse to taking a closer look."

"What? Like I'm a patient kind of thing?"

"Oh no, I don't think so." She smirked, pulling his head down so his lips were just a whisper away from hers. "And definitely not an experiment. But maybe," she added, "something very special."

His lips gently brushed across the top of hers. "I like the idea of *special*," he murmured.

"Yeah, me too. ... It seems like a very long time since I had something special in my life."

"You and me both," he muttered, as he gently kissed one corner of her mouth, then the other, followed by her cheekbone, then the other.

She moaned gently. "You know something? This is beyond nice."

"It would be nicer in New Mexico."

She burst out laughing, then threw her arms around his

neck and said, "I'll consider it."

"Good. ... I don't want to push you."

"Like hell you don't," she countered, with a snicker. "You can't wait to get out of this town and to get me away from here too."

"Guilty as charged." He lifted his head, so he could look at her little easier. "Is that wrong?"

"No, not wrong, but I still want to take some time to think about it."

"Good, as you should." Then he lowered his head and whispered, "You have at least five minutes." Then he kissed her, and her toes curled.

"Wow," she mumbled, when he lifted his head. "I know it's been a while for me, but holy crap."

"Me too," he muttered.

As he shifted, she felt his erection pressing against her and said, "I think we still have too many clothes on."

"We do," he confirmed, "but I'll take a little bit of time to take yours off." With a waggle of his eyebrows, he slowly lowered his head, so he could kiss her chin and her neck and on down to her collarbone. All the while his hand was doing things that made her dizzy with delight. As she moaned beneath him, her tank top came up over her head, and he took one of her nipples in his mouth and suckled it deeply.

She shuddered with joy and whispered, "You can't keep that up."

"Oh, I think I can." He laughed against her belly.

"No," she murmured, "because I want access too."

"Next time. It's been a little too long for me to let you have too much access."

"Hey, it's been a little too long for me too," she noted.

"In that case ..." he murmured, as he lifted his head and

worked his way slowly back up to her lips, "we'll need to spend a lot of time over the next couple days in bed."

"Isn't that what the doctor told me to do?" she asked, raising her eyebrows.

"Perfect. For the first time we'll strictly follow doctor's orders." And laughter filled his voice.

When he shifted up to kiss her gently, she wouldn't have anything to do with gentle. "No need to be gentle," she murmured. "I want to feel every ounce of passion you have inside you." He shuddered, and she whispered, "Don't you *ever* feel bad about who you are and what you look like now."

He smiled, his lips curling against her mouth, and he whispered. "I wasn't planning on it. Believe me. I can still make you happy."

"I *am* happy," she replied. "What I really want now is a little bit of satisfaction."

And, with that, he lowered his head and kissed her until she couldn't see straight. He whispered, "You mean like that?" Then he did it again and again, until she came apart underneath him.

She shuddered and cried out, "God, I don't know what you did to me, but I just had an orgasm. Wow, that was amazing."

"Get used to it. We'll do that time and time again." He chuckled gently, as he kissed her a few more times and then finally shifted his body atop hers.

"Not a problem," she whispered, as she opened her thighs and made room for him. "Besides, we've got all day."

"Except for Chica."

And, with that, he slid deep inside Sabrina, and she shuddered, coming apart in his arms again. He followed her soon afterward, and she felt the moment as he climaxed too.

When he finally relaxed beside her, she held him close and whispered, "I wish Chica was here with us now, so we didn't have to move."

He raised up on his elbow, looking down at her. "Why don't we just go get her, then come back?"

"And how will you do that?"

"Hopefully today she's ready. It's been getting better, day after day. But this time, she might be ready."

Landon put on his prosthetic, they got dressed, not bothering to shower as they pulled on the same clothes they had worn earlier. Landon noted, "I'll have to go back to the hotel and grab my clothes at some point. I could really use a shower, but maybe this way Chica will recognize me faster."

"Yeah, and even me now too," she added.

He laughed. "It's not a bad way to help her get used to both of us. The combined smell will be something she'll have to figure out."

"That doesn't sound good." Sabrina frowned, wrinkling up her nose. "Can't say I like the idea of me *smelling* at all."

He just smiled as they went downstairs. "Will we really not eat something here first?" she asked.

"We can pick up something on the way back. Unless you didn't want to go."

"No," she replied immediately. "I'm not planning on being alone here for quite a while yet," she declared. "Besides, it's all about Chica right now."

"It is." Landon checked to make sure he had enough dog food and treats. Then he loaded his dogs and helped Sabrina and her dogs into the truck and said, "The dogs are handling this pretty well right now."

"Yeah, though it's hard to say how it would be in their

own surroundings," she noted, "but they seem to be handling it fine so far. Patches and Snowball are easy going and have taken to yours just fine. Although, once you have Chica, it could be a bigger issue."

He shrugged. "I won't worry about it right now." He drove back out to the park and quietly led her to the place where he always sat. He put dog food down a little bit closer yet again. "I don't know how she'll handle you being here," he mentioned.

"Probably just fine. Maybe she'll take her lead from these three." And, sure enough, Larry, Curly, and Moe were all quite happy to be back at their favorite spot. Sabrina watched and just relaxed, as Landon sat here with the coffee they'd picked up on the way.

"At least we got coffee," he murmured.

"We did, and, on the way back, we can always pick up something to eat, although we probably should have grabbed something as it is."

"We're good," he said. He watched the tree line and then whispered, "She's coming."

At that, Sabrina turned casually to take a look and saw a sight that made her heart break. "Oh my God. She's so thin."

"Yep, and injured and all alone," he added.

"Yeah, I know how that feels."

He reached down, squeezed her hand, and said, "You and me both."

She looked up at him and smiled. "Is this thing between us real?"

"It is as far as I'm concerned," he replied calmly. "But, if you need a little bit longer, you can have another five minutes."

She chuckled. "I suspect you'll give me as long as I need."

"I will because I don't want to lose you."

There was something rough in his voice as he admitted that. She squeezed his hand.

Just then Chica limped a little bit forward.

"She needs to go to the vet," Sabrina muttered.

"I know," he agreed, "but first we must get close enough to put her on a leash."

Sabrina's heart broke, as she watched Chica move, obviously in pain, traumatized, and suffering. "I wonder how much longer she would have lasted."

"Hopefully that's not a question we ever have to ask," Landon said. "I really just want to take her home now." As it was, the dog came forward another step and didn't seem to be too bothered at all that Sabrina was here. He could see not so much acceptance but maybe a sense of surrender in Chica. He told Sabrina, "Stay here."

He got up with the leash in a big loop over his arm, then took two steps forward, crouched down in front of Chica, and asked, "Are you ready to give it up, girl? You really don't need to be worried. I'll be the best thing ever for you. I promise you that."

Her tail wagged slightly, and, while he still saw the fear in her eyes, he also saw something else—acceptance. She was done. She couldn't fight this anymore, and, whatever happened now, she desperately hoped she was making the right decision.

Landon felt a burning in the back of his own eyes, tears for this valiant animal who had been through so much and who was struggling so hard to survive. As he remained crouched in front of her, he reached out a hand, the loop still tucked over his arm, and gently placed it on her head and stroked behind her ears.

Her head lowered, and she just sat here for a moment.

He managed to get the loop down over her neck and tighten it ever-so-slightly. And, with that, he stood slowly and took a step forward, then bent to put his arms under her and picked her up. He looked at Sabrina. "Can you grab them?" he asked, with a nod toward the other dogs.

She already had their leashes in hand, as she looked at the beautiful War Dog. "Oh my God, I'm already bawling my eyes out."

"That's why we're taking her straight to a vet. Now the question is, do you want to go to your vet or another one?"

"We can go there," she said. "Dave is good."

"Good enough." Landon nodded.

"Do you want me to drive?" she asked.

He looked at her and then nodded. "That's not a bad idea. Are you okay to drive the truck?"

"Yep. I've never driven something quite like this before, but I do feel less fuzzy. So, right now, I'm all about doing whatever I can to help. Plus Chica clearly feels safe with you, so let's not rock the boat." And, with that, they headed out, and soon their motley crew arrived outside the vet clinic.

"If you can hang on here for a few minutes, I can go get a gurney, and we'll take her inside."

He shook his head. "I'll just carry her. It's probably easier."

"They should be ready for us, since we called on the way," she noted, and, with that, she hopped out.

She opened up his door and saw that Chica's head was tucked against his arm. "Will she make it?" she asked, with pain in her voice.

"I hope so," he replied. "But she did just give up. It's like she's gone all in with me and is just hoping she made the right decision."

"I just want to kill whoever did this to her," Sabrina said. "She is far too sweet and beautiful to have anybody treat her so badly."

"Part of it could just be her circumstances," he noted. And, with an unspoken signal to the other dogs, he headed toward the back door of the vet clinic, already open for them.

The vet stepped outside, took one look, and whistled. "That's her, *huh?*"

Landon nodded. "Yeah. We need to check her over and see what's up. She's in a lot of pain though."

"I can see that. Let's get her in here." Then he led the way to one of the rear surgery rooms. He took a quick look and said, "That leg doesn't look very good."

Landon nodded. "I'm afraid there's BB pellets of some kind in her because she's in way too much pain for it to be her old injuries."

Dave nodded, as Landon laid Chica down gently. "Let me get something into her for pain right now," Dave said. "Better yet, I'll start an IV and put her out, so we can do a full and thorough exam."

And while Landon still held her more or less in his arms, half on and half off the table, they quickly administered the drugs, and then he released her and took a step back. "I'd like to stay, if I could."

"I understand, but it will just slow us down," Dave said. "We'll get right back to you, as soon as we know a little more."

And, with that, Landon nodded and stepped through to

the waiting room. There he found Sabrina, talking with another woman. Sabrina walked over to him, as soon as she saw him. "How is she?"

"Dave's got her sleeping, so he can do a thorough exam and some tests to see what kind of shape she's in."

"We'll take good care of her," the other woman said, as she disappeared into the back.

"Was that your friend?"

She nodded. "That's Angela."

"And?"

"She apologized again, and I think she was sincere enough"—Sabrina shrugged—"but it just feels different."

"Different doesn't have to mean bad, so give it some time. Give yourself some time."

She nodded. "I guess." And then she smiled up at him and reached out her hand. "But, hey, we've got Chica. Good job!"

"And that's huge," he agreed, wrapping an arm around her and pulling her close enough to drop a kiss on the top of her head.

"Now my questions are, how bad is she, and what does she need for care? Then there's the money aspect," she added, looking at him.

"It's covered," he replied, with a negligent shrug.

"And, if it wasn't, you would cover it, wouldn't you?"

"Absolutely I would." He smiled at her. "No way I would leave a dog after what she has been through." And, with that, they sat quietly in the waiting room, until the vet finally came out and sat down beside them.

"You're right on a couple counts. She's injured. She's hurting. She's dehydrated, and she's obviously been starving for a very long time. She does have three pellets in her hide.

One is infected. Another one has gotten into a joint. I'll have to go in and get it out. She also has a newly broken leg," he added. "So, everything is doable. It's her overall condition that is worrisome. Hopefully she'll be strong enough to make it through the surgery. I don't dare wait to get her in better overall shape because of the infection. If you'll excuse me, I need to go check on her, as we've got antibiotics streaming into her right now, and I'm prepping her for surgery." Dave looked over at Landon. "I hate to bring this up, but there's that delicate issue of budget."

"You do what you need to do, Doc," Landon stated.

Dave looked over at Sabrina, with a smile. "So I gather you are the reason he brought her here?"

"Absolutely. Landon's been looking for Chica for several days now. Please, just do everything you can to keep her alive."

"I'll do my best," Dave said. "Then you'll need to convince Chica that better days are coming and that it's worth fighting for."

They sat here in the waiting room for another three hours, with just a break to walk the three Chihuahuas. Finally the vet came back in again, looking tired but smiling. "She did fine. The pellets are out. The leg is as good as it can be. She was really dehydrated. She'll need a couple days before we really see how it'll go. I'd like to keep her sedated for the rest of the day. Then, in the morning, we'll wake her up and see if we can get her back up on her feet."

"So when can we see her?" Landon asked.

"Maybe in the morning. We'll see." Dave asked Landon, "Are you keeping her?"

"Yes, I am."

"Good." Dave nodded. "There must be a bit of a bond

between you, or you would have never gotten her this far, and I'd hate to see that get broken."

"Me too," Landon agreed, with a smile.

And, with that, Sabrina and Landon headed out, made a stop at the motel for his things, made a quick run into the grocery store, and even picked up her car. Then they spent the rest of the day together. She called in sick for the next day, really needing a little bit longer to recover from everything that had happened, and, by the time the next morning dawned, she was feeling a whole lot better herself.

When they got to the vet clinic, Sabrina saw Angela, gave her friend a tentative smile, and asked, "How's Chica doing?"

"She had a quiet night," Angela said, smiling back. "She looks to be doing very well."

"Good. We'd like to see her."

"Yep, not a problem," Angela replied. And, with that, they were led into the back, where they found Chica in a cage, awake, but struggling to lift her head.

Landon crouched in front of the cage, opened it up, and reached out a hand to gently stroke her. "It's okay, sweetheart. We'll get you fixed up," he murmured. Her tail wagged, and he just smiled. "You work on getting healthy. That's all we ask. Just fight for your life a little bit."

And, with that, Sabrina crouched down beside him. "She's so beautiful."

"No, she's not," he disagreed, with a laugh. "She's ugly, thin, and much too smelly right now, but, hey, she'll clean up nicely."

She laughed at him. "Yeah, well, that's the last time you get to say she's ugly." She glared at him, but it soon turned into a smile.

He grinned back and nodded. "She will be beautiful again, but she'll also need to build up a little more faith in humanity."

"That will take time," Sabrina noted, "but she'll get there. She's got you, and she's got me, so that's a pretty top-notch team, right?"

He looked over at her. "So is that an answer to my question?"

"What question?" she asked. Then she remembered and smiled. "It's a yes, if we're talking about moving."

He nudged her chin toward him and whispered, "Thank God for that. I was prepared to give you another five minutes, but that was it." Then he kissed her.

ONE WEEK LATER he pulled up in front of his house, then looked over at her and smiled. "It was pretty nice that you had vacation time coming."

"Nice for me but not for the hospital."

"It sounded like they had people coming back from vacation anyway," he noted, "so it worked out well."

"Maybe. I do have to go back though."

"Unless they find somebody to replace you."

"Yeah, that was the agreement, but I'm not holding out hope. Also, with Grandma fading away faster, it seems, I'll need to make a trip back soon anyway." She swallowed down her grief and took a look at the huge old farmhouse. "Wow, Landon. This is beautiful."

"Not only beautiful, … it's mine," he reminded her. "Joe left me one hell of a gift."

"But then you gave him one hell of a gift too," she noted. "Nobody should die alone."

"Oh, I agree with you there, and that was part of my philosophy at the time, but it was about more than just not dying alone. I didn't think he should spend his last few years alone either."

He hopped out of the truck, opened up the gate, then unclipped the Chihuahuas, who raced around, delighted to be home again. Grabbing up the bags in the back— including the one she'd brought along for the short visit she'd arranged, before she finished her commitment at the hospital—he got the rest of her stuff moved. "Welcome home."

"I'm glad to be here," she said, as she looked around with interest both Patches and Snowball clipped onto leashes for the moment. "It looks like a beautiful place to stay," she added, then turned to look around, but he was already helping Chica slowly get down out of the truck. He placed her inside the gated area so she could wander and hobble on her own.

"She's doing so much better," Sabrina noted, with quiet joy. Indeed all the dogs seemed to understand Chica's health issues and were giving her space but staying in the vicinity. She unclipped her dogs as Landon watched them all interact.

"So far so good." She said with a bright relieved smile.

"I know. Good to see." Then he grabbed the last of the bags and carried them up to the house. He dropped them inside the living room and then stepped outside to join Sabrina, placing an arm around her shoulders. "Just look at her." They watched as Chica went to the bathroom, then walked over and sniffed a patch of grass. "The antibiotics really have kicked in."

"Yeah, she needs fattening up now," Sabrina added,

"then some conditioning to get her muscle mass built back—when she's able. I can't wait."

He chuckled at that. "She needs love. She needs care, and she needs a bit of time."

"Yeah." Sabrina smirked. "And, knowing you, you'll give her at least five minutes."

And that, he burst out laughing, wrapped Sabrina up in his arms, and replied, "She can have a little more, if she needs it. I'm never giving up on her."

Sabrina threw her arms around him and asked, "What about me?"

"I'm never giving up on us," he murmured. "This is just too perfect."

She smiled. "Absolutely," she agreed, with tears in her eyes. "I'm so grateful that you came into my life."

He placed a finger against her lips. "We can thank Chica for that." Then he lowered his head and kissed her. Turning, he looked out at the dog. "Thank you, Chica. We'll repay the favor by looking after you, and making you happy for the rest of your life too."

EPILOGUE

K AT LOOKED OVER at Badger. "That worked out better than I thought."

"You're not kidding." Badger stared at the door, where Landon and Sabrina and the four dogs had just exited. "With the FBI's tip line and the cadaver dogs going over that area, they fully expect to find a killing field of rape victims, including the body of Jared's mom. They'll update us as their investigations continue. I'm particularly interested in the DNA results of the child born to one woman, so far, who became unexpectedly pregnant. I'm hoping that'll be a nail in the coffin for Smith, his ass-wipe son, and the sheriff."

Kat shook her head. "That trio was date-raping their way through their community, which is a complete misnomer, as that was no *date* when your sexual partner is drugged into unconsciousness and submission. And by two officers of the law? It's horrid."

"Yeah, but"—Badger chuckled—"justice came for them all. That punk kid was beaten up pretty badly in jail, enough that he may stay in the infirmary for about a week. The deputy has already been outed as law enforcement and a rapist, so he's been targeted too by the inmates. And the sheriff? He's in solitary, but he can't hide there forever."

"That's more good news to come out of that nasty business," Kat replied.

"I really like Sabrina," Badger said.

"Me too," Kat agreed, with a bright smile. "I'm so glad we're making more friends as we do this."

He chuckled. "Most of them don't live close to us though."

"No, but I think it's great that this couple is settling here. Besides, it'll take several fittings to work on Landon's foot," she noted, her mind already on the problem of Landon's prosthetics. "He's a special case."

"Sure." Badger chuckled. "I'm pretty sure you say that about every one of them."

She gave her husband a sheepish smile. "Maybe, but everyone deserves to have prosthetics designed to work the way they need them to. Sometimes the smaller prosthetics are trickier than the larger ones. Regardless it's important for him to have a working ankle without pain."

"Agreed. Now that brings us to the next problem."

"What's that?" she asked, pulling her attention back to him.

"The next dog," he noted.

"You know, if we had ten guys ready and available, we could do ten at one time?" she mentioned. "But instead we wait for one to get solved and then go on to the next."

"And part of that," he noted, "is the reality of the funding."

She nodded. "I know. And really, in some of these cases, it seems like we're waiting forever to get intel on where to even look for the dogs."

"If we get any intel at all," Badger added.

At that, the phone rang. She looked down, then smiled. "Hey, Harper. How are you doing?"

"I'm good. I wanted to thank you for the job you did on

my brother."

"What job?" she asked in a joking manner. "The prosthetic is still to come."

"I know, but he's a different man. He went out lost and looking for something, but he came back found—and in a way which I hadn't expected."

"Neither did we," she agreed. "Badger is here on Speakerphone."

"That's the other thing," Harper added. "I just kind of wondered ... God, it's really arrogant of me to even ask."

"Ask away," she prompted him. "You never know what's too much until you ask."

"Well, my surgery has been postponed for six months," he shared, "and believe me. I'm not thrilled about it, and I'm frustrated as hell. But it has kind of left me with, you know, nothing to do."

"Meaning?" She frowned, as she looked over at Badger, who just shrugged.

"I just wondered if you needed somebody to go after another dog."

"Ah." She gave her husband a beaming smile. "We still have a couple cases that we need to handle. But I don't want to stress your body. You know as well as I do how important all that rest is for getting your body shipshape, both pre-op and post-op."

"I understand. I just don't know whether the cases are particularly stressful or not. This last one didn't seem to be."

"It certainly had some stressful moments, but it was a different kind of case," she noted. "Some have been pretty ugly though, so if what we had turned into an ugly one, I wouldn't feel very good sending you out there."

"Yet you know yourself that there's no way to know beforehand, not until we get there."

"Isn't that the truth." She gave a heavy sigh. She looked over at Badger and asked him, "What do you think?"

"We had asked him before, but he was due to have surgery," he noted, looking at Kat. "So is there any reason to discount him now?"

"I hope not," Harper spoke up. "It kind of sucks when you think about it because we already tend to do enough discounting of our own."

"Yes," Kat agreed. "I get that." She looked over at Badger. "I don't know anything about this case though."

He rustled a bunch of pages. "This one?" He glanced at the paperwork. "No, it looks like maybe it's pretty tame."

"Tame is good," Harper replied cautiously. "But I don't want you to give me something so tame because you think I can't handle it."

"I would never do that," Badger stated. "Plus we sometimes have very little, if any, knowledge going into these, so there's no foolproof way to predict what we'll find. So, even something that might look like it's pretty mellow could end up butt ugly, and we'll have no way to warn you ahead of time."

At that, Harper laughed out loud. "Butt ugly," he repeated. "That sounds kind of like me right now."

Kat asked, "Are you up for this? How are the wounds, the scars?"

"The scarring is there," Harper admitted. "But, if I'm dealing with animals, I won't have to deal with people."

"People are always an integral part of these jobs," Badger noted, frowning.

"Yeah," Harper agreed, "but at least I'll have a purpose that has nothing to do with people."

"You can't avoid them though," Kat emphasized. "You do know that, right?"

"Part of the surgery I was hoping to get done already is to make sure this face of mine isn't quite so ugly."

"It's beautiful as it is," she stated instantly.

He burst out laughing. "Liar. This is a face only a mother could love—or possibly a good friend. Listen. I appreciate the vote of confidence, but you and I both know that this scar on my face is pretty rough. Not to mention the rest of me—missing a hand and foot."

"It's all still healing, and of course the injuries to your face can't be hidden so easily. Those look angrier and redder than normal, yes," she agreed, "and the prosthetics will be adjusted as needed, but that doesn't mean it's bad news all the way."

"No, it doesn't have to be, and I'm really hoping that, over time, maybe I'll find somebody who's not quite so adverse to my particular brand of beauty," he admitted, with a note of humor. "But you and I both know it'll take that surgery to make me look anywhere near presentable."

"You look very dashing," Kat said. "Very much an *ancient warrior* vibe."

"Yeah, well, most people don't like ancient warriors," he noted, with a laugh. "But my brother did get through his job pretty well, and he came out with a whole lot more than I expected. Honest to God, I'm a little jealous of Landon. If I'd known that getting the girl would be part of this, I'd have tried to reschedule the surgery myself," he joked.

"I've got to tell you," Kat added, "that has happened more times than not."

"What's happened?"

"That the guys going out after these War Dogs have also

found somebody for themselves."

"Seriously?"

"Yeah, but there's absolutely no guarantee for that, and we have no hand in that. It just seems to work out that way."

"That's even better," Harper declared. "Sign me up. Give me a chance to go out and see if there's a girl out there who can handle my face."

"Hello, it's not about the girl."

"It's not about the girl," he immediately repeated. "But, hey, it's about the girl."

She smiled. "As long as you realize there is no guarantee."

"No, not at all. What do we know about the dog?"

"It's a female," Badger piped up, "an older one …" Then he stopped and frowned. "I think this case is about two dogs, one male and one female."

"Two dogs?" Harper repeated.

"Did you have K9 experience?"

"Yeah, plenty. The War Dogs don't usually get adopted out at the same time, do they?"

"No, but these two were both injured at the same time, and apparently their recovery was fairly interdependent on each other, so they were adopted at the same time."

"Wow, so where did they go?"

"They were eventually shipped to a training center out of Louisiana," Badger read from the file. "I think it was because of that specific facility's successes that the two War Dogs were heading there. Unfortunately, at the first center in Mississippi, the male was not quite healed, and it looks like maybe there were some issues in terms of getting him the specialized vet care he needed. He wasn't responding all that well in that first facility, and there was talk of separating them. Now, whether the dogs knew what was going on or not, I don't know. We often put human qualities onto dogs, however I'm not sure that was the case in this instance."

"Okay, keep talking. So what happened?"

"The sick male dog was sent to Louisiana for more specialized care, and, once that happened, the female supposedly took off."

"Ah, crap," Harper said. "Yeah, if they're bonded, and one has any idea where the other one has gone, then I can see a dog trying to follow."

"And the male separated for treatment in Louisiana isn't doing well at all. Recovery is going badly, and there is even talk of putting him down."

"Oh, hell no. Come on. Don't give me a job guaranteed to break my heart."

"There is always the chance that you could end up with two dogs out of the deal."

"Hey, I'm not sure if I have the time or the energy for even one. Is keeping the dog part of the deal? I thought it was a retrieval," he asked in confusion.

"It is a retrieval," Badger said instantly. "If you find a scenario where either dog has made a good life with somebody, and it's going well, we've left them in place. Or if both dogs come back with you, and it's not a good fit for whatever reason, we find them a home. It's all about what's happening when you find the dogs."

"Right, so if the scenario is good, the dogs can stay, or, if there's an alternative scenario that comes up, we can look at that as well."

"Exactly, but, when in doubt, you contact us, and you stay close."

"At least I can get my fill of crawfish." Harper chuckled.

"Yeah, you can at that. And we do cover expenses, but, of course, there's no payment for this job otherwise."

"No, I got that the first time around, and I'll take it. It will give me something productive to do, while I'm waiting for my surgery. Besides, my brother said it was a great experience."

"I'm glad to hear that," Kat replied, "but I think Landon's point of view may be greatly influenced by the fact that he got the girl."

"Yeah, he got the girl," Harper repeated, with an exaggerated sigh. "I want to get the girl."

"Make an effort and go get the girl then," Kat said, chuckling.

"The effort is not the problem," he noted. "The fact that I chase away all the girls? … Now that's the problem."

"Make note that the female War Dog went missing from Mississippi, and the male War Dog went to the specialized Louisiana facility, so you may need to bounce between the two of them," Badger warned.

"That's fine," Harper said. "Haven't been out of state in a long time, but I'm totally okay to travel."

"As long as you're sure you're healthy enough," Kat reminded him.

"I was healthy before," he stated, "as you well know. And I promise I'll get down there and back and see what the problem is."

"We already know what the problem is," Badger said. "The question is, can you go find us a solution?"

"Right." Harper chuckled. "Send me the file. I'll do my best." And, with that, he hung up.

Kat looked over at Badger. "What do you think?"

"You tell me. What's his mental health like?"

"He didn't sound too good about the idea of losing the male dog."

"Neither would anyone else. We haven't had to deal with that so far, but we must expect that it could happen, especially in this case," he muttered. "I don't want to be responsible for this guy taking a mental tumble, should he end up in a tough spot with either dog."

"Got it." Kat nodded. "And you're right. I don't either." She frowned as she thought about it, then added, "I think he'll be okay. Let's give him the best chance that he's got. And, hey, maybe if he's lucky, he'll get the girl," she said, with a bright smile.

Badger looked at her, frowning.

She shook her head. "I know there are no guarantees in life, but we've had so many miracles happen. So why can't we ask for still one more?"

"Because maybe we're being greedy."

"And maybe there's no limit," she suggested gently. "And this guy needs it. You may not remember what his face looks like, but I do."

"I remember," Badger stated instantly, "and it always pissed me off that anybody could see a wound like that and laugh or mock him."

"Harper has been through a lot of that," she murmured, "so will he find somebody? I don't know. I'll tell you what though. If he does find someone, while looking like he does right now, that person is gold. When he does get that surgery, he'll look a hell of a lot better, but it'll take some time to heal."

Badger nodded. "All surgeries are a bitch, but, if we can get through it, we often end up much better on the other side."

"Often, yes," Kat agreed, "but there are no guarantees."

"Nope, same as with our War Dogs." He closed the top file and patted it, long after the telephone conversation with Harper had ended. "But you're right, we have done really well. So let's keep hoping that our streak of luck continues."

She grinned. "As far as I'm concerned it already has. Now we must give them time to make it work."

This concludes Book 18 of The K9 Files: Landon.

Read about Harper: The K9 Files, Book 19

THE K9 FILES: HARPER (BOOK #19)

Welcome to the all new K9 Files series reconnecting readers with the unforgettable men from SEALs of Steel in a new series of action packed, page turning romantic suspense that fans have come to expect from USA TODAY Bestselling author Dale Mayer. Pssst... you'll meet other favorite characters from SEALs of Honor and Heroes for Hire too!

With his surgery postponed, Harper can finally take on a War Dog case to help out Kat and Badger. Harper knows it is short-term, a fill-his-time thing. Considering his stage of life, that is perfect. Finding out he needs to find two dogs is a surprise, but he doesn't expect to track one dog in order to keep another alive.

As Saffron works to keep Beast alive, she knows how important it is to find Beauty, his bonded partner. The pair of War Dogs had come to Saffron for medical treatment. Beauty had thereafter been released, supposedly taken to a huge training facility in Mississippi, while Beast hadn't been healthy enough to leave Saffron's care. With Beauty missing, finding Harper on Beauty's trail is both a relief and a distraction. Saffron can't ignore the dynamic Harper, even as injured and as scarred as he is. Not to mention the work he's doing is so close to her own.

As Harper gets closer to Beauty's location, it becomes obvious that someone wants to make sure the War Dog doesn't reach her destination. But why? And how far will this person go to take down the dog?

Find Book 19 here!

To find out more visit Dale Mayer's website.

https://geni.us/DMHarperUniversal

Author's Note

Thank you for reading Landon: The K9 Files, Book 18! If you enjoyed the book, please take a moment and leave a short review.

Dear reader,

I love to hear from readers, and you can contact me at my website: www.dalemayer.com or at my Facebook author page. To be informed of new releases and special offers, sign up for my newsletter or follow me on BookBub. And if you are interested in joining Dale Mayer's Reader Group, here is the Facebook sign up page.
http://geni.us/DaleMayerFBGroup

Cheers,
Dale Mayer

Get THREE Free Books Now!

Have you met the SEALS of Honor?

SEALs of Honor Books 1, 2, and 3. Follow the stories of brave, badass warriors who serve their country with honor and love their women to the limits of life and death.

Read Mason, Hawk, and Dane right now for FREE.

Go here and tell me where to send them!
https://dalemayer.com/masonfree/

About the Author

Dale Mayer is a *USA Today* best-selling author, best known for her SEALs military romances, her Psychic Visions series, and her Lovely Lethal Garden cozy series. Her contemporary romances are raw and full of passion and emotion (Broken But … Mending, Hathaway House series). Her thrillers will keep you guessing (Kate Morgan, By Death series), and her romantic comedies will keep you giggling (*It's a Dog's Life*, a stand-alone novella; and the Broken Protocols series, starring Charming Marvin, the cat).

Dale honors the stories that come to her—and some of them are crazy, break all the rules and cross multiple genres!

To go with her fiction, she also writes nonfiction in many different fields, with books available on résumé writing, companion gardening, and the US mortgage system. All her books are available in print and ebook format.

Connect with Dale Mayer Online

Dale's Website – www.dalemayer.com

Twitter – @DaleMayer

Facebook Page – geni.us/DaleMayerFBFanPage

Facebook Group – geni.us/DaleMayerFBGroup

BookBub – geni.us/DaleMayerBookbub

Instagram – geni.us/DaleMayerInstagram

Goodreads – geni.us/DaleMayerGoodreads

Newsletter – geni.us/DaleNews

Also by Dale Mayer

Published Adult Books:

Shadow Recon
Magnus, Book 1

Bullard's Battle
Ryland's Reach, Book 1
Cain's Cross, Book 2
Eton's Escape, Book 3
Garret's Gambit, Book 4
Kano's Keep, Book 5
Fallon's Flaw, Book 6
Quinn's Quest, Book 7
Bullard's Beauty, Book 8
Bullard's Best, Book 9
Bullard's Battle, Books 1–2
Bullard's Battle, Books 3–4
Bullard's Battle, Books 5–6
Bullard's Battle, Books 7–8

Terkel's Team
Damon's Deal, Book 1
Wade's War, Book 2
Gage's Goal, Book 3
Calum's Contact, Book 4
Rick's Road, Book 5

Scott's Summit, Book 6
Brody's Beast, Book 7
Terkel's Twist, Book 8
Terkel's Triumph, Book 9

Kate Morgan
Simon Says... Hide, Book 1
Simon Says... Jump, Book 2
Simon Says... Ride, Book 3
Simon Says... Scream, Book 4
Simon Says... Run, Book 5
Simon Says... Walk, Book 6

Hathaway House
Aaron, Book 1
Brock, Book 2
Cole, Book 3
Denton, Book 4
Elliot, Book 5
Finn, Book 6
Gregory, Book 7
Heath, Book 8
Iain, Book 9
Jaden, Book 10
Keith, Book 11
Lance, Book 12
Melissa, Book 13
Nash, Book 14
Owen, Book 15
Percy, Book 16
Quinton, Book 17
Ryatt, Book 18

Spencer, Book 19
Hathaway House, Books 1–3
Hathaway House, Books 4–6
Hathaway House, Books 7–9

The K9 Files
Ethan, Book 1
Pierce, Book 2
Zane, Book 3
Blaze, Book 4
Lucas, Book 5
Parker, Book 6
Carter, Book 7
Weston, Book 8
Greyson, Book 9
Rowan, Book 10
Caleb, Book 11
Kurt, Book 12
Tucker, Book 13
Harley, Book 14
Kyron, Book 15
Jenner, Book 16
Rhys, Book 17
Landon, Book 18
Harper, Book 19
The K9 Files, Books 1–2
The K9 Files, Books 3–4
The K9 Files, Books 5–6
The K9 Files, Books 7–8
The K9 Files, Books 9–10
The K9 Files, Books 11–12

Lovely Lethal Gardens

Arsenic in the Azaleas, Book 1

Bones in the Begonias, Book 2

Corpse in the Carnations, Book 3

Daggers in the Dahlias, Book 4

Evidence in the Echinacea, Book 5

Footprints in the Ferns, Book 6

Gun in the Gardenias, Book 7

Handcuffs in the Heather, Book 8

Ice Pick in the Ivy, Book 9

Jewels in the Juniper, Book 10

Killer in the Kiwis, Book 11

Lifeless in the Lilies, Book 12

Murder in the Marigolds, Book 13

Nabbed in the Nasturtiums, Book 14

Offed in the Orchids, Book 15

Poison in the Pansies, Book 16

Quarry in the Quince, Book 17

Revenge in the Roses, Book 18

Silenced in the Sunflowers, Book 19

Toes in the Tulips, Book 20

Lovely Lethal Gardens, Books 1–2

Lovely Lethal Gardens, Books 3–4

Lovely Lethal Gardens, Books 5–6

Lovely Lethal Gardens, Books 7–8

Lovely Lethal Gardens, Books 9–10

Psychic Vision Series

Tuesday's Child

Hide 'n Go Seek

Maddy's Floor

Garden of Sorrow

Knock Knock…
Rare Find
Eyes to the Soul
Now You See Her
Shattered
Into the Abyss
Seeds of Malice
Eye of the Falcon
Itsy-Bitsy Spider
Unmasked
Deep Beneath
From the Ashes
Stroke of Death
Ice Maiden
Snap, Crackle…
What If…
Talking Bones
String of Tears
Psychic Visions Books 1–3
Psychic Visions Books 4–6
Psychic Visions Books 7–9

By Death Series
Touched by Death
Haunted by Death
Chilled by Death
By Death Books 1–3

Broken Protocols – Romantic Comedy Series
Cat's Meow
Cat's Pajamas
Cat's Cradle

Cat's Claus
Broken Protocols 1-4

Broken and... Mending
Skin
Scars
Scales (of Justice)
Broken but... Mending 1-3

Glory
Genesis
Tori
Celeste
Glory Trilogy

Biker Blues
Morgan: Biker Blues, Volume 1
Cash: Biker Blues, Volume 2

SEALs of Honor
Mason: SEALs of Honor, Book 1
Hawk: SEALs of Honor, Book 2
Dane: SEALs of Honor, Book 3
Swede: SEALs of Honor, Book 4
Shadow: SEALs of Honor, Book 5
Cooper: SEALs of Honor, Book 6
Markus: SEALs of Honor, Book 7
Evan: SEALs of Honor, Book 8
Mason's Wish: SEALs of Honor, Book 9
Chase: SEALs of Honor, Book 10
Brett: SEALs of Honor, Book 11
Devlin: SEALs of Honor, Book 12
Easton: SEALs of Honor, Book 13

Ryder: SEALs of Honor, Book 14
Macklin: SEALs of Honor, Book 15
Corey: SEALs of Honor, Book 16
Warrick: SEALs of Honor, Book 17
Tanner: SEALs of Honor, Book 18
Jackson: SEALs of Honor, Book 19
Kanen: SEALs of Honor, Book 20
Nelson: SEALs of Honor, Book 21
Taylor: SEALs of Honor, Book 22
Colton: SEALs of Honor, Book 23
Troy: SEALs of Honor, Book 24
Axel: SEALs of Honor, Book 25
Baylor: SEALs of Honor, Book 26
Hudson: SEALs of Honor, Book 27
Lachlan: SEALs of Honor, Book 28
Paxton: SEALs of Honor, Book 29
Bronson: SEALs of Honor, Book 30
SEALs of Honor, Books 1–3
SEALs of Honor, Books 4–6
SEALs of Honor, Books 7–10
SEALs of Honor, Books 11–13
SEALs of Honor, Books 14–16
SEALs of Honor, Books 17–19
SEALs of Honor, Books 20–22
SEALs of Honor, Books 23–25

Heroes for Hire

Levi's Legend: Heroes for Hire, Book 1
Stone's Surrender: Heroes for Hire, Book 2
Merk's Mistake: Heroes for Hire, Book 3
Rhodes's Reward: Heroes for Hire, Book 4
Flynn's Firecracker: Heroes for Hire, Book 5

SEALs of Steel

Badger: SEALs of Steel, Book 1
Erick: SEALs of Steel, Book 2
Cade: SEALs of Steel, Book 3
Talon: SEALs of Steel, Book 4
Laszlo: SEALs of Steel, Book 5
Geir: SEALs of Steel, Book 6
Jager: SEALs of Steel, Book 7
The Final Reveal: SEALs of Steel, Book 8
SEALs of Steel, Books 1–4
SEALs of Steel, Books 5–8
SEALs of Steel, Books 1–8

The Mavericks

Kerrick, Book 1
Griffin, Book 2
Jax, Book 3
Beau, Book 4
Asher, Book 5
Ryker, Book 6
Miles, Book 7
Nico, Book 8
Keane, Book 9
Lennox, Book 10
Gavin, Book 11
Shane, Book 12
Diesel, Book 13
Jerricho, Book 14
Killian, Book 15
Hatch, Book 16
Corbin, Book 17
Aiden, Book 18

The Mavericks, Books 1–2
The Mavericks, Books 3–4
The Mavericks, Books 5–6
The Mavericks, Books 7–8
The Mavericks, Books 9–10
The Mavericks, Books 11–12

Collections
Dare to Be You…
Dare to Love…
Dare to be Strong…
RomanceX3

Standalone Novellas
It's a Dog's Life
Riana's Revenge
Second Chances

Published Young Adult Books:

Family Blood Ties Series
Vampire in Denial
Vampire in Distress
Vampire in Design
Vampire in Deceit
Vampire in Defiance
Vampire in Conflict
Vampire in Chaos
Vampire in Crisis
Vampire in Control
Vampire in Charge
Family Blood Ties Set 1–3

Family Blood Ties Set 1–5
Family Blood Ties Set 4–6
Family Blood Ties Set 7–9
Sian's Solution, A Family Blood Ties Series Prequel
    Novelette

Design series
Dangerous Designs
Deadly Designs
Darkest Designs
Design Series Trilogy

Standalone
In Cassie's Corner
Gem Stone (a Gemma Stone Mystery)
Time Thieves

Published Non-Fiction Books:

Career Essentials
Career Essentials: The Résumé
Career Essentials: The Cover Letter
Career Essentials: The Interview
Career Essentials: 3 in 1

Made in United States
North Haven, CT
05 December 2022

27979138R00163